KILLER'S GUN

The horse lay where it had fallen. It shuddered, tried to raise its head, trembled again and died, as a hard distant crack echoed along the rain-emptied street. The distinctive thump of a heavy rifle, its sound trailing behind the bullet it had sent.

Even before the shot was heard, Stillwell was bellied down behind the dead paint, peering over the mud-spattered rim of his saddle. Eyes that missed nothing scanned the street and everything along it. But there was nothing to see.

A Sharps or one of the 45-90's, Stillwell guessed. A long range rifle probably mounted with a telescopic sight. A gun to deliver sudden death, unexpected and unseen.

An assassin's weapon.

Stillwell put away his Colt and a knowledge colder than rain crept down his spine.

Goldie Locke had found him, and had opened the match.

DAN PARKINSON
DRIFTER'S LUCK

ZEBRA BOOKS
KENSINGTON PUBLISHING CORP.

For those who wondered what happened after
Brother Wolf . . . *and*
especially for those who asked

ZEBRA BOOKS

are published by

Kensington Publishing Corp.
475 Park Avenue South
New York, NY 10016

First printing: May, 1991

Printed in the United States of America

Prologue

He awoke to darkness and the smell of impending rain. For a long time he lay there, a soot-blackened figure sprawled on scorched black ground under a night sky. He didn't think about that. He didn't think about anything except the delicious coolness of a fresh breeze that washed over him. He drew the breeze into him, deep into scorched lungs. He could almost feel the soothing caress of it there as it began its healing.

The night sky was clear to the east but black in the west and overhead . . . black now not with the driving smokes of prairie fire but with rolling cloud that muttered soft thunders. Lightnings danced there, within the clouds, displaying bright cloudscapes that shifted and grew.

I'm all right, Mattie, he thought vaguely. In the best of health and enjoying my travels. Hope you are well, too.

Distantly, the rolling clouds seemed to answer him. A fat raindrop splattered in the ash an inch from his nose, and made him blink. Another fell cold and wet behind his ear.

He knew he had fainted . . . from lack of oxygen, probably. That and the heat. He had burns on his hands, his face and his legs, burns that throbbed dully now, warning of greater pain to come. The burns would need attention. But they would heal. The other wounds would heal, too, he decided. The bleeding wounds where bullets had scored him. Those would heal, because if they weren't curable he would already be dead.

How long had he been unconscious? He didn't know, but when he turned his head he could see a trace of light on the eastern horizon. Far away. Prairie fire, still visible in the distance? Or was it the promise of morning?

He sat up, a groan escaping as agonies swept over him. Starlight showed him a black velvet land where nothing moved — a land that was dead, that would remain dead until the rains came and brought new green grass to stand above the runneling ash and begin the recovery of the prairie.

Finally he got to his feet, hurting everywhere — hurting, but alive. What had once been a heavy serape hung for a moment from his shoulders, then fell away, nothing left of it but ash and tatters. Beneath it, his other garments were charred.

He didn't try to remember just then. There would be time for remembering. It was enough now just to be alive. He wondered vaguely if anyone else had lived, then tried not to think about that. The quick, taunting memories that flashed before him were akin to nightmare — walls of fire raging across a dry land, fire that ran with the wind and made its own winds as it went. Berserk images of fire where men rode, with guns in their hands and blaze all around them . . . the dull barking of their guns as they blossomed with fires brighter than the leaping flames of blazing grass. He saw the flares, saw their brilliances and felt again the bullets finding him even as he made fire of his own with his Peacemaker. Again and again he saw them falling as he fired.

Was it over now? He wondered. It should be over. Double D had been stopped. But was it over? Was anything ever really over? A nagging, dull worry clung to his thoughts, vague and distorted but real. A name . . . a name that was synonymous with dread. And with sudden death. Goldie Locke. Goldie Locke was unaccounted for. But who was Goldie Locke?

There would be time later to remember, time to sort it all out. He would let it come in its own time. But there was something, aside from the things he needed to remember. Aside from the lingering dread, there was a feeling of peace—a sense of completion that lingered above all else. Almost a sense of completion, though accounts remained to be settled and things remained to be done.

Can I go back to Patty now? The thought toyed with him, teasing him. Now will there be time to share separate pasts, maybe even time to consider a shared future? No, the dread told him. Not now. Not yet, and not like this. Not while the land lies dead and black, and some will know it was my hand that started the fire . . . the fire of vengeance for a dead man, the fire that stopped Double D. And not while Goldie Locke remains—a faceless, unknown threat. No face—only the eyes of death, seeking him out.

Now is not the time to go back, the wind whispered. In a season the rain will have come and the new grass grown and the ashes will be hidden. And maybe, sometime, forgotten. In a season maybe things will be resolved. Then will be time enough to go back.

Wind gusted, stirring the dark ash all around him. He stood and savored the wind's coolness.

Then something moved. Distantly, a hint of brightness moved in the dark. He walked toward it.

It was a painted horse, limping, its head down as it came, reins dragging on the black ground. The saddle it carried was dark and sticky, matted with blood. He took up its reins and rubbed its head and neck, pressing his burned face against the animal's cool hide. Chako's horse. A good friend's horse, its saddle sticky with a good friend's blood.

Chako. The name stirred other, fresher memories. Not

9

only enemies had died among the flames of raging prairies. A friend had died, too.

Chako wouldn't have grieved, he thought. The Comanche would spurn grief, preferring the memory of savage vengeance to the insignificant fact that he had died in the process. It had been his way.

But I'm not Chako, he thought. And I'm not Comanche. I will miss you, my brother Wolf.

The memories brought grief, and he felt a wetness in his eyes that he had not known in a very long time. He looked back the way the horse had come, seeing nothing but darkness there, and the hurt that welled inside him was as real as the hurts of burns and bullet wounds.

"Go, Brother Wolf," he muttered. The cool wind gusted and carried the words away.

Chapter One

In sunlight, to a good eye, the old sign might have read: Mullinsville. At dusk of a rainy evening it was only a weathered slab nailed to a scrub-oak tree and might as well have been blank.

But to the lone rider plodding past on a weary horse, it didn't matter. He slouched in his saddle. Rain dripped from his hatbrim to splatter on the pitted surface of a naked iron saddlehorn and soak the knees of his faded britches when he turned his head one way or the other. The old poncho hanging from sloped shoulders was frayed and torn, its corners flopped back over the stained cuffs of a battered flannel shirt. Large hands held patched reins in the manner of a rider accustomed to long trails — one hand doing the work, the other keeping slack. They were big hands, scarred and calloused — one wrapped to the knuckles in greasy linen, the other shiny with the scar tissue of recent burns.

Beyond the sign, the muddy trail widened where another trail forked into it and the two became a rutted road. The rider clicked his tongue and touched back on the reins, moving only the fingers of his clutch-hand. At the touch, the horse — a short-coupled paint with the rangy look of an Indian pony — raised its ears and halted. Both man and horse were motionless for long seconds, heads up and cautious as they tested the air.

11

For both it was long habit . . . for the man, a reflex not to go into anything or any place without first sizing it up, for the horse an instinct honed by long miles of weary travel where each turn might bring the need to run. Each in his way, they paused and listened. Then the man hauled back on the reins, backing the paint into the deep shadows of a rain-wet copse beside the trail.

"Hold," he whispered, leaning low over the horse's neck to stroke the animal gently beneath one ear.

From the right came sounds. Sodden hoofbeats on wet ground, low voices coming near . . . and brief laughter. Three riders came into view, not hurrying, just trotting toward the town ahead. The one in the lead hesitated for an instant where the trails merged, glancing around. Then he went on, the other two just behind him, abreast.

"See that jigger's eyes go wide back yonder?" one said, and giggled.

"Never expected us, I bet," the other grinned. "How much we get?"

"Dunno. Elgee's got it. Hey, Elgee . . . !"

They were past then, and going away. The man in the shadows watched them fade into the darkness and the rain, and shook his head. Reluctantly, then, he reined the paint to the right, back the way the three had come.

It wasn't very far. He found the horse first, a spooky chestnut wearing an old cavalry saddle. It stood facing him, and skittered back a few steps at his approach. But its reins dragged in the mud, and it obeyed its reins. It halted and held, and he caught up its leads and went on. Just beyond, a man lay sprawled in the mud. The rider on the paint looked down at him curiously, then swung stiffly from his saddle, wincing as he did. Each movement pained him, each brush of clothing against half-healed burns an agony. Holding both sets of reins, he bent over the fallen man, then squatted beside him. The man was dead, but still warm. The blood that pooled in his open mouth and ran down the side of his head was fresh and steamy where the cold rain pocked it.

"Beat to death," the crouching man muttered. He sighed, braced himself and lifted the dead man's shoulders, wincing as sharp pains ran up his left leg and across his shoulders — pain of wounds too recent to ignore, protesting his movements.

Long, agonizing minutes passed before he had the body slung across the chestnut's saddle, and he panted from the exertion. I'm shaky as a two-day drunk, he thought. I wouldn't be a match for a fresh-weaned pup just now.

For a moment he clung to the paint's saddle, feeling sick and dizzy. But it passed. With a muted groan he climbed aboard again, turned the horse and headed for the town he knew was somewhere near.

"Might have been better to lay over in Fort Worth," he muttered. "Just lay low for a while and got some rest." He sighed, slouching tired shoulders. He couldn't "lay over" anywhere, he knew. Not yet. He needed distance, and time to think. Time to plan. He didn't know for sure that anyone was behind him, but instinct said they were.

He grimaced as a new pain made itself known. He reached beneath the poncho to press a careful hand against a tender spot on his side. Distinctly, through the fabric of his shirt, he could feel the scab of the deep cut where a bullet had creased him, barely a week past. Like his other wounds, it ached and aggravated him. But the pressure of his hand made it no worse. He nodded. It was healing, and had not broken open. Nor had the bullet holes in his leg and shoulder, though right now they ached like sin.

"That sawbones in the Nation was right," he told himself. "I'm *not* in shape to travel."

A sardonic grin tugged at stubbled cheeks. Been nice, he thought, if there had really been a choice in the matter.

"Hope there's decent law in that town," he told the paint, glancing back at the dark shadow of the led horse with its burden of death. He shrugged. "More than that, I hope there's a decent bed."

He saw the town then—a strung-out little place with no more buildings than a man could count, most of them dark and defeated-looking, squatting in the rain.

Midway along a deserted street, a hitchrail fronted a low building with lamplight filtering from board-shuttered windows. There was no sign, but he had seen plenty of such places before. He got down, looped both pairs of reins and limped to the door. It opened at the pull of a drawstring, and a man in rumpled shirtsleeves swiveled a creaky chair toward him. A sallow, tired-looking man with drooping mustaches.

The rider stepped in. "I'm looking for the local law," he said.

"You've found him." The man stood, tired eyes assessing the newcomer. "I'm Johnson. Marshal of Mullinsville. What can I do for you?"

He flipped a thumb toward the door. "Dead man outside. Beat to death and likely robbed. I found him where the roads fork, just north of here. He was still warm when I got there. Three men did it. One of them's a thin, nervous type with a fancy hatband. The other two called him Elgee."

Johnson stared at him. "You saw them kill a man?"

"No, but I saw where they came from, and what they left is just outside there, belly-down on a chestnut horse with a Circle Six mark and a cut-down cavalry saddle. Man about fifty, five-eight or nine maybe, hundred and fifty pounds and not much face left on him. Looks like those boys had some fun. Anybody you recognize?"

Johnson nodded, looking bleak. "Fred Blake," he said. "I told him he shouldn't carry cash money. Wasn't any secret that he did, though. Just asking for trouble."

"He got it," the newcomer said. "What about the others?"

"What about them? The ones you described are Elgee

Folger and two of his brothers. I know them." The marshal looked tireder than before. "I guess you'll be willing to swear out a statement about what you saw, Mister . . . ?"

"Stillwell. Byron Stillwell. Yes, I'll give a statement, but I'd sure like to get a night's rest first. Where can I find a bed around here?"

For the first time, the marshal seemed to notice the newcomer's exhaustion. "Are you all right, Mr. Stillwell? You don't look very good."

"Nothing I can't sleep off," he said. "But I sure need to get to it soon."

"Help yourself to a cell, then." Johnson pointed at an interior door. "They're both empty. Take your choice." He stepped to the street door and opened it, peered out and then looked back. "The paint yours?"

"Yeah."

"I'll get somebody to tend him. You go ahead and rest. I'll send word to the sheriff, and we'll get your statement tomorrow.

"The Folgers," he added, as though to himself. "Well, it was bound to happen . . ." He closed the door behind him and Byron Stillwell went looking for the nearest cell . . . and the quilt-draped cot which was all he wanted at the moment.

Dimly, he heard voices in the street beyond the office—Johnson's voice, and others. There'd be a crowd soon. Even on a rainy night, a man brought in across his saddle would always draw a crowd.

He pulled off the sodden poncho and draped it over the top of the open cell door. He hung his battered hat on the lock bolt, brushed back unkempt dark hair and ran rueful fingers over the stubble on his cheeks. "Good thing you can't see me now, Mattie," he muttered. "I'm sure not fit for polite company just now." Probably time to send a wire, he thought. Mattie Stillwell had given up worrying

15

about her errant son years ago . . . so she said. He knew better. Mothers always worried.

There'd be a Western Union somewhere along the way. He would send a message when he could. "Seeing some country, Mattie. In excellent health and having a wonderful time."

There were more voices out on the street now. The crowd was growing, as crowds always do. He unbuckled the shell belt across lean hips and folded it carefully, pausing for a moment to draw and inspect the Colt .45 Peacemaker. The gun was worn and patinaed, but it was clean and its mechanism clicked smoothly as he checked hammer and cylinder action.

He returned it to its holster and sat down on the hard bunk to pull off his boots. There was no pillow, but a pair of boots laid soles-out with the tops overlapping was as much pillow as he would need.

With a groan and a sigh, he stretched six-feet-plus of hurt on the bunk and closed his eyes. Rain on the roof, and distant voices. The voices blurred, became other voices—voices of other times and other places. He slept.

Vague, lingering dreams taunted him. Dark dreams full of smoke and fire—walls of fire marching across a black land beneath a black sky, where men appeared among the flames, brighter flames growing from the muzzles of the guns in their hands. Flowers of brilliance that licked at him, tormenting . . . dream thunders, and a thunder that shouldered through the dream and was real. Like the gray light from the jail-cell window was real, and the face at the cell door . . .

"Christ, Mister!" The door creaked as the boy there backed against it, flinging up his hands. "Don't shoot! I didn't do anything . . . !"

The adolescent voice brought him full awake. He was crouched beside the cot, his Peacemaker trained on the youngster in the doorway. A boy, barely into adolescence, his eyes huge with sudden fear. Stillwell lowered his gun,

16

eased the hammer down and took a deep breath. "Don't come up on a man like that, son," he rasped. "Some folks aren't used to it."

There were voices outside, as there had been the night before. But they sounded different now . . . excited and aroused.

Stillwell stood, groaning at the stiff pains that radiated from his wounds. The boy was still staring at him, wide-eyed. After a moment, the man sat on the bunk and started pulling on his boots. Every motion brought fresh aches. "Well," he said, "did you need me for something?"

"I . . . I didn't know who was in here," the boy piped, struggling with his voice. "Are you the one that brought Mister Blake in?"

"That's right. I'm supposed to give the marshal a statement. Where is he?"

The boy's lips trembled. "He . . . he's dead, Mister. Elgee Folger just shot him, not but a minute ago, out there on the street."

Stillwell sat motionless for a moment, then got to his feet and strapped on his rig. "I see," he said. Then, "All right, son. You've warned me. Now get out of here."

"They know about you, Mister. They'll be lookin' for you . . ."

The man sighed, shrugged and stifled a groan. "I know. Now you heard me. Get away from here. Now!"

"Yes, sir." The boy turned and ran.

Stillwell got his poncho off the cell door and shoved his hat onto his head. "Damn," he muttered. Outside the open street door, the shouting voices had stilled. He rubbed his eyes with hard knuckles, rolled his shoulders and winced, then took a deep breath and sighed. Some people just couldn't let a thing rest.

The street beyond the open door was empty now, and suddenly silent except for the echoes of slamming doors and shutters. Deserted except for some tethered horses, a stray cat and the body of a dead man sprawled against a horse trough. A dead man with a badge on his shirt.

Stillwell sighed, dark eyes going bleak, and the staring blind eyes of windows on the street echoed the silence. Not much of a town, he decided. Might be better to hold off contacting Mattie until he could write to her from someplace more memorable.

Of the three men he had seen, on a rainy road the night before, he guessed that the fancy hatband—Elgee—was the most dangerous. The other two likely had killed the man on the road. Fists and boots would be their style. But Elgee had the look of a gunman about him . . . and the boy had said it was Elgee who shot the marshal.

Up the street, northward, batwing doors creaked in the morning breeze and harsh laughter sounded.

"Is that where they are?" he asked, his voice level.

A pause, then the boy's voice, somewhere behind him. "That's Morey's. They went in there. How did you know I was here?"

"At your age, I would have been. Now stay out of sight, and maybe you'll live to be my age." Without looking back, he stepped into the street. He felt eyes watching him, but not a soul was in sight now. The only other movement on the street—besides himself—was a half-grown yellow kitten. A tramp cat in search of a morning meal. Stillwell walked toward the saloon. A face appeared there, above the batwings, then was withdrawn and there was a shout. A moment later the batwings opened and a burly figure stepped out.

"By God," the taunting voice came clear, "Look what we got here, Lee. A damned scarecrow."

Another came out to join him. The two followers . . . Elgee Folger's brothers. Lee gawked at the approaching man, said, "He must be the one," and turned to call through the doors. "Hey, Elgee, I think we found the tattletale."

"Then kill him," someone inside snarled.

Together, grinning their delight, the two stepped off the

18

boardwalk and spread to brace Stillwell. He slowed and tossed back his poncho.

"Oh, my," Lee said. "Scarecrow's got a real, big gun."

"Well, so have . . ." the other started, his hand diving for his holster.

Both of them got their guns out, and both fired . . . but the shots were wild. Random shots discharged by dead men. Byron Stillwell's Peacemaker spoke twice and the two spun like string-dolls, dead before they fell.

In the silence as the echoes died, Elgee Folger's voice came from Morey's door. "Well? Did you drop him?"

Byron Stillwell stepped over the sprawled Lee, feeding a pair of cartridges into the smoking Peacemaker. Beside the saloon door he paused, called, "They missed, Elgee. I guess it's up to you," and spun through the batwings. A bullet clipped the frame beside him, and another tugged at his poncho. Then the Peacemaker roared . . . once, and again . . . and Elgee Folger crashed back against the keg-top bar. Wild eyes stared for a moment, as a gun slipped from useless fingers. Then his feet slid out from under him and he went down. The bar's edge knocked his hat off and it fell atop him—a fancy hat with a fancy band, hiding the two little holes an inch apart in his chest.

Byron Stillwell sagged against the saloon wall, reloading. When a man crawled from behind the bar, he asked, "Who's the local law, now that Johnson's dead?"

The man got to his feet, staring.

Stillwell pinned him with eyes as bleak as epitaphs. "Well?"

"Uh . . . well, I guess it's the sheriff, but he's over at Proctor. That's the county seat."

"Are you Morey?"

"Y . . . yes, sir. Morey Mc . . ."

"Fine. I'm going back to the marshal's office to write out a statement, and when I finish it I want you to see to it that the sheriff gets it. Do you understand?"

"Uh . . . well, yes, sir, but . . ."

19

"Do you understand?"

"Yes, sir." The man was trembling visibly. "You know Pack Folger's going to hear about this, Mister."

"Who is Pack Folger?"

"He's a . . . well, he's a bad 'un. Last I heard he was in prison over in Arkansas, but he won't be there forever. These was his brothers."

"I expect he'll be upset, then." Stillwell sighed. "But if he wants a chance at my hide he'll just have to wait in line. There's others with prior claim." He pushed through the batwings, groaning beneath his breath. The man followed him, scampering to keep up.

"You don't look good," he allowed. "Did one of them hit you?"

"I'm all right. Just some old bumps and bruises. I'll be fine, with a little rest."

"You could stay around here," the man suggested. "At least 'til the sheriff . . ."

"I don't think so," he grunted. "I don't like this place. But you tell the sheriff I'll get in touch with him when I light someplace, in case he has questions."

He wrote his report then found some breakfast at a smoky little place with a sign that said only, *Eats.* No one else entered while he was there. There were just himself, the cook and that stray cat from the street. But he felt others watching him, eyes on him through the open door and the dusty window. When he had finished, he had the cook chop up some raw calf liver and pour goat milk into a bowl. These he set on the floor, and sat for a time watching the cat put them away. Half-starved, it seemed, but when he reached toward it the animal hissed and swatted at him with businesslike claws that grazed his fingers. It didn't welcome any foolishness, and made that very clear. He grinned, paid his bill and left.

The boy from the jail was waiting with the paint, and Stillwell slung his possibles aboard, mounted stiffly and looked down. "Obliged, son," he said.

20

He didn't look back as he rode out of Mullinsville, nor for a half-mile beyond, until a sound behind him brought his head around. The yellow kitten was tagging after him, panting from its efforts to keep up. When he looked around, it made a mewing sound and hurried toward him.

He sat stiffly, looking down at the little creature. It stared back, and repeated the sound it had made—a soft, articulated sound that could almost have been querulous words of complaint.

"I swear," he muttered. Then he unrolled his poncho and let it hang from his hand, its frayed end nearly reaching the ground. "So you're a grubliner, huh? Well, if you want a ride, you'll have to climb up because I'm too stove up to come down after you."

Chapter Two

Ennis was a town with a future. It had a bustling new rail yard, a brand new opera house, a pullman-car contract, three grain mills and a stockyard district. Affluence was afoot, and all the trappings that went with it.

And the town had four things that Byron Stillwell wanted: a man he hoped to find, a Western Union telegraph office, a doctor he knew and trusted . . . and a decent hotel with doors on the rooms.

His first stop was the telegraph office. He was aware of the curious appraisals of passers-by, some only glancing while others stared openly as he looped the paint's reins at the hitchrail in front. Aside from a brief look around, he ignored them. He knew how he appeared. A prairie fire and a showdown with most of the Double D spread's gunmen — followed by three hundred miles of hard travel — didn't do much for a man's wardrobe. And burn scars and bullet holes tended also to single a man out.

He tipped his battered hat to a pair of matrons carrying shopping baskets, and kept a straight face as they sidled away from him and hurried on their way, glancing back only for a second view of the yellow cat asleep on the paint's saddle. Stillwell crossed the wide walk, stepped into the telegraph office and nodded at the man in sleeve garters who frowned at him from behind a littered desk. "Can you handle a bank draft by wire?" he asked.

22

The man nodded, grudgingly. "If it's a regulated bank. No remote drafts on territorial banks without a transfer voucher."

"It's a state bank. But not the state of Texas. It's in Kansas."

"I see." The man stood, walked across to a bookcase and took down a thick volume. He put it on a table, opened it and glanced up. "A chartered bank?"

"A chartered bank," Stillwell assured him. "The First State Bank of Hays. Look on page 14 of the Kansas State register. It's there."

The telegrapher looked and nodded. "It's here." He straightened, still looking doubtful. "I can wire a draft for you, but you'll have to give me your account number, Mr . . . ,"

"Stillwell. Byron Stillwell."

The man wrote it on a small square of paper, then looked up. "Your account code number?"

Stillwell eyed him, a slow perusal by unreadable eyes in a darkly sardonic face. "Are you bonded?"

The man blinked. "Well, of course I'm bonded! Every telegrapher with the Western Union Company is bonded."

"What's your name and bond number?"

"Name's Michaelson. You want my . . . ?"

"Not really. I just felt like pointing out that I don't have any more reason to trust you than you have to trust me. But I'll take your word for it."

The man blinked again, then grinned and Stillwell recited the number of a bank account in Hays. "Make the draft for one hundred dollars plus the cost of the transaction." He leaned idly on the counter while the telegrapher noted the information and took it to his key table.

Beyond the window, people passed by, some pausing to glance at the tired-looking paint horse with the worn-looking saddle—and at the half-grown cat atop it. The cat opened its eyes, stared coolly back at a curious townsman, then stretched luxuriously, yawned and sat upright. Its disinterested perusal of the town around it was as brief as Stillwell's had been. Finding nothing of interest to look at, the creature began washing its face with a paw.

Several riders with various brands on their horses cantered along the street and reined in nearby. One of them, a youngster with long red hair and big buck teeth, stood for a moment looking at the cat on the paint's saddle, then stepped over for a better look. Even from behind, Stillwell could see the grin widening his cheeks. He turned to call over his shoulder, the words muffled but clear through the window, "Hey, Jude! You ever see the likes of this? Give this cat a hat and a shell-belt, he could prob'ly ride fence-line for any of them hill spreads."

Still grinning, the redhead reached for the cat . . . and drew back abruptly as the animal's ears flattened and a lightning-fast paw raked his fingers with needle claws. The grin disappeared, and the youngster held up his hand. Little drops of bright blood welled along two fingers. The kid stared at the cat, his hand dipping by reflex toward his holster.

Behind him, the telegraph office door opened and a low, matter-of-fact voice said, "If you pull it, you'd better be looking this way."

The kid spun around, and stared at the battered-looking man standing there, his fingers an inch from the butt of a big gun at his hip.

"Be better all around if you just forget it," Byron Stillwell suggested. "I don't think that cat takes to socializing."

For an instant a feral light shone in the kid's pale eyes, a look of intense anticipation. Stillwell had seen the look before. But it was only an instant. The kid relaxed and his grin returned. He held up his scratched hand and chuckled. "I guess you're right, mister. I'm just not used to bein' out-slicked by a critter. That your cat?"

"No, but that's my horse, so I suggest you just leave it alone."

His grin widening, the kid spread his hands and backed away. "No harm done an' none intended." With a touch of his hatbrim he turned away, walked a few steps and turned back. Stillwell hadn't moved.

Despite the grin, the youngster's eyes were bright and curious. "You don't look to be up to bracin' folks, mister. What would you do if I was to draw on you?"

"Kill you," Stillwell said.

"Maybe if you was as fast as that cat, you might." Somehow the notion seemed to amuse him, and his eyes took up his grin. "Maybe one of these days we'll find out."

He walked away, and some of the others who rode in with him followed along. Their glances at Byron Stillwell were not friendly. Stillwell watched them go, then went inside again. The telegrapher had been watching from his window.

"Young rowdies, but a hard bunch," the man said. "You came off lucky, I'd say."

"Did I?"

"I'd say so. Some of those young toughs that drift through here would as soon shoot a man as look at him, and for my money Coby Shanks may be the worst of the bunch." The telegraph key clattered and he listened, then walked back to his desk to write on a pad. "Your draft is cleared, Mister Stillwell. I'll give you a cashier's order. You can cash it at the bank. Just around the corner."

"You don't keep cash here, I gather."

The telegrapher glanced at his window, frowning. "Not these days," he said. "Too risky. Ennis is a good, solid town, mister, but it is a railroad town."

"Then deduct two more telegrams from the cashier's order. And I'd like you to write them down for me." He raised his bandaged hand and shrugged. The telegrapher got his pen.

"One to Mrs. Mattie Stillwell. Care of the Rosenthal Trust, Baltimore Conservatory of . . ."

25

The man looked up. "Mattie Stillwell? The singer?"

Stillwell nodded. "My mother. Conservatory of Music, Baltimore, Maryland. Just say, 'Gone to Texas for a while. Doing fine and staying out of trouble. Will let you know where to write when I am settled. Don't worry about anything you might hear. Stories get twisted around. Love, Byron.' Got that?"

The man nodded, counting words. "And the other one?"

"Is to Patty Mills . . . that's *Mrs. Patricia* Mills, in care of Mr. Silas Rutledge, Fargo Springs, Kansas. The message is, 'Don't believe everything you hear, and don't forget *Scheherazade* and sherbet some rainy evening in Philadelphia. I'm counting on it.' And sign it, 'By'."

Again the man counted words, then he wrote a cashier's order and handed it across. "So Mattie Stillwell is your mother," he said. "Didn't she sing at that new opera palace out in California?"

"San Francisco. The Pavilion. That was a couple of years ago. Have you heard her sing?"

"Wish I had," the man said. "Critics say she's . . ."

"They're right," Stillwell said. "She is." He paused, then nodded toward the note pad. "One more message. To the county sheriff at Proctor. Say, 'Stopping at Ennis. Wire if you have questions about Mullinsville. Sign it Byron Stillwell. I guess that's all of them."

"What happened to your hand?"

"Just a burn. How much do I owe you?"

The man added word counts. "Six dollars and eighty cents. Be a lot cheaper to write."

"Make out my voucher," Stillwell said. "If any responses come, I'll be at that hotel over there."

From the Western Union office, he led the paint along busy streets until he found a boarding stable. The cat rode, perched imperiously on his saddle until the paint was in a stall with feed. Stillwell began stripping off the saddle then, and the cat leapt down and disappeared into the shadows.

"You tend this horse right," Stillwell told the stabler. "He's come a long way. You have a farrier?"

"Blacksmith," the man nodded. "He contracts for us."

"Then get shoes put on him, if it can be done in a day or so."

"I'll tend to it. Where did your cat get off to? I don't want these animals spooked."

"It's not my cat. But don't worry about it. Most horses like cats. I've seen stables that keep cats around, just to calm the stock. That and mousing."

From the boarding stable he went to the bank to cash his voucher, then to a general merchandise store from which he carried parcels to a barber's shop with a bath house behind it. The attendant who brought water for the tub stared at the man stripping down to bathe and muttered, "Jesus!"

Stillwell turned. "What?"

" 'Scuse me." The man turned away and poured hot water. Then he glanced back. "Mister, I seen some men with gunshot wounds, but you look like you been used for target practice. How'd you get all them marks?"

"Generally by being in the way when there was shooting." He stepped into the tub and eased down until the water covered him to the shoulders. "This is just fine," he said. "Don't hurry back. I mean to soak for a while."

The attendant left, shaking his head. He was an old man, and had seen a lot of strange things, but he had never before seen a man take his gun into the tub with him.

When the water had gone cool, Stillwell toweled off and dressed himself in new, store-bought clothes that smelled of starch and still had the shelf-creases in them. The boots he pulled on were stiff and proud, but they fit and would break in eventually. He dried the Peacemaker, rubbed it with oil from a lamp base, slid it into its holster and strapped on his shell-belt. Then carrying his new coat, new hat and a new leather valise, he went through into the barber shop for a shave and shearing.

The man who stepped out onto the street would scarcely have been recognized as the one who had gone in, except on close scrutiny. A ragtag, trail-weary drifter had gone into the tonsorial parlor. The man who came out was trimmed and neat, a tall, muscular man of about thirty, dark-eyed and dark-haired with just a trace of silver at the temples. All that remained of two weeks' growth of whiskers was a short mustache, carefully trimmed above a mouth with traces of sardonic humor at its corners and a jaw whose scars just made it seem more rock-hard.

One of the packages from the store had held a leather valise, which he carried now. Inside were the rest of his purchases.

At the hotel he requested—and got—a back room, and carried his valise upstairs, pausing only to turn and call back to the desk clerk, "There may be messages for me. Just keep them at the desk, will you? I'll be resting."

"Yes, sir, Mr. Stillwell," the clerk waved. "Have a nice rest. You won't be disturbed."

"Thank you." He went on up the stairs, found his room and went in. The single window had a thin net curtain through which he could see the back lot and an alley, and the buildings beyond on the next street. He opened the window and leaned out, noting which window it was, then closed it and let the curtain fall into place. From his valise he took a hat—his old, battered hat—and set it on a bureau top beside the window. He pulled back the bed's covers, realigned the two thick down pillows and covered them with sheet and blanket. At a glance, it looked as though someone were sleeping there.

Satisfied, he left the room quietly, locked the door and went down the back stairs and across the alley. At a boarding house beyond, he paid for a room and registered himself as Charles Dance of Mobeetie, a track surveyor. The second-floor guest rooms were along a hall that led to

28

a balcony.

"I may be coming and going a bit," he told the landlady. "Business, you know. But I'll be careful not to disturb any of your other guests. Also, I won't be taking meals here, so don't trouble yourself about me."

Frederick James Cathcart, M.D., had a two-room office over the Emporium, with a sign at street level and awninged stairs. Stillwell watched the stairs from across the street for a time, until the door at the top opened and a man came out with his arm in a sling. He watched the man descend the stairs and walk away along the street, then he crossed and went up.

A cowbell clanked as he entered, and moments later a thin, balding man with wire-rim glasses appeared at the inner door, started to speak, then blinked and stared. "You," the doctor said, finally.

"Me," Stillwell shrugged. "How's the salve holding out, Doc?"

"Come in," Cathcart motioned, holding the door open. "My God, By. I'd heard you were dead. That big fire up in the Strip . . ."

Stillwell went into the treatment room and Cathcart closed the door. "For your records, Doc. list me as Byron Dance. From Mobeetie. Just a precaution."

"All right, By." Cathcart paused, then his eyes narrowed. "Dance? That was the name of the man you went looking for, wasn't it? Did you find him?"

"I was too late." Stillwell pulled off his coat and began unbuttoning his shirt. "They killed him, Doc. I never even got to see him."

"I'm sorry." Cathcart turned away to arrange instruments on a cloth-covered table. "He was the one, then? He was . . . ?"

Stillwell nodded. "My father. Yes. Mattie's blue soldier, from the war. Sam Dance."

"Does Mattie know?"

"She knows. I found her old hymn book among his

29

things. I sent it to her so she'd understand." He removed his shirt, peeled his long johns to the waist and perched on a tall stool. "I've got three new bullet-scars, Doc. New and recent. Couple of weeks, I guess. And some burns. I stopped to see a sawbones up in the Nations to tide me over, but I'd appreciate your services. I still have a ways to go."

The doctor turned, looked him over and pursed his lips in a low whistle. "By, it's a pure miracle you're still alive." He examined the crusted scar on Stillwell's side, then walked around him to see the one on his back. "I see two. Where's the third?"

"Left leg. It wasn't so deep, though. It's about healed over."

Cathcart shook his head in disbelief. He walked around in front of him again and pointed. "There's another one I hadn't seen. Within the year, I'd judge. How come that one didn't kill you? It's right over the heart."

"Serape slowed the ball, I guess. The man who gave me that *thought* I was dead. That's why I'm still alive."

"I see. And him? The man who thought you were dead?"

"He *is* dead. Him and a few others like him."

"What was it all about, By?"

"It was about a lot of things. Things usually are. Mainly, I guess it was because a fellow decided that he'd like to have a territory—or a state, maybe—all his own. He tried to push a herd across the Strip into Kansas, to break down the quarantine. He'd been setting it up so those west border counties would lose their charters when he did. Had some judges and the like on his payroll. He'd have wound up with pieces of two states and a couple of territories, that he could reorganize to suit himself. That's why Sam Dance was killed. He'd started putting two and two together and they had to get rid of him."

The doctor was peeling bandages off Stillwell's hands. "I'm sorry, By. I really am. How'd you get these burns?"

"Playing with fire."

"I see. Well, they're healing. You must have the constitution of an ox. I . . . fire? That big range fire up in No Man's Land, few weeks back? Did you . . . ?"

"It was my fire. I set it. Only way to stop Double D."

Cathcart gawked at him. "Double D? Old man Dawes . . . from Mobeetie?"

"Peter Lewellyn Dawes," By nodded. "It was his game that was being played."

"My God, By! That old man's got influence everywhere! Where are you going to find a hole deep enough to . . . ?"

"To hide from Dawes?" Stillwell shrugged. "If I started hiding from him and his, I'd be hiding the rest of my life. No, if he wants to find me, he can. I leave a plain enough trail."

"It won't be him, By. He'll send others. You know the kind of men he can hire."

"I know one who might already be working for him. Did you ever hear of someone named Goldie Locke?"

"Not that I know of."

"Just as well. I got wind in Kansas that Locke was mixed up in that mess somehow, but I never ran into him. If he was there, though, he might be looking for me now."

"You could go back east, you know. Wait for things to blow over."

"You know better than that, Doc."

"Yes, I know." Cathcart sighed and began salving his patient's wounds. "Byron Stillwell only knows one way to go and that's straight ahead," he recited, angrily. "But there'll come a time when Byron Stillwell's way isn't anything more than a way to die. You'll stop one bullet too many, son, and there won't be anything left to patch up. I hate to think about that, because when it happens it will break Mattie's heart."

Stillwell shrugged. "My mother knows how it is with me, Doc. She accepts it."

31

"Maybe she does, but I don't!"

"You still love her, don't you."

"I guess I always will," Cathcart sighed. He rewrapped the burned left hand, and draped cheesecloth dressing over his patient's shoulder to cover the oily salve, tying it off with brown fabric tape. "That's all I can do, for now. I don't suppose there's anything busted up inside you, or you'd never have made it here. I *could* tell you to go find a bed and stay in it until those scabs begin to curl, but it wouldn't do any good, so I won't." He turned away. Byron noted how age was setting in, how the man's movements seemed slower and more deliberate than he remembered. "I don't suppose you came to Ennis just to see me."

"Partly," Stillwell smiled. "Also I want to look up a man I heard was here A retired judge from Mobeetie, Arthur Knox. Know him?"

"I know him. Good man. He lives over on Elm, a block off Union. But someone said he was out of town. Social call?"

"Just wrapping up some business . . . for Sam Dance."

"You'll be leaving soon, then?"

"Soon as I can. I want to see if anybody is following me yet."

"How will you know that?"

"I'll know." He put on his shirt and his coat, paid a modest fee and stepped out into the waiting room. A woman was there, with two children. He nodded, strode to the outer door and turned back. "Thanks for seeing me, Doctor. I feel a whole lot better now."

Cathcart stared at him, shaking his head. "Just remember what I said, Mr . . . ah . . . Dance. The kind of allergy you have can be very serious. It's better just to avoid the cause of it if you can."

Chapter Three

Later in the evening there would be a crowd in the Steel Rail, but now only a few gathered there. At a back table a brace of switch yard hands just in from shift was nursing a pair of mugs of cellar-cooled beer. A few townsmen and a couple of farmers sat or leaned here and there in the big, ornate gaming room, ignoring some hard-eyed stockmen who gathered at the far end of the bar as though defending a territory.

Two young gun-toters sat at a game table, turning cards with a bored faro dealer for a nickel point. One of them was red-haired and buck-toothed, with pale eyes in a smiling leprechaun face.

The other raked a handful of coins across to the gartered dealer, his face twisting into a sullen sneer. "We're wasting time in this burg, Coby," he muttered. "I'm ready to move on and see if we can't find some real action."

"We'll be travelin' soon," the redhead said, casually. "One more turn, Clancy." He nodded at the dealer, then raised a hand. "No, I tell you what. We'll cut three ways for what's on the table."

"Can't do that," the dealer shook his head. "Rules of the house. No trail camp games in here."

The redhead pinned him with eyes that held no trace of the careless grin below them. "I don't recall askin' you," he purred. "What I recall is *tellin'* you. We'll cut three ways."

33

The dealer glanced around, nervously, his eyes going to the empty chairs behind the overhead rails where shotgun enforcers would sit later in the evening when there was a bigger crowd. "One round cut," he conceded. "Then I'm out. I have to get my records in order for evening count." He shuffled the deck expertly, laid it on the table and tapped it. "Go ahead," he said.

"You first," Coby Shanks grinned.

"All right." The dealer ran his fingers part way down the deck, hesitated, and cut, keeping the card to himself.

"Go ahead, Jude," Coby said.

Jude cut the remaining deck, drew his cut into closed hands and shifted impatiently.

"Now me," Coby said. He cut almost to the bottom of the remaining cards and turned his find over. Jack of hearts. He tossed it on the table, and Jude's eight of spades fluttered down beside it. The dealer looked at his cut, then turned it up. It was the king of spades. He raked in the scattered coins on the table and got to his feet.

"Table's closed, gents," he said. "Open again at seven." He walked away and Coby Shanks watched him go, still grinning.

"How come you let him get away with that, Coby?" Jude snorted. "You saw him rake that cut, as well as I did."

" 'Course I saw him. So what?"

"So how come you let him get by with it?"

"Felt like it," Coby shrugged.

"Been a day of that, seems like." Jude's sullen face twisted into a leer.

"What in hell is that supposed to mean?"

"I mean it's just like this morning when you let that beat-up drifter brace you down. It ain't like you, Coby."

"You think I should have wasted a bullet over that? Over a damn cat?"

"I've seen you shoot for less cause."

"Trouble is with you, Jude, you're trigger-happy." Coby

gazed across at him, coolly. "I don't believe you know the difference between shootin' for cause and shootin' for the hell of it. This is a good town to come back to. I'd as soon keep it that way."

"Did you know that drifter went to the bank and cashed a voucher for near a hundred dollars? And checked into the hotel just like a seed drummer would? Sharkey saw him."

"So he's got an angle on somethin'." the redhead stretched and stood. "I said forget it, Jude. We ought to be thinkin' about more profitable things than bracin' drifters."

"Well, I got an idea about that, too."

"Like what?"

"Like I found out when the cotton gin down at Tightwad cashes its crop voucher, and how the money is carried."

"Crop money?" Coby frowned. "It ain't anywhere near cotton harvest, Jude. That's months off. Besides, who ever heard of robbin' a cotton gin?"

"Not the gin," Jude's eyes narrowed, becoming furtive. "And keep your damn voice down. Just one man . . . two at the most. Old boy that owns the gin, he'll go to the bank at Waxahachie to get the money. Then he'll head back toward Tightwad."

"So he'll have a little money," Coby wrinkled his nose. "That's penny ante, Jude. If we're goin' after somethin', I'd as soon it was somethin' big."

"I don't call four-five thousand dollars exactly small change."

"That much?"

"That much, at least. Could tide us over real nice 'til somethin' better comes along. So what do you say, Coby? Worth lookin' at, ain't it?"

"I don't know . . ." the redhead hesitated.

Jude stared at him, speculating. "You ain't goin' soft on us, are you, Coby?"

35

"Do you want to try me on for size, Jude?" Coby's voice was a purr, his fingers brushing the butt of his gun.

Jude backed off, shaking his head. "I didn't mean nothin' by that, Coby. I only think we ought to have a look at that cotton money."

Coby nodded. "We can have a look. Then I decide. Pass the word to the boys to stay sober. We'll be takin' a little ride tomorrow."

Byron Stillwell walked along Union Street until he came to Elm, and asked a woman sweeping a porch for directions to the home of Arthur Knox.

She pointed. "It's the red two-story over there, but the judge isn't home. He's gone over to Waxahachie. Might be gone a spell, too. He's holdin' court."

"Court? He's retired, isn't he?"

"Still keeps his hand in, I reckon. He goes sometimes when they got their dockets full an' need an extra judge. Are you kin?"

"Not kin," Stillwell said. "I just wanted to deliver something to him. It can wait. Thank you." He tipped his hat and went back toward the main thoroughfare. A closed carriage rolled past, slowing, but it went on by. When he glanced back, the carriage had stopped. The woman with the broom was talking to someone inside.

Disappointing that Judge Knox wasn't here. Finding the old man wasn't the only reason he had come south after the fire, but it was a thing he had set himself to do.

That, and find out who was left from the Kansas conspiracy, who might be trailing him even now. To find out—and a dull dread lingered with the thought—if Goldie Locke was after him. He shook his head, to dispel the ominous feeling. If Goldie Locke wanted him, he would know it when Goldie Locke came for him . . . if he lived long enough.

Somehow he was sure that Locke would be looking for

him. A hunch, and nothing more, but he had learned to listen to his hunches. And a second hunch said that Locke wasn't behind him, at least not following his trail. It said Locke would be ahead somewhere, waiting, somehow knowing where he would pass and when.

As for others who might be on his trail, the best way to find them would be to let them find him, but on his own terms. Then he'd know who was out there and what they had in mind. The game was played out in Kansas. Peter Lewellyn Dawes, for all of his wealth and power, would never again have the opportunity to separate the Panhandle lands from their constitutional domains, to build a territory of his own.

Others might try, at another time. The notion of splitting off a corner of Kansas, a wedge of Texas and the Cimarron Breaks region of Colorado and New Mexico, with the lawless Neutral Strip as the bonding center—of forcing the creation of a new territory or state, right in the middle of the continent—was a thing that many in the high plains had considered. But not soon. Not in the lifetime of the cattle baron of Mobeetie, Peter Lewellyn Dawes.

Still, a lot of people had been hurt in the stopping of Double D. Some wouldn't forget. Up in the Nations, they said nearly four thousand square miles of range had been blackened by that fire. Mostly in No Man's Land—the Neutral Strip between Kansas and Texas, where no court had jurisdiction and no law prevailed except the law of the gun—but there had been burn across the Kansas line too, and into the Nations. There were few enough who might know that the fire had been deliberate and not just some act of nature. But there would be some, and some of them would come for him if they could.

Yet what better chance to finish his business with the Double D crowd, than to have them come to him?

He was content with that idea, mostly. Except for one point. If one of those coming for him was Goldie Locke, he might never know it in time. Goldie Locke killed people, for money. He was very good at it. And no one—not even those who hired his services, knew where Goldie Locke was. No one even knew what Goldie Locke looked like. The man might have been a ghost, for all anyone knew . . . except ghosts didn't leave trails of dead people behind them.

"You can't back away from anything, can you, By." Mattie Stillwell had said it, years ago. Not a question, just a statement of fact. "There is a fierceness in you that isn't temper or whim, and I guess it's just part of you, like breathing. I don't understand very much of it, the drive you have to wander, the thing in you that makes you strike out when you see a wrong. I can't begin to fathom that . . . that awful thoroughness in the settling of scores. I can't understand . . . but I accept it. It is just how you are. Maybe he was like that, too—your father—but I never had the chance to find out. But I love you, By. So I just have to accept how you are."

Mattie accepted him the way he was. Of course she did. A mother accepts her young. But he knew she had always recognized the price he must pay for being as he was. Images played in his mind as he walked . . . images of another pretty face, accepting him also, and trusting him, a face he had kissed, and talked with by candlelight. But Patty Mills must wait. The price of being Byron Stillwell was—always, it seemed—to keep great distances between himself and those he loved. The price of being Byron Stillwell was to be alone . . . to be a drifter.

If people came looking for him, with ready guns and vengeance on their minds, they must find him far away from the ones who mattered to him . . . the innocents who could so easily be caught up in what must follow.

He had turned from the roadway, onto a footpath that angled across a brushy vacant lot. Evening was at hand, the sun only a rim of fire on the western hills, and a cool breeze touching the weedy tops of untended brush.

And there were footsteps behind him. He turned.

At first he didn't recognize the two young men who stopped five paces away, grinning at him while intent eyes studied him. Then he remembered. These were two of the pack that had been with the tough young redhead earlier in the day, when the redhead had stopped to have fun over the cat sitting on the paint's saddle.

"Clothes do make the man," the nearest one said, tauntingly. "You were right, Sharkey. I wouldn't hardly have knowed that this fine-lookin' specimen is the same no-account grubliner that tried to start trouble with Coby today. Sure looks different all duded up, don't he?"

"Aw, I don't know, Sim," Sharkey shrugged. "To me he still looks like the bottom side of a hog waller. But I bet he'd be willin' to make a donation to a good cause, if we explained it to him. How about it, drifter?" The look he turned on Stillwell was pure malevolence, "You still got some of that money you took out of the bank this mornin'?"

Stillwell looked from one to the other, getting their measure. A pair of cocky young toughs, both wearing guns but not wearing that certain look of one who intends to draw. No, if they had sport in mind, it was of a more direct kind than the exchange of bullets. He turned and walked on, not hurrying, just ignoring them.

"Hey!" Sharkey called, surprised and angry. "You deaf or somethin'? We ain't through talkin' to you."

Without changing his pace, he glanced back. "You boys are out a little late, aren't you? Your mamas might get worried."

"Well, by damn," one of them breathed. Then he heard the scurry of their feet, overtaking him, spreading to flank him. He listened to their breathing, to the sound of their boots . . . and turned abruptly, crouching. The nearest one was an arm's length away, closing, one hand reaching and one cocked to throw a punch. Stillwell let the tough double himself over a stiff forearm, then came upright.

39

His left hand closed like a wolf trap on the attacker's left wrist and he twisted, shoving the pinioned arm up behind the kid. In the same instant he drew his .45, brought its heavy barrel down across the kid's right forearm in a crippling blow, then turned the gun and thrust its muzzle into the kid's mouth just as it opened to scream.

"I tried to tell you boys it's dangerous out here after sundown," he drawled. "You, Dribbledrawers! Take out that gun and put it on the ground."

Sharkey stared at him for a second, then did as he was told.

"Now back away from it," Stillwell said.

"Mister, you're gonna be sorry . . ."

"You'll find out what sorry means if you don't back off. *Now!*"

Sharkey backed away, pure hatred in his eyes. Sim was struggling in Stillwell's grasp, moaning and gurgling, his mouth full of cold gunbarrel. Stillwell paused for an instant, then withdrew the Peacemaker, shoved Sim away from him and disarmed him in the same movement. Holding Sim's gun in his left hand, he put his own away, stooped to retrieve Sharkey's, then threw both guns as far as he could, into shadowy brush beyond the vacant lot.

"You boys shouldn't carry such things," he said evenly. "You could hurt yourselves."

Sim was bent over, blubbering and trying to cradle a broken arm. Sharkey sneered at him, then advanced on Stillwell. "I don't need a gun to handle the likes of . . ." He never saw the hard fist that came from knee level to lift him to tiptoes and lay him out on the weedy ground.

"When you get around to it," Stillwell told the blubbering Sim, "you might give some thought to how lucky you boys were this evening. Some folks get mean when youngsters forget to be polite. Now pick up your friend. I know where there's a good doctor." He turned and started on, not looking back.

"I can't pick him up!"

He turned back. "You gonna leave him there like that?"

"You broke my arm, you son of a . . ."

Sim didn't finish it. A fist like an anvil collided with his skull.

Stillwell looked down at the unconscious pair. "You boys are a real problem," he muttered.

It was full dark by the time he delivered both of them to the foot of Doctor Cathcart's stairs.

He left them there, and went on his way.

He entered the hotel's back door quietly, went up the stairs and let himself into the back room. His old hat was still where he had left it. The covered pillows on the bed had not been disturbed.

Setting his new coat and hat aside, he went into the hall in shirtsleeves, and down the stairs. The clerk on duty, dozing at the registration counter, was not the one who had been there earlier. The only other person in the lobby was a dark-coated man lounging at the open front door, looking outward. When Stillwell came down he glanced around. A bright copper shield glinted on his lapel. Stillwell nodded at him and went to the desk.

"I'm Stillwell," he told the clerk. "Have I had any messages?"

The clerk scanned his book, then peered at the beehive key-cabinet behind him. "Looks like one," he said. He handed the folded yellow paper across. It was from Patty Mills, in Liberal, Kansas. So the wire has reached the new town, he thought. It's past Arkalon. The message was brief, and guarded: "Wonderful to hear from you. Glad you're there. Not healthy here now. Guthrie says be careful, By. He says to watch your back, and Texas law. I won't forget about *Scheherazade*. Love, P.M."

He felt the lawman's eyes following him as he went upstairs again. In his room he checked again the things he had left there, then put on his new coat and hat and his gun.

"Shifty-looking law hereabouts," he muttered. He

found a lamp, lifted the mantel, lit the wick and trimmed it down to a soft glow, then replaced the mantel and set it on a spindly-looking table by the wall, near the window. He lifted the cheesecloth curtains and tied them back, out of the way. Then he let himself out the back entrance, making sure no one saw him, and crossed the back lot to the boarding house on the next street.

The landlady was clearing dishes from a table. "Good evening, Mr. Dance," she said. "You missed supper, but there is still some roast beef and part of a loaf of bread. And the coffee is warm. Just help yourself."

He took his sandwich and coffee upstairs, looked in on his rented room, then went out onto the back balcony and settled himself on a wicker settee. Fifty yards away were the windows of the hotel, and he had a clear view of the room he had left. The soft lamplight even showed him the old hat on the dresser top where he had left it.

He hoped that no one in the boarding house was in the habit of whiling away the evenings on this balcony. He didn't know what might happen, but his instincts told him that the badge-toter in the hotel lobby didn't just happen to be there . . . instinct, and the fact that there had been no message from the sheriff two counties over, with questions about the shootings at Mullinsville.

The written statement he had left at Mullinsville was accurate, but he had left out a couple of minor points . . . points that any honest lawman would want to ask about, to complete his report.

How long were the arms of Peter Lewellyn Dawes? It was time for him to begin finding out.

Chapter Four

He almost dozed off, several times. The wounds that still troubled him, the exertions of the day, all of these conspired against him in league with the delicious coolness of the night breeze, the quiet of the nearby neighborhood, even the distant, raucous noise coming from the saloon strip down the street from the hotel. Sleep welled in him and struggled for dominance, and the melancholy wail of whistles in the distant rail yards only added to the struggle.

I could just disappear for a while, he told himself. No problem to do that. Disappear and take life easy and just rest. But then I'd have to start all over again, laying out a trail to see if anybody happens to follow it.

And it has to be done, before I can go back to anyone who matters. Patty knows that. Her telegram as much as said so. She understands . . . like Mattie understands. A man with carnivores on his scent doesn't lead them home to meet the family. He waits them out. Identifies them. Deals with them, one way or another.

Then he can go home. But not before.

Home. The word hung drowsily before him, and it was only a word. What do drifters know about home, he thought, his cheek twitching sardonically. I don't any more have a home to go to than that grubliner cat. Or have any more use for one, either. What does a man do with a home? Sit in a rocking chair on the porch and wait for company to come calling? The twitch became an ironic grin. Sure, Stillwell. Sit in a rocking chair and clean your gun, because if company shows up you'll need it.

Social occasions, he thought. That's exactly what a .45 Colt is for. Social situations. Memorable occasions, one and all.

The thought intrigued him and he toyed with it. At least it was something to keep the drowsiness at bay.

Frederick James Cathcart had barely gotten to sleep when Deputy Marshal Roy Pye banged on his door to wake him up. A bachelor, Cathcart's home was a tiny side room off his office, with an entrance on the same landing as his office door. The banging sounded again, and Pye's voice: "Cathcart? Come on, open up. You got customers out here!"

He slipped his feet into a pair of old shoes and fumbled for a lamp, grumbling. He had no liking for Roy Pye. The man was an animal, a strutting bully who enjoyed hurting people. No better than a common criminal, despite the badge he wore. Cathcart despised the man, and had never hesitated to tell him so . . . or to file periodic complaints about him with city and county officials. As a doctor, he had seen examples of how Roy Pye dealt with those unfortunate enough to find themselves in his custody. The man was a throwback to dark old days when it was hard to tell a lawman from an outlaw in Texas. The man almost certainly lined his pockets with petty bribes and connived with gamblers and their ilk. Cathcart had a deep suspicion as well that some of the killings Pye had done—Cathcart knew of four, personally—may have been pure assassinations for pay, rather than the keeping of the peace.

With his lamp lighted, Cathcart opened his door. "Do you know what time it is? What do you want?"

Pye sneered at him, then stepped back and pointed. Cathcart lifted his lamp. On the stairs were two sprawled figures, one near the top, the second a few steps down. One was rocking back and forth, groaning. The other just lay there. Cathcart went to them for a better look, recognizing them vaguely . . . two of the young hardcases who had taken to hanging out at the Steel Rail the past few months. Young toughs who made a lot of noise but always seemed to stop just short of crossing the line between hard looks and jail cells.

Both were injured. One had a badly swollen, oddly distorted arm. Fractured right tibia, he decided. Some complaint in the left shoulder, as well, but it seemed to be only a sprain. As though the shoulder had been almost dislocated but not quite. The second gave all indications of a mandibular fracture, possibly multiple. Probable concussion, as well, though his respiration and the dilation of his pupils when lamplight touched his eyes indicated only minor implications. A livid bruise colored his chin, and Cathcart frowned. Whoever had hit this one either had intended to kill him . . . or was an expert in stopping just short of it.

He looked up at the leering Pye. "Did you do this? You ought to be run out of . . ."

Pye glared at him. "I didn't lay a hand on these jaspers, you damned old fart. I found them here. Noticed them earlier, about dark, down at the foot of the stairs, but I figured they was just sleepin' off a load. Then I got busy and didn't come back by here until just now. You'll have to argue with them about your fee. No money on either one of 'em."

Of course not, Cathcart thought. If there ever was any, it's in your pocket by now. He kept the notion to himself and stood. "Well, help me get them into the office so I can have a look at them."

"Not my problem, Doc." Pye started down the stairs, stepping over one figure and around the next. "I done all I

45

need to. It's your concern now." He paused then and turned, squinting against the lamplight. "By the way, did you have any new patients the past day or two?"

"I have patients every day."

"The one I'm lookin' for is a big jasper, a six-footer about thirty years old. Word is he might have some bullet creases, maybe some burns like from a fire. Goes by the name of Stillwell. You seen him?"

Cathcart stiffened. "My patients' ailments are their own business, Pye. Not yours. And I don't intend to waste my time helping you find strangers."

"Oh, I don't need help findin' him," the deputy grinned. "I know where he is. He's stayin' at the hotel. I'd just like to know what kind of shape he's in before I . . . you still haven't said if you've seen him."

"I have seen no one who used that name," Cathcart snapped.

Pye's grin became a sneer. "No, I don't guess you have," he said. He went on down the stairs and turned toward the "parlor" strip. Cathcart watched him go, then set his lamp on the rail and went to work, half-dragging the injured hardcases into his office. Both wore belt holsters, he noticed, but neither had a gun.

"Probably decided to hooraw the wrong people," he muttered. "Serves you right, both of you." Some intuition suggested to him who that "wrong people" might have been, and he shivered as though a chill breeze had touched him. He had seen it before, in another town . . . the marks of sure, methodical reciprocation on an injured man who had made the mistake of messing with Byron Stillwell.

Your son is a mirror image of you, Mattie, he thought bleakly. So help me, I believe By is an honest man, but I'll never understand how an angel like you ever produced a . . . a curly wolf like your son.

A thorough examination, a brace and splint and a wrap to keep the broken jaw closed, then he dosed them with

46

laudanum, bedded them on cots and hurried into his own room to dress. A few minutes later he crept down the stairway, looked up and down the dark street, and hurried eastward.

Scuffing footsteps brought him fully awake and he sat motionless, uncertain of what he had heard. Then the spring on the balcony door creaked, and someone peered out into the night, a dark figure silhouetted by dim lamplight.

"Hello?" A woman's voice. "Is someone out here?"

He relaxed. "It's only me, Mrs. Clay. Byron Dance."

She turned toward him, holding up the lamp. She was wrapped in a nondescript night dress with a drawstring robe, and had a cap on her head. "Mr. Dance? My goodness, I didn't know anyone was awake. Are you all right?"

"Just fine, Mrs. Clay." He yawned. "I was enjoying the night air. I suppose I dozed off. Hope I didn't startle you."

"Oh, no. I just got up to get my husband's medicine from the cabinet—he complains of chest pains and fever sometimes, and a bit of quinine helps him—then I noticed a shadow out here. It is quite late, so . . ."

"Yes, Ma'am. I'm sorry I worried you. Good night."

"Ah . . . good night, Mr. Dance. By the way, you *did* say you are from Mobeetie, didn't you?"

"Yes, Ma'am. That's what I said. Why?"

"Oh, nothing. Just a coincidence. Mobeetie is quite a distance from here, yet just today I've encountered its name twice. First when you arrived, and then shortly after when Mr. Pye—he's the deputy town marshal, you know—received a telegraph message from there. It *is* quite a coincidence, isn't it?"

"It certainly is. But I don't believe I know Mr. Pye. Does he room here?"

"No. He has a room with the Cutshalls next door. But

47

there was no one there just then, so I held his messages for him until he came by."

"I see. I suppose he received it, then."

"Oh, yes. I gave it to him myself. I assume he was expecting it, because he showed up shortly after it arrived. He seemed very cross, that the telegraph had sent it over here instead of holding it for him . . . but then," she sighed and shrugged, "Mr. Pye is not always, ah . . . pleasant. I suppose a man like that is necessary, though. For the good of the town."

"It takes all kinds," Stillwell agreed. Movement in the distance caught his eye. Across the back lots, someone was approaching the back entrance of the hotel. "Mobeetie," he said again. "Yes, that is quite a coincidence, Mrs. Clay. I don't think I know anyone around Mobeetie named Pye, but I'm away quite a bit, on business."

"Oh, I don't think it was from family. I've heard that Mr. Pye has no family . . . or mentions none. This was from someone named Dawes . . . was that it? Yes. A Mr. Dawes. Of course, anyone can read that on the envelope. I don't make a habit of inquiring into people's private affairs."

"Of course not." Across the back lots light shone for a moment as the hotel's service door was opened and closed. "Well, good night again, Mrs. Clay. I hope Mr. Clay feels better soon."

"Yes. I do, too. Good night, Mr. Dance. Please latch the door when you come in."

"I will. Good night, Mrs. Clay."

Though the woman couldn't realize it, never once through the conversation had his eyes strayed from the shadowy rear of the hotel building, less than a hundred yards away. And still they fixed there, intently. After the first dull gleam of the service door opening and closing, it had happened again. A second dark figure had followed the first inside.

It might mean anything . . . or nothing. He could only

48

guess at the routines of the hotel and its guests. But it was the sort of thing he had watched for, and now his eyes held on the lighted window, beyond which an old hat rested on a bureau top. And his eyes were no longer sleepy. They were slitted with speculation.

It had always been likely that Peter Lewellyn Dawes—if he lived—would be searching for him. Now there was no question of it. He had laid a plain trail, and men were following it—men in the employ of Dawes. And in Texas, Dawes pulled a lot of strings. Peter Lewellyn Dawes was Double D, and Double D was an empire to itself.

In the lighted room across the back lots, something was happening. The hall door remained closed, but something white appeared beneath it. A piece of paper, he guessed, pushed through from the hallway beyond. A message? He waited, watching.

Moments passed, and the ground-level service door opened again. This time he recognized the man there, and frowned. Stay out of it, Doc, he thought. This is my game, not yours. You could get hurt.

In the lighted window on the second floor, there was movement. The door opened a crack, then was flung full open and a dark-clad man was in the room, training a pistol at the pillow-stuffed bed. Stillwell nodded, sadly. The same badge-toter he had seen earlier in the hotel lobby, the man with the copper shield. And now he knew a name. Pye. Deputy Marshal Pye.

The man in the lighted room stepped to the bed and threw the cover back, then swung around, taking in the rest of the room at a glance. His gun still in hand, he crouched to pick up the little piece of paper by the door, glanced at it, then stepped to the window and threw open the sash. Doc Cathcart was still there, just walking away, and Stillwell saw him turn at the sound. And saw Pye spot him from the window. The deputy's gun came up and Stillwell surged to his feet, shouting, "Doc! Look out!"

The words were lost in the harsh, flat crack of Pye's revolver. A tongue of flame stabbed out, and Cathcart was flung backward to sprawl unmoving in the patch of dim light from the lamp in the window. Stillwell's gun was in his hand, but Pye was no longer there in the distant room. Stillwell caught a glimpse of him, scurrying into the hall beyond. Ignoring the balcony door, he swung over the balustrade and dropped, doubling over, flexing his knees to absorb the impact of the drop. He hit ground and went to one knee, then was up and running. In the hotel, another window or two showed light, and there were voices here and there—curious people, awakened or startled by the gunshot.

Before Byron reached the alleyway, there were already people in the hotel's back lot, one or two bending over the sprawled figure on the ground, a few others gawking around, others arriving. He paused in shadows, watching and listening.

"This man's dead," someone said.

"Who is he? Can you . . . ?"

"I know him. He's that doctor, the one that has an office over on . . ."

"What happened?"

"He's shot. Dead center. Somebody shot him dead."

"Stand back! Clear away!" The deputy marshal was there then, coming from the far street in front of the hotel. "That man . . . is he dead?"

"Sure is," someone said. "What happened."

"I saw the whole thing," Pye said. "I was just over at Moore's store, checkin' the locks, and this fella came runnin' out of the back door of the hotel. Then somebody shot him, from that open window right up there. Cold-blooded murder, looked like to me. But I was too far away to catch the shooter, an' there's nobody up there now. I looked."

In shadows beside the alley, Byron Stillwell sighed. So this was how the deck was to be stacked, then. Some innocent bystander had to die, so that a corrupt lawman could trade favors with Peter Lewellyn Dawes.

Why did it have to be you, Doc? The hard realization clawed at him. By trying to deliver a warning—certainly it was a warning of some kind—Frederick James Cathcart had become that innocent bystander. A man who owed him nothing, who probably didn't even like him and certainly could never have approved of him. A man whose only attachment to him was that it had been his misfortune to fall in love with the singer, Mattie Stillwell.

I came to this town, Doc, because I can't let death trail me to anyone who matters. Yet I came here and death followed me . . . and found you. You deserved better, Doc. He eased farther into the night, then turned and hurried away. Behind, he could still hear the voices, but he didn't need them. He knew how the cards would be played: Whose room is that? Name of Byron Stillwell. Drifter or something. Keeps to himself, seems like. Only came here yesterday. Well, we'll need warrants. Doc was a good man. We'll find his murderer.

They had his scent now, those who followed him. They had him at the disadvantage. Wanted by the law. And nobody would care if he was never brought back alive.

At the silent hostelry he retrieved the paint and his saddle and gear, leaving a few dollars behind to cover the hostler's fee and the cost of the new iron shoes on the horse's hooves. He led the animal along dark streets to a secluded alley near the railyard, then made his way back into the dark town. He climbed to the balcony of the Clays' house, went inside—latching the door behind him—and picked up the belongings he wanted from the room he had never slept in, then left a fair payment behind and crept downstairs and out the guest door.

Here and there, at various distances and intervals, he heard the voices of searchers—men looking for him.

It was very late and the town was virtually silent again, when Stillwell finally found what he had waited for. Roy

51

Pye, alone, still searching the town after most others had given up. He needs to find me, Stillwell thought. He didn't plan what happened. It was just an opportunity and he took it, and now he needs to find me before anyone else does. He needs my dead body to complete his little scheme.

For a moment he almost felt sympathy for the deputy. The man had acted on whim, and was having to make up a plan as he went along . . . and he lacked the intelligence to do it right.

"I'd enjoy having you answer some questions for me, killer," he muttered. "You probably don't have any information that I really need, but I'd enjoy getting it out of you, anyway."

Along dark streets he stalked the man, just watching and waiting. At one turn he thought he had lost him, then saw him again at a distance, a shadow among shadows, going toward the rail yards. Just a shadow of movement, touched by dim reflections from yard lamps, and the glow of lanterns on a horse-drawn carriage standing beside a loading platform. There was no one in the carriage.

He watched, aware that it would soon be morning. Little time remained for blind stalking. There would be nothing more to be learned. He detoured a block, retrieved the paint, saddled it and packed his gear, then judged the time and led the horse along silent streets toward the railroad yards.

He hated to leave matters like this, hated to have to turn tail and run with nothing resolved—nothing concrete to tell him who or what else was out there, waiting. But time was running out. One swing through the yards . . .

It was only luck that let him find the deputy before someone else did. Luck and the swinging lamps of a hand of rail cars being switched for reassembly.

He did find him, though, and in pre-morning gloom he stood over what was left of Roy Pye.

"You never told me anything," he muttered. "Except

maybe you did. Maybe what you told me is that you should have left well enough alone and not tried to be smart. You should have settled for a little fee, deputy. Somebody else is out to collect the big money, and all you wound up doing was getting in the way."

Pale sky silhouetted the eastern hills when Stillwell strode into the freight shed beside the mainline dock of the Midland Junction Railway Company, pausing for a moment to look to the east where lanterns were converging upon a track juncture in the switching yards. Steam whistles and bells were making a racket over there, and men were running.

"I have a package to ship," Stillwell told a sleepy clerk.

"Our shipping office is downtown," the man pointed.

"I know, but it won't be open for hours. Can't I consign this here? I'll pay for it." The package he held out was small, a thin four-by-six inch parcel wrapped with butcher paper and string, with a name and address printed on it.

The man took it and shrugged. "To Mobeetie? I guess I can put it aboard the seven-ten. Two dollars will cover it."

Stillwell handed over the money. "What's all the fuss out there in the switch yard? Looks like people all over the place."

"Some damn fool got himself killed," the clerk shrugged. "Charlie said it looked like he'd gone to sleep under a span of freight cars. Five cars and a switch engine ran over him. Not enough left to recognize, Charlie said."

"That's terrible."

"Some drunk, probably. It happens."

"Well, thanks." Stillwell walked out into the darkness, glancing back to see his package disappear into a stack waiting to be loaded aboard an early westbound.

In the package was a piece of copper that once had been a lawman's shield. Now it was a flattened, distorted bit of metal, thin as a hatbrim and as wide as a rail, pounded down by iron wheels. With it was a brief note. "You paid for this badge," it said. "It's right that you should have it."

The addressee was Peter Lewellyn Dawes, at Mobeetie.

He was a mile or more west of Ennis, the paint rested and covering ground, when something moved at his elbow. He jerked and twisted away, looking down. Then he grinned. "So it's you," he said. "Where were you, sleeping in the saddlebag?"

At the approach of his hand, the cat's ears went back and it bared sharp teeth in a hiss.

"All right," he shrugged. "I feel a little that way, myself, sometimes."

He turned away and the cat sprawled comfortably across the saddle-skirt behind the cantle. Within moments it was asleep.

Chapter Five

Jude Meece, Tandy O'Neill and Ollie Chadwick were waiting at the water tank when Coby Shanks rode his favorite steeldust past Fletcher's Chutes and turned onto the county seat road. He hauled up facing them, and turned, looking back toward town. "Where's Sharkey and Sim?"

"Dunno," Jude said. "Nobody's seen them since yesterday."

"Weren't they plannin' to go with us?"

"I thought so," Ollie shrugged. "I told 'em we was goin' for a ride this mornin'."

"Did you tell both of 'em? That damn Sim can't remember anything from one day to the next."

"I told 'em both. Ran into 'em headin' uptown the past evenin'. Sharkey said they were goin' after some beer money, but they never showed up at the Steel Rail."

Shanks frowned, shading his eyes against the morning sun as he looked back toward town. For a year or more he had run with this bunch. More to the point, they ran with him. He had been the leader since the day Winch Bodine pushed him too far . . . and then went for his gun. Not since that day, when Winch Bodine lay face down in the dust outside Ignacio's Cantina at San Antonio, had any of them disputed Coby's right to lead. Sometimes he felt as though Jude Meece was just waiting for the right moment, but Jude didn't have the gumption to face him and challenge, any more than Sharkey did. The rest . . . well, they just went along. At nineteen years of age, Coby Shanks was undisputed leader of his bunch. And one of the rules he set down was that when the bunch went on a job, everybody went.

"Maybe somethin' happened to them," Tandy O'Neill offered. "*Something's* been goin' on in that town. I heard there was a shootin'.'"

"Yeah, last night," Coby said. "Somebody shot a doctor. But that's got nothing to do with us."

"Maybe they pulled out on their own," Jude suggested. "Ol' Sharkey, he ain't been too happy layin' around that damn town, you know. No more than I have."

"Maybe they did," Coby turned to fix Jude with eyes that bored into him, a trick Coby had learned early—lay the hardeye on a man, chances are he'll just fold up and turn away. "Did you tell them where we're goin', Jude?"

Jude tried to return the gaze, then blinked and looked away. "I didn't tell anybody, except you, Coby." He glanced at the other two. "You boys can back me on that. I didn't say where we're goin', did I?"

"Not to me," Ollie shrugged. "I still don't know."

Tandy shrugged. "Me, too. I reckon we could go back an' look for 'em."

Coby made his decision. "We'll go on. If those hooraws can't show up, that's their lookout. But they're no part of this now." He looked from one to another. "Y'all understand? Long as I'm callin' the shots, any man that isn't in is out."

They all nodded. "Where *are* we goin', anyway?" Tandy O'Neill asked.

Jude Meece grinned at him. "Waxahachie," he said.

"Not Waxahachie," Coby said flatly. "We're goin' over to Tightwad." He nudged the steeldust and took the lead, westward.

* * *

Jack Raney was, or so the betting went, the last town marshal the city of Ennis would have. He knew it, and most everybody else in town did, too. The town was twenty years old, solid and settled . . . and growing. And along with growth came cultural progress. The decision had been made months ago that, come next election day, the city of Ennis would decide whether to eliminate the elective office of city marshal. It was generally expected that the proposition would pass easily. In place of a marshal, the city fathers decreed, a chief of police would be employed, and a proper police force established, answerable directly to the mayor.

Progress, most agreed. A new century was just around the corner . . . less than eight years away. Modern times called for modern ways. It was time, the civic thinkers said, for Ennis to shake off the dust of the past — old ideas, old appearances, old ways. Words like *town marshal* tended to remind folks of earlier times . . . times that too often had been lawless and violent. Times older than the town itself, times that had the musty scent of gunsmoke about them. Ennis was no brawling cowtown. With nearly 1,600 people in residence, Ennis was a city to be reckoned with, so said the Boosters' Club.

There was even thought of persuading some of the immigrant families who had come to build the rails, those whose tenements and shacks contrasted painfully with the bright new houses of merchants and planters, to consider finding their futures in other places. Real estate values and business investments were, it was felt, better served by immaculate streets and painted houses than by reminders of other times and other standards.

And, of course, once certain elements were no longer part of the civic scene, then areas like Hays Street and the Parlor Strip would just fade away.

With progress and prosperity at hand, there would be no further need for anachronisms like Jack Raney . . . and certainly not for such seedy types as the gunhappy deputy marshal, Roy Pye.

For his part, Jack Raney hoped they were right on all counts. But sometimes he wondered whether the fine cloak of civilization went any deeper than the bright paint on the big new houses over on the west side.

This was one of those times. He sighed and rubbed a callused hand through thinning silvery hair as he looked at the mess in the switch yard. It had been a bad night in Ennis. Doc Cathcart was dead, and there were more questions than answers. And now in the light of day he was called on to identify another dead man.

"It's Roy," he nodded. "That's his boot, and the ring on that hand . . ." he shuddered, pointing at a hand that wasn't attached to anything, "that's the ring he bought . . . *said* he bought . . . from Lefty Miller. And that's his gun. I doubt there's another one like it in the county. Bulldog .41."

"Any idea what he was doin' out here?" someone asked.

Raney glanced around. It was Homer Sillsbee, publisher of the *Herald-Dispatch*. Raney shook his head. "I don't know why he was here. Town ordinance says the deputy marshal has his own authority. He didn't tell me what he was doing."

"I heard he was planning to organize a search for that drifter," Sillsbee said. "The one who killed Doctor Cathcart."

Raney sighed again, then said softly, "Be careful about that, Homer. We don't know just yet who killed the doctor."

"Is there a doubt?" Sillsbee's eyes narrowed. "Didn't Roy say he saw the whole thing?"

"He may have," Raney nodded. "But do you see an eyewitness here? All I see is bloody meat."

"You aren't sure, then? What other evidence is there to consider?"

"When I know that, you'll know, too, Homer. I expect there'll be more to go on by the end of the day."

It was all he was going to say, right then. Maybe they were right. Maybe a younger man should take over the task of peacekeeping in this town. And maybe he should wear a uniform with sewn lanyard loops and a bill cap, like the lawmen did now in places like Dallas and Wichita Falls, and maybe he should have the title of chief of police and have a few other young bucks dressed just like him to salute him and patrol the streets. Maybe it *was* time for progress to take place.

But no uniform could tell a man what make and caliber of gun had fired the shot that woke him up three blocks away. Only experience could give a man the sure ear to tell the difference between the thump of a Colt .45 Peacemaker—which was what four witnesses so far had said the drifter carried—and the hard slap of a Bulldog .41.

And the sound that had interrupted the sleep of Marshal Jack Raney in the wee hours of that morning *was* the sound of a Bulldog .41.

He had sent for Doctor Rosenthal, to have a look at Frederick James Cathcart's body. He would know more, soon. Then he would have a chat with the high sheriff over at Waxahachie, and probably with the district judge. There were some interesting things in the private file which Raney and Sheriff Matt Kingman had collected on Roy Pye.

They had held off from bracing Pye about his dealings, though it had galled Raney to wait. Kingman had a notion that more and bigger snakes might turn up, if they dug further.

But Pye was gone now. Probably it was time to let in some light. Ennis was a decent town, for all the follow-the-leader foolishness of its civic leaders. Even the determination to put the old warhorse out to pasture was not without kindness. They were through with him and all he meant, but they *had* passed the hat for a retirement fund.

Maybe it's the least I can do, he thought. Clean house a bit. Give the shiny new police department a clean start, and maybe they won't get hurt too bad before they learn how towns *really* work.

It occurred to him that he should ask Rosenthal to look at what was left of Roy Pye, too. Investigations should be thorough.

From Ennis to Waxahachie was almost twenty miles, a journey of rolling hills and cotton fields, a pastoral land where the only traces of a wilder past were the trail herds that still came up from the south—up the Chisholm Trail heading for Fort Worth and the big stockyards.

To some, the most exciting thing that had happened in recent years in Ellis County was the christening of the ornate new courthouse at Waxahachie. It was how the county liked to see itself, and thus how it was seen . . . if one didn't look too deeply. Prosperous, pleasant and free of all the ills of humanity. Sheriff Matt Kingman understood that, but he had no personal illusions, either about his county or about the people in it.

Morning sun was a handspan above the hills ahead when he turned in his saddle to look back to the west, the way he had come. The two young deputies following him also looked back. They had come half a mile from the headquarters of Half Moon Cross, and were alone.

He waved the deputies forward and gazed at them thoughtfully, first one and then the other. Two of a kind, he thought. Jaybirds. Both were young and green, and he had taken them along on this social call to have a look at how they worked in the field. Buck Mabry was a chunky, grinning kid barely past his teens. John Henry Taylor was the nephew of a county commissioner.

Bright-eyed and bushy-tailed, both of them. Likable kids, who still had a lot to learn about their jobs and—he was sure—about life itself.

Probational deputies . . . and it was up to Matt Kingman to make lawmen of them.

They edged their mounts in close alongside and he squinted at them. "Where did you boys get off to back there? Seems to me I told the both of you to just hang close and listen."

"I went up in the haybarn," John Henry said, narrowing his eyes as one who expects approval.

The sheriff gazed at him. "Why?"

"Well, shoot, Sheriff, that's a tough bunch back there. Everybody knows that. I figured if . . . well, if any of them taken a notion to get a drop on you, maybe I could sort of even things up."

"I see." Kingman looked past him, at Mabry. "And you? Where were you?"

Mabry grinned. "I noticed that Injun and the kid weren't around, so I went to look for them."

"Did I ask you to do that?"

"Well, no sir, but I thought you wanted to talk to the whole crew. I mean, with Cap Freeman dead that way, and you investigatin' . . ."

"Did you find them, then?"

"Not a sign."

"Marvelous," Kingman breathed. "Now both of you, hear me good. If I want you to do something, I'll tell you so. If I don't tell you to do something, then don't do it. Do you understand?"

"Yes, sir," they said together. Buck looked suddenly contrite. John Henry looked as though he would think it over.

Kingman held John Henry's gaze. "Just why did you think any of those boys might go for a gun?"

The deputy blinked. "I don't know. It's just . . . well, you bein' the sheriff, and some of that bunch bein' gunslicks . . ."

"Deputy, do you know what *gunslick* means?"

"Oh, sure. Everybody knows that. A gunslick . . ."

"Is a person with skill in the use of a gun," Kingman cut in. "That's all the word means. It doesn't mean anything else. It doesn't mean gunhand, or gunman, or gun-slinger, or . . ."

"Gunfighter?" Buck Mabry suggested, helpfully. "Like that fellow you got the wire from the sheriff at Proctor County about? That Stillwell jasper?"

"How come you to know about that wire, Deputy?"

"I read it. Wasn't I supposed to? It was on the desk."

"On *my* desk. But all right, yes. I know about Byron Stillwell. And yes, he is a gunfighter. He also happens to be very slick with a gun, so he's a gunslick. But that doesn't mean . . ."

"Are we gonna go over to Ennis and get him?"

"For what?"

"Well . . . for bein' a gunfighter, I guess. That wire said he killed three men at Mullinsville."

The sheriff breathed deeply, shaking his head. "Tell me somethin', Buck. Say you were riding along here just minding your own business and some jaybird popped out of that brush over yonder and commenced to shoot at you. What would you do?"

Mabry shrugged, grinning. "Why, I guess I'd shoot back."

"You'd shoot back. Do you know what that answer makes you, Deputy?"

"What?"

"A gunfighter. Now hush up when I'm talking!"

"Yes, sir."

John Henry frowned, trying to follow all that had been said. He asked, "Are you mad at us about something, Sheriff?"

Kingman took a while to answer. Finally he sighed and shook his head. "No. I reckon you'll learn, all right. It just seems like you both have a ways to go."

"Yes, sir."

"In the first place," Kingman stretched upright, shading his eyes. Waxahachie was in sight ahead. "In the first place, we didn't go out to Half Moon Cross to *investigate* anything. I already know how Cap Freeman died, and it was an accident. In the second place, just because that bunch out there has a reputation for being tough, that doesn't mean they're bad. Cap Freeman wouldn't have kept an outlaw on the place."

"Why did we go, then?"

"Because they'll all be in for the funeral and I don't want any trouble. If you jaybirds had stayed around to listen, you'd know what I told 'em. And in the third place, about Byron Stillwell . . . if he's wanted for anything, I don't know about it, so therefore where he goes is his business and not mine, or yours, either, unless . . ."

Kingman's voice trailed off. He rubbed a hard hand across a stubbled chin, frowning.

"Then how come you're frettin' about him, Sheriff?" Buck wondered.

"Because I know him. Know *about* him, anyhow. From other lawmen. Byron Stillwell's got a reputation for trouble. They say it follows him around just like his shadow does."

Mabry looked back the way they had come, and pointed. Half a mile back, riders were coming along the road, a line of horsemen following behind them. A dozen or more—too far away to get a count, but Kingman knew they would all be there, heading for town. The crew of Half Moon Cross, on their way to Grace Cemetery to pay their final respects to Cap Freeman.

Chapter Six

Stillwell's shadow rode ahead of him as he topped the rise called Gingerbread Hill, just across the "east shunt" cow-trail from the city of Waxahachie. Morning sun was warm on his shoulders. The road here became a wide boulevard lined on both sides with saloons, dance halls, gaming places and various other establishments catering to the cravings of the male citizenry of three counties, as well as the drovers who pushed the big herds northward along the Chisholm Trail. Gingerbread Hill was almost legendary among the more opulent of Texas "recreational" enterprises — a double row of pleasure palaces decorated in the gaudiest of design and the brightest colors of paint available.

The two largest buildings on the street faced each other across its width, each flanked by open-doored taverns. Somewhere a piano tinkled lazily. Women in shifts and open robes peered from several upstairs windows, some of them waving at him as he passed. At this quiet hour on a weekday morning, he was the only rider on the street in this, the section of Waxahachie that many citizens pretended did not exist. Gingerbread Hill, it was said, was an embarrassment to some elements of the county seat of Ellis County.

Byron grinned at the waving women, and touched his hatbrim.

"Oh, look!" one shouted. "He has a cat! Lookee there, ridin' up behind him proud as you please!"

Other voices joined in: "My, ain't that just the cutest *thing?*" "Here, kitty-kitty-kitty!" "Stop off, Mister, I'll tend to you an' your kitty-cat both!"

And then a familiar voice, slicing through the rest, "By? My Lord, is that you, By Stillwell?"

He turned and reined in. Just above, a gaudy sign proclaimed "Cotillion Club." Beside it, a shapely bare leg was thrust from a window, followed by piled strawberry blonde hair, blue-robed shoulders and another enticing leg. She sat on the windowsill and arched a quizzical brow at him. "It *is* you! But you look older or something. How are you, By?"

He pulled off his hat and grinned at her. "Can't say the same for you, Daisy. You haven't changed a minute's worth. What are you doing here?"

"Same thing I was doin' up at Leadville the last time I saw you. Makin' a livin' the best way I know how. Only the climate here is better. Land, By, you *are* a sight! How long's it been? Two-three years?"

"More like five, Daisy. Time flies."

"Well, don't just sit there grinnin'," she said, sliding her bottom outward on the sill. The movement exposed even more of a graceful set of long legs. "Sidle up here and say howdy."

He nudged the paint forward onto the narrow boardwalk and stood in his stirrups, reaching upward. The girl slid out of the window, stepped a bare foot into his raised hand, lowered herself to his shoulders and then into his lap. Warm arms went around him and she kissed him lingeringly, full on the mouth. She smelled like fine perfume, freshly applied.

"You didn't have this cookie-duster last time I saw you," she said, holding his face in both hands while she looked him over. "I kind of like it, though. Where did you go from Leadville, By? I didn't know if you were alive or dead, 'til I heard . . ." Abruptly, she stopped and grinned. "Listen to me run on! By, I never did really thank you. About Leadville, I mean."

"Long ago and forgotten, Daisy," he said quietly. "Not worth remembering."

"But you saved my life, By. That Slick would have killed me. He'd already killed my best friend."

"It wasn't anything, Daisy. Forget it. Anyway, I heard Slick turned up dead right after all that. Somebody back-shot him, they said."

"With a heavy rifle, yeah. Couldn't have happened to a more deserving skunk." Her lustrous eyes glittered coldly, at momentary memories.

"How about you now?" he asked. "You haven't got any new claims on you, have you?"

"After Slick? Not a chance. I'm a free agent, By. See this house here? Cotillion Club. I own it. And *nobody* owns me. Not ever again." She wriggled suggestively and hugged him. " 'Course, I'd be willing to consider . . ."

He shook his head, smiling gently. "Best to know when you're well off, Daisy. You don't want any part of my life."

"You might be surprised." She leaned around him to peer at the young, yellow tabby preening itself on his saddleskirt. "Lot of things can change in five years, you know. Who's your partner?"

"He isn't mine," Stillwell shrugged. "Just a grubliner from upcountry. I gave him a feed, so then I had to give him a ride, too."

"What's his name?"

"Don't know that he has one. He doesn't say much. But I wouldn't . . ." He glanced around. "Be damned," he breathed. Daisy was stroking the cat, rubbing its ears and chucking it under the chin. It slitted its eyes, its nose and tail twitching. It was flattened in an odd, defensive crouch, its eyes watching her every move. But it held still for the petting.

Daisy hugged him again, then put her bare foot atop his booted one and climbed down. "Had your breakfast? Either one of you? I've got a cook here that can burn bacon with the best of 'em."

"Best offer I've had this morning." He swung down, barely hearing her voice behind him.

"No, it isn't," she breathed. "But I guess you'll never know that." Then, more loudly, "Come on inside, By. Tables yonder by the back window. I'll get some clothes on and be down in a minute."

She disappeared through the open front door. He led the paint to a hitchpost beside a trough, and loose-reined it. The cat gazed at him, slant-eyed and distrustful, though its odd posture of moments before was no longer apparent.

"Well," he told it, "you heard the lady. Let's eat."

He went inside, the cat padding along beside him. Critter knows about riding the grubline, he thought. Never miss a chance for a handout.

It was a big, ornate room—tapestries hanging here and there on walls heavily draped in red velvet, a three-tier crystal chandelier glistening above a waxed hardwood bar, freshly-mopped wood floors—a place where plenty of cash could change hands in an evening. A man with a wool vest paused at the door as he entered, frowned at him, then left behind him. No one else was in sight except a pair of swampers, a big jasper who might be a night bouncer, and a sleepy bartender.

The bouncer was gaudily-dressed and had a face like a gravel road, ruts and all. He looked vaguely familiar, but only vaguely.

Beyond the bar a curving staircase with carpeted risers led to a lacquer-railed landing that went around three sides of the building. He counted fourteen numbered panel doors leading to rooms beyond.

"First time I ever . . . uh . . . seen a man bring a cat to a cathouse," a gravel voice said.

The speaker was the bouncer, leaning against the bar. A big man, face lumpy with knuckle tracks, squinty eyes below a brow of scar tissue, and a nose that had been flattened too many times.

Stillwell glanced at him and started past, aiming for the rear wall where little tables and chairs were set in front of a row of sash windows. A large hand gripped his arm. "I'm talkin' to you," the man said.

Stillwell half-turned, a quick, almost casual-seeming move, then stepped past the man and pivoted. Suddenly the man found himself standing on tiptoes, his right arm caught in an iron grip while a hard hand pressed his fingers back against straining joints.

"I don't like to have my arm grabbed, Mister," Stillwell explained, quietly. "It's poor manners, you know."

The man struggled, but couldn't get out of the grip. "Let loose!" he breathed through clenched teeth.

"Whatever you say." Stillwell released him and backed away a step. "Just don't grab folks that way. Some of us are touchy."

"Yeah." The man glared at him, rubbing his sore hand. "I'd say you are, all right. You could have just . . . uh . . . answered me, you know."

"You didn't ask me anything." Stillwell turned away and went on back to the window tables. By instinct he chose the end one, and selected a chair where he could see both the room and the window, and have a wall at his back. He turned the chair and sat astraddle of it, looking up at the big man, who had followed him.

The man stayed a few steps away, still rubbing his right hand. "Miss . . . uh, Miss Daisy, she called you By Stillwell," he said.

Stillwell nodded. "I didn't hear anybody call you anything."

"I'm Taffy. I look after things around here, for Miss Daisy."

"Sounds like a high callin'." By peered at him.

"Do I know you from someplace?"

"You ought to." Taffy glared at him. "I spent . . . uh . . . time at Folsom because of you."

Stillwell studied him, then smiled. "Taffy! Sure, Taffy Bates. You used to work for Chuey Camargo. I remember."

"You *should* remember. You busted me up."

"I busted Chuey Camargo," Stillwell corrected. "You were just in the wrong place at the wrong time, Taffy. And on the wrong side. Things like that happen." He fixed Bates with a cold gaze. "You feel like you have a score to settle with me?"

The man's glare wavered. "I just . . . uh . . . I never knew why . . . uh . . . why you did that to Chuey an' them. You weren't law, were you?"

"I did it because it needed doing. Camargo wasn't a nice person, Taffy. He hurt a lot of decent folks. One of them was a friend of mine."

"But that . . . uh . . . what you did — th' blastin' powder stunt!" Taffy's battered face seemed more puzzled now than angry. "You killed sixteen men, down in that canyon. I know. I heard about it."

"I killed one Chuey Camargo," Stillwell said, quietly. "The rest killed themselves by being with him. It was their choice, Taffy. Like it was yours to work for him. Do business with skunks, you wind up stinking."

The big man sighed and lowered his head. "Long time ago, I guess. I don' think about it much any more. But when Miss Daisy . . . uh . . . she said your name . . . then I remembered."

"Best forgotten," Stillwell nodded. "No hard feelings, Taffy?"

"Hard feelings about what?" It was Daisy, clad now in a silvery gown that would have been the envy of any lady in Denver or Philadelphia. She stood just at the foot of the curving stairs. "Do you two know each other?"

"Well, uh . . . yeah," Taffy looked puzzled. "This is

69

Byron Stillwell. I thought I . . . uh . . . told you about him. Didn't I?"

Stillwell stood, removing his hat. "Taffy and I met once, Daisy. A long time ago. About the same time I met you." He grinned. "Daisy, I believe the sight of you could cure a man's ills."

"Thank you, kind sir." She strode to the table, a tall woman, maybe near thirty years but appearing far younger. Her alert, searching eyes and strong, no-nonsense walk only emphasized her beauty.

Taffy backed away another step and gazed at her with undisguised adoration. " 'Morning, uh . . . Miss Daisy. We was just talkin'. Uh, I never knew he was a friend of yours. You never said."

"He certainly is, Taffy." She sat in the chair Byron offered her. "A good friend, from when I was at Leadville."

Taffy's gaze lingered on her a moment more, seeming puzzled, then turned to Byron. "Well, then, I guess he's . . . uh . . . mine, too. Mister, you saw th' fella that left when you . . . uh . . . come in?"

"I saw him."

"He's law, y'know. Town law. Zeke Albert. Ought to watch for him."

"I'm not dodging, Taffy."

"Oh. Well, that's good, 'cause he sure was . . . uh . . . cypherin' your numbers when you rode up." Taffy turned away abruptly and went back to the bar.

"Taffy's a little sweet on me," Daisy explained.

Stillwell grinned at her. "I'd never have guessed it," he said.

Breakfast was platters of bacon, fried eggs, biscuits and peach preserves, with cream. Under the table, the cat had its own platter—a gold-rimmed china plate with meat scraps from the kitchen and its own bowl of cream.

Daisy leaned aside to watch the animal for a moment, smiling. "Where did you pick him up?"

"Place called Mullinsville. I guess he was out

70

of work. How long have you been here, Daisy?"

"Couple of years, I guess. Maybe three. I knocked around a little, then decided I'd had enough of that. Came into some money, and I had an opportunity to visit Waxahachie a while back. I decided to move here, so here I am. Waxahachie's a nice town, and the cattle trail gives me a good, regular profit. And I'm free to . . . well, travel when I feel like it, or do anything I want to do."

He looked appraisingly at the fashionable gown, the exquisite bracelet on her wrist, the fine pearls at her throat. "This place must turn quite a profit."

"Oh, I have some other ventures, too. I told you, I came into some money. But tell me about yourself. I want to know where you've been, what you've been doing, why you're here . . . everything!"

"Not much to tell. I've just been drifting around, doing whatever comes to hand. The reason I'm here is, I'm just passing through."

She looked startled for an instant, then simply disappointed. "You're not staying, then?"

"I don't think so. I'll look around town a little, then head on out."

"Where will you go?"

"I don't know. West, I guess."

"Well, I suppose you just never change, By." She looked across at him with shrewd eyes. "I won't ask any more about what you've been doing. I see the scars . . . even those I can't see. Still getting involved in other people's troubles, I gather."

"Not other people's," he shrugged. "Just my own."

"There's a woman, too, isn't there." It was a statement, not a question.

Her perception brought creases to the corners of his mouth. "Yes, there is."

"Then how come you're not with her?"

"Enemies, Daisy. My enemies, not hers, and I want to keep it that way."

71

"Who is she? Will you tell me about her?"

"No."

She toyed with her food, gazing at him. "Men do hate to tell women anything," she said. "But I guess it's just how you all are." Moments passed, then she asked, "You said you'd look around town before you go. Does that mean you *are* here for a reason, By?"

"Nothing much. Just making a delivery, some loose ends to wrap up. Then I'll drift."

"I hope you'll be careful."

"I'm always careful, Daisy. I'm still alive."

"Sure, you're still alive. So far." The tone of her voice seemed odd . . . almost teasing. But it passed as quickly as it had come. "I know you're careful." She gazed at him intently, as one who has seen wounds—and the shadows of wounds—reflected in the eyes of many men. Little traces of pain etched into the features each time a man was hurt, small signals that became part of the face and never went away. "If you need a doctor while you're here . . ."

The look that passed across his eyes was brief, but it cut her off. It was a chill, far-away look, bleak as winter snow. She had said he looked older . . . this look was older still. "I've seen a doctor, Daisy. I only wish to God I hadn't."

It passed as quickly as it had come, and he said no more about it. The meal passed in light conversation, and a feeling of finality. When he was ready to leave she stopped him for a moment, then stood on tiptoes suddenly and kissed him. An odd, lingering kiss that tasted of finality. As though she were saying a last goodbye to someone she knew she would never see again. She kissed him, then turned and climbed the stairs, not looking back.

Strange, he thought, how trails that cross tend to cross again. Taffy Bates, and Daisy—he realized he didn't even know her last name. Never had known it. Different times

72

and different places, yet people often turned up again. And things changed but somehow didn't change. Daisy had been a prostitute, but he recalled she had wanted to learn a trade. She had mentioned a mail-order course for women, and learning to operate machinery . . . yet here she was. Financially successful, by all appearances, and the owner of a brothel. The ways of the world can be strange, he thought.

And Taffy—likely she had hired him on before she ever left Leadville. Not a bad idea, either. In rough times and rough places, a beautiful woman could use a strong man who was devoted to her. And if he wasn't too bright, maybe that was all for the good.

He half expected the cat to stay. The critter and Daisy had seemed to hit it off, but it sat and watched her go, then followed him outside. When he crossed the narrow boardwalk to take up the paint's hitch, the animal padded along beside him. And when he swung into the saddle, its imperious *mao-o-ow* was a command. He leaned down and let it climb his sleeve to get to its place on the saddle-skirt.

"This free ride isn't going to last much longer," he rasped at it. "You are not my cat. I don't have a cat."

Near the end of the street an aproned saloonkeeper was sweeping his porch. Byron reined toward him and stopped. "You wouldn't happen to know where I can find a Judge Arthur Knox, would you?"

The man glanced up. "Never heard of him, but I guess the place to look for a judge would be at the courthouse. No, wait." He paused, glancing at the high sun. "Lot of people will be at Cap Freeman's funeral today, I imagine. Old rancher, died a couple of days ago. Say a breed bull busted its chute and stomped him. Everybody around here knew him. If I was you, I'd go by the cemetery. It's on the way, and you might save a trip to the courthouse."

73

The man returned to his broom. Stillwell rode westward, toward the main town of Waxahachie a mile or so away.

At the house on Gingerbread Hill, Taffy Bates stood aside as Daisy came down the stairs again. She had changed clothes, and now wore a stylish day dress with suncap and a shawl. Taffy nodded at her, his eyes adoring her. "Sure nice you came out this morning, Miss Daisy. Don't see you here too often any more."

She shrugged and stepped past him. "Have my carriage brought around, will you, Taffy? I have things to do today."

"Yes, ma'am. Sure was nice, though, how you happened to be here when your friend showed up. Otherwise you might have missed him."

"Yes," she said. "That would have been a shame."

Chapter Seven

It was only a mile from Gingerbread Hill to the outskirts of Waxahachie, across the expanse of the cattle trail, and between the trail and the town was a maintained road that ran northward between cotton fields. Beyond the first field on the right was Grace Cemetery, and a crowd was gathering there. Maybe a hundred people, Stillwell estimated as he paused at the turnoff to let a procession pass. The man being buried today was an important man.

Freeman, the man had said. Cap Freeman. Stillwell had never met the rancher, but he knew of the brand. Half Moon Cross was a respected outfit . . . one of the early spreads in the upper Brazos country, and one of the few big spreads to survive the coming of King Cotton to these lands. Most of the cow operations were long since broken up for farming, but Half Moon Cross still shipped beef—high-bred beef fattened on rolling range almost within sight of the Nations Trail where dusty riders from the south pushed scrubland herds northward, heading for Fort Worth and beyond.

A good man had died. A tough, smart old man who had kept a ranch—and plenty of related businesses—alive through changing times. Therefore, an important man. And folks were turning out for the burial.

The procession coming from Waxahachie would increase the cemetery crowd by half. There were a dozen or more carriages, cleaned and shined and draped in black, and the funeral hearse with its glass sides and top-hatted driver, a long dozen riders following close behind. Stillwell knew them at a glance, for what they were. The crew of Half Moon Cross. Tough, weathered men dressed now in whatever finery each owned. A hard-looking crew. And probably a good one.

As the hearse turned onto the northbound road, he removed his hat. Some of the following riders glanced his way, and some of their gazes lingered, measuring him. A stranger, with a look about him they had seen before. A man to be measured and watched. He lowered his eyes, understanding what was in their minds. Understanding, and respecting it. More than once over the years he himself had done the work these men were molded for—and molded by. Cowboys. To some, a derisive word. But not to him.

Beyond them the procession continued—more carriages, a few plain wagons and more riders. Solemnly the line turned northward, toward the cemetery. He scanned faces as they passed, wondering which of the older men among them might be Arthur Knox, if any. He had never met the old judge.

Three riders near the end of the line slowed and paused, looking at him. A man of middle years and a pair of strapping youngsters, all wearing bright badges. He put his hat back on his head and walked the paint toward them, stopping a few yards away. " 'Morning, Sheriff," he said. "I wonder if you could tell me whether Judge Arthur Knox is out here today."

The man studied him for a moment, the searching gaze of a long-time lawman. Finally he asked, "Mind telling me who wants to know?"

"My name is Stillwell," he said. "Byron Stillwell."

The two deputies' eyes widened, and the nearest one's

hand strayed toward his gun. "Easy, Buck," the sheriff said without looking around. Then, to Stillwell, "Yeah, I had a notion you might be. Heard you were in the county. What's your business with the judge?"

"I have something for him," he nodded. "A memento from an old friend. Is he here?"

"He's here. Does he know you?"

"No." He glanced at the nervous deputies. "Something botherin' you fellas?"

The sheriff looked around. "You boys go ahead and escort that procession."

"But, Sheriff . . ." the second began.

"You heard me!"

They went.

"Buttons!" the sheriff muttered. Then he held out his hand. "I'm Matt Kingman. And those two are green as grass. Don't worry about them."

"I don't," he said. He eased the paint closer and shook hands with Ellis County's high law. The sheriff blinked at sight of the cat riding behind him, but made no mention of it. There were other questions on his mind, and Stillwell could see him trying to decide how to approach them. "You said you'd heard I was around," he said. "Mind saying who you heard it from?"

"Sheriff up at Proctor. Been some shooting up there, I understand."

Stillwell nodded. "I'm glad you heard from him. I thought I might, but I didn't. Yes, there are four men dead at Mullinsville . . . well, five, really. Three owlhoots robbed and killed a man, then killed the town constable. They were coming after me next, because I would have been a witness. Three brothers named Folger. They're dead now, too."

"All three?"

"All three. Self defense. They all three fired first, and there were witnesses. I left an affidavit for the sheriff there."

"He said you did. Left out a couple of things, though."

"Yeah. That's why I thought I'd hear from him. When I didn't it worried me."

Kingman sat in silence for a moment, then nodded. "Testing?"

"Being careful. Did you get word from Ennis lately?"

"Should I have?"

He nodded. "There was a murder there last night. A doctor. He was shot and killed by a man named Roy Pye. Deputy town marshal. Pye was all set to make out that I did it, but it was him."

The sheriff's eyes narrowed. "Pye? Do you know him?"

"Not until yesterday."

"Why would he want to pin a murder on you?"

"Roy Pye was on a private payroll, Sheriff. I imagine others are, too. And I have reason to think the man holdin' the purse-strings wants me dead."

"I don't suppose you'll mind having a little visit in my office?"

"I'd have been surprised not to," he grinned. "But would it be all right if I find Arthur Knox first? That's why I came."

Kingman thought it over, then nodded. "I'll go along with you, of course."

Stillwell grinned again. "Want to hold my gun?"

"You aren't under arrest . . . unless there's some reason why you should be. Is there?"

"Sometimes that's hard to tell. But I don't believe there are any warrants out on me."

"There aren't," the sheriff said. "I checked, yesterday."

Arthur Knox was a man of seventy or more years, lean going to frail but with bright, inquisitive eyes in a face that carried the shadows of all that the eyes had seen, all the decisions made and all their consequences.

Sam Dance's friend, Stillwell thought as Sheriff Matt

Kingman introduced him. I wish I could have heard him talk about you, known how he truly felt about what you did for him, instead of just putting it together from the notes and clippings of a dead man.

"Stillwell," the judge said. "I've heard your name, sir. but I don't think we've met."

"We haven't," he said. "But you knew my father, I believe. He was a young lawman at Mobeetie when you were judge there. His name was Samuel Dance."

"Dance?" The bright eyes studied him more closely. "Yes, I remember. You even look something like him, I believe. But as I recall, Sam Dance's son was named David. David Dance. Sam married the Dawes girl. But they had only the one child."

Remarkable memory, Stillwell observed. All of that had been a quarter of a century ago.

"He never knew about me, sir, He and my mother met during the war. I use her name. Stillwell. It was only a year ago that I learned who and where he was."

"And did you find him?"

"I wanted to. At least to see him. But I was too late."

"Sam's dead?" The old man's eyes went sad. "I'm sorry about that. I truly am. He was a good man and a fine lawman. But I'd lost touch with him. How did it happen?"

"He was murdered, sir. By people sent to Kansas by Peter Lewellyn Dawes."

Over at the fresh grave they had hoisted Cap Freeman's coffin from the hearse and set it atop poles laid across the hole. People were moving in around the site, and Matt Kingman said, "They're ready to begin the service, Judge."

"Can we visit later?" Knox asked.

"If you'd like." Stillwell thrust his fingers into a coat pocket and drew out a small package. "I just came to give you this."

The judge received the package and unwrapped it. It

was a simple lawman's badge, inscribed: *Marshal—City of Mobeetie, Texas.*

"It belonged to Sam Dance," Stillwell said. "I think he was proud of it once, then it became a burden. I think you helped him to be proud of it again. I think he'd have wanted you to have it, now he's gone."

Knox gazed at the old badge, turning it in his hand. "I did nothing for him," he said, as though to himself. "It was a matter of law. He enforced it and I administered it. That was all."

"You showed him that he wasn't alone in respecting the law."

The crowd had sorted itself out, assembling around the gravesite. A sun-shade had been erected and chairs set out, enough for the several women in the crowd and some of the older men. One of Kingman's deputies was holding a chair for Knox, and the judge walked away toward the shade, still holding Sam Dance's badge in his hand.

"I heard about that sheriff that was shot down up in Kansas last winter," Kingman said. "Didn't know him, myself, but I hated to hear it. He had a good name. Your father, huh?"

"Yeah."

"Sorry."

One of the young deputies—the wide-shouldered one— appeared at Kingman's side. He pointed. "That Injun is here, Sheriff. And the kid. They just showed up."

Stillwell looked where the deputy was pointing. Near the gravesite, the Half Moon Cross crew had lined up, holding their hats in work-hardened hands. Bareheaded, they seemed even more of a breed, hatlines separating their foreheads into two shades—sun-dark faces below, fish-belly white above.

Cowboys, Stillwell noted. The first thing they put on of a morning and the last thing they take off at night . . . their hats.

A few steps behind the ranch crew stood two more, obviously part of the crew but not like the rest. One was an Indian, and Stillwell's eyes narrowed. No Tonkawa, this. Dressed as a rangehand, the Indian was broadly-built, barrel-chested and sturdy on short, slightly bowed legs. A wide, high-cheeked face, raven hair that fell to collar level beneath a twisted headband of faded cloth. Black-almond eyes that sensed his own eyes watching and glanced up in quick response. And at his hip a big Colt in an oiled holster, looking like it was part of him. For an instant, Stillwell felt his shoulders tighten. Chako, he thought.

But Chako was dead. All that was left of Chako was the paint horse he had ridden the last time Stillwell saw him.

"What's a Comanche doing in these parts?" he asked Kingman.

"That's Willie Birdsong. He worked for Cap Freeman. The kid next to him did, too. But if he's got a name he's never told anybody what it is."

The kid was a wild-looking youngster, scrawny and loose-jointed. Thin hair so pale it was almost white wafted around his ears. Pale eyes, pale skin, he looked washed-out in the bright sunlight. The kind of kid a person might not even notice at first glance. Stillwell had seen the type—drifting through the Nations, hanging around places like Tombstone and Wichita and Tascosa—often never being noticed at all, until somebody learned abruptly that noticing would have been a good idea.

The west was full of such kids—hungry-looking, quiet kids without names. Some were decent kids, some not. But any of them could be dangerous.

Kingman had glanced at the newcomers, then stretched tall to look over the crowd. "There's a few boys from Tightwad over there," he told his deputy. "You and John Henry ease over yonder and keep an eye on them. I'll tend to this side."

"Trouble?" Stillwell asked, quietly.

"Not if I can help it," the sheriff said. He headed for the two newcomers. Stillwell shrugged and followed.

At the gravesite a preacher was talking to the Lord about Cap Freeman, while everybody near stood with bowed heads. Kingman eased around the line of Half Moon Cross waddies and stood just behind the Indian and the kid. Stillwell stopped a few feet away, just watching. The pair both knew the sheriff was there, but they didn't raise their heads until the preacher said, "Amen." Then both of them looked around.

"I'm glad you boys came in for the funeral," Kingman said quietly. "Shows respect for the old man."

"Good man," Willie Birdsong said. "Never rode for a better."

"That's fine," the sheriff nodded. "Too good a man to have his funeral get out of hand, I'd say."

"We ain't here for trouble," the kid squinted. "No more than any of the rest."

"I already talked to the rest, this morning. But you two weren't around. You boys bring any grudges with you?"

"There are grudges," the Indian said, "but this isn't the time or place for them."

"Been a whole lot more of Mister Freeman's beef served up down at Tightwad than ever was sold there," the kid muttered, looking across the crowd to where the two young deputies now flanked a group of twenty or so men who stood a little apart from the Waxahachie crowd. "But Willie's right. This ain't the time to think about accounts."

"Good," Kingman said. "We have no problem, then."

The Indian was looking at Stillwell, ebony eyes taking his measure, and now the kid turned to look at him, too. "This somebody we ought to know?" the kid asked.

"Nobody to do with you," Kingman said.

They both turned their attentions back to the funeral service.

82

Kingman eased off a few steps, giving the Half Moon Cross crew some room, and Stillwell backed away with him, raising a brow.

"Cap Freeman didn't leave any family, far's anybody knows," the sheriff explained. "So the crew is sort of closest kin, for these purposes. They'll do the honors."

Stillwell nodded, scanning the crowd. An old habit with him, so automatic that he was barely aware of it. From moment to moment, his eyes saw and his mind registered how the crowd stacked up . . . who was where, how they acted, what seemed to be on their minds.

He felt eyes on him and glanced aside. A man with a wool vest stood a few paces away, watching him intently, not even trying to seem not to. The same man who had left the cathouse on the hill as Stillwell had entered. Town law, Taffy had said.

"Excuse me," he muttered to Kingman, then walked quietly over to stand by the wool vest. "Something special you want with me?" he whispered, "Or are you just curious?"

The man blinked. "I'm . . ."

"I know. You're Zeke Albert, and you're paid to be curious. And I'm Byron Stillwell and I don't mind, except that if you want to stare at me, do it from in front. Otherwise I get nervous."

"I don't want you in my town, Stillwell," the man said flatly. "I like it here, and I don't like trouble. I know all about you, Byron Stillwell. You draw trouble like a windmill draws lightning. I don't need you here."

"Well, that's plain and to the point."

"Just stay out of my jurisdiction," Albert muttered.

"It's *his* jurisdiction, too." Stillwell tipped his head toward Matt Kingman. "Talk to him about it." He drifted away quietly, into the crowd, and a moment later Kingman was beside him.

"What was that about?" the sheriff asked.

"Nothing. I just don't like to be stared at. That's a nervous type there."

"Zeke Albert? He's all right. Don't worry about him."

"I don't," Stillwell said. "But that's a man with somethin' eatin' at him. Something he can't put aside."

Beside Cap Freeman's grave, the preacher was holding forth, extolling the virtues of the old rancher—virtues magnified now beyond likelihood, as funerals and large crowds inspire preachers to do. Wry looks were exchanged among those who had known Freeman, and one of the Half Moon Cross hands leaned toward another to whisper hoarsely, "Dang shame Cap ain't here to hear this. He'd laugh for a week, most likely."

A crisp wind had come up, suddenly as winds do in the Crosstimbers and Valley lands, and dark clouds were climbing from the west. The air smelled sweet, like spring rain. When thunder rolled overhead the preacher glanced up and began winding down. There was another rambling prayer, then the usual ashes and dust verse, and the preacher put away his book. Men knelt beside the grave, slid ropes under the casket and lifted it an inch while others took the poles away. Then Cap Freeman was lowered to his final rest. The preacher looked toward the Half Moon Cross crew, nodding. A tall, square-set cowhand stepped forward, squatted on the heels of fresh-slicked boots and tossed a handful of soil into the grave.

"Stoke Winburn," the sheriff whispered to Stillwell. "Half Moon Cross ramrod. A good man."

Another of the crew followed, tossing his handful of farewell, then another. The Indian and the kid had joined the line of crewmen. Across the way, a few voices were raised above whispers. Stillwell noticed that the young deputies flanking the Tightwad delegation looked nervous. Trusting his own instincts, he scanned them one by one—rough men, men who thrived on trouble. The kind of men one expected to find in the borderline places, like Tightwad. A dozen or so men, tight-wound as though waiting for something to happen.

The voices grew in volume as Willie Birdsong neared the grave, following in line.

Stillwell frowned, then eased aside and crossed behind the main crowd.

When the Comanche's turn came, he knelt beside the grave and picked up a handful of soil. He hesitated a moment, dark eyes looking into the hole, then tossed in his handful of respect.

At the fringe of the Tightwad crowd a big, bunchy-looking man said, loud enough to be heard, "I don't like to see a thing like that."

The nearest deputy, John Henry Taylor, spun toward him. "Like what, mister?"

"Why, that redskin! The notion of an Injun puttin' dirt over a white man. I don't hold with that."

He might have said more, but suddenly he was unable to speak. A hand like a wolf-trap closed on his shoulder, a boot kicked his feet out from under him and he found himself dangling, held painfully upright by iron-hard fingers that pressed into his flesh, suspending him by sinew and collarbone. Other fingers were at his throat, pressing in and upward just below his jaw. At his ear a voice rumbled, "I don't hold with folks interrupting funerals." Then the world of his vision narrowed, became a reddish tunnel, and winked out.

Gently, Byron Stillwell lowered the man to the ground as people all around gawked, wondering what they had seen.

The young deputy stepped up, blinked at Stillwell, then squatted beside the inert man on the ground. "What happened to him?"

"He fainted." Stillwell said quietly. "Happens sometimes if a body doesn't get enough blood to his head. He'll be all right after he's rested."

"You had hold of him," the youngster whispered. "What did you do?"

"I let him down easy, so he wouldn't get hurt." He

straightened the unconscious man, crossed his arms over his middle, and stood, glancing around with narrowed eyes that had no nonsense in them. "Go on with what you were doing, Deputy," he said, letting his voice carry. "There isn't going to be any trouble here. Not any at all."

Chapter Eight

Steady rain was falling by the time the Ellis County Courthouse lay before them, its elaborate central clock tower rising garish and grand above a four-level complex of courtrooms, libraries, land and transfer repositories, petition and clerical offices and county functions. Byron had heard of Waxahachie's new architectural marvel. So had everyone else within hundreds of miles, who had access to newspapers.

At least two other Texas counties already had plans for courthouses just like it.

A county with plenty of money, in an age of architectural embellishment, Ellis County had built for itself *the* courthouse. Craftsmen had been imported from Italy to transform mute red granite—imported from Greece—into Texas' most eminent example of garish opulence and Romanesque Revival construction. Spires upon peaks, peaks upon porticoes, porticoes crafted by sculptors and framed by Roman arches upon Gothic columns, the new courthouse was acclaimed by some as the epitome of elegance . . . and by others as a monstrosity. Opinions varied, but hardly anyone who saw it . . . or even its likeness in the new gravure pages of newspapers . . . didn't have an opinion.

Waxahachie was justly proud of its new courthouse, which it considered its very own, to the sullen disapproval of other county towns which could boast no such edifice but still had to share in the cost of it.

There were even legends growing around the monument. It was said, for instance, that the sculpted faces adorning its tower—faces which gradually changed from angelic cupids to leering gargoyles as they progressed around the structure—were a chronicle of the ill-fated love of one of the Italian sculptors for the daughter of his landlord. The final, hideous visage was completed— they said—on the day that the landlord's comely daughter married a lawyer from Fort Worth.

And some whispered that among the stoneworks adorning the south portico were representations of human reproductive organs. Some even said they could see them, among the myriad Gothic curlicues.

In all, a monumental structure. And in this spring of 1892 every streetcorner facing the new courthouse held at least one saloon done out in the garish grandeur of the time.

"This is the courthouse," Matt Kingman said offhandedly as they reined in on the Ferris Street side. "Buck, you tend the horses. Come on in, Stillwell. We need to have us a talk. Come along, John Henry."

Stillwell followed the sheriff inside, John Henry Taylor tagging along behind, still keeping a respectful distance from the newcomer. Neither of the young deputies had found much to say since the funeral. Both of them had seen the quick, methodical silencing of the troublemaker from Tightwad, and neither had seen anything like that before.

The sheriff's office was a large, comfortable room behind a busy common room shared by staff workers and deputies of both the sheriff and the clerk of the district court.

"Come on in," Kingman beckoned, holding the door open. "You, too, John Henry."

Inside, Stillwell settled himself into a leather-upholstered sofa and the sheriff turned to the deputy. "Now tell me what happened out there," he said.

John Henry swallowed, then stood at attention. "Well, sir, me an' Buck . . . uh, Deputy Mabry, I mean, we was . . . were observing the citizens from Tightwad like you told us to. Then when that Injun from Half Moon Cross . . . uh, Willie Birdsong, sir, when he tossed dirt into Mister Freeman's grave, one of the Tightwad citizens—Mister Tim Sullivan—took a notion to get offended about it and there was fixin' to be just one hell of a . . . uh . . . some, uh, unwarranted confrontation between them Tightwads and them tough hands from Half Moon Cross."

The sheriff sat behind his desk. "Get to the point, John Henry. Just tell me what happened."

"I don't exactly know, Sheriff." The deputy's stiff stance eased. "All I know was, this . . . uh, Mister Stillwell here, he moved in behind Mister Sullivan, and kind of took him by the neck and shoulder, and then Mister Sullivan, he just sort of went to sleep."

"Did you see grounds for a complaint on the part of Mister Sullivan?"

"Well, sir, I don't know if I hold with Injuns throwin' dirt on white men's . . ."

"*Legal* complaint, Deputy! Any grounds for a complaint against this department, or against Mister Stillwell?"

"Oh, no, sir! Why, if anything, it looked to me like Mister Sullivan an' his friends was about this far from gettin' their asses whooped by Half Moon Cross, right there in the middle of Mister Freeman's funeral, if Mister Stillwell hadn't . . . uh, did whatever I didn't rightly see him do."

"All right, John Henry," Kingman nodded. "Wait for me outside."

"Yes, sir." The deputy slipped out and closed the door.

Kingman sighed. "Buttons," he muttered.

"It's part of learning," Stillwell said.

"What exactly *did* you do to that man?"

"Got his attention, and cut off the blood to his brain. Just long enough to put him to sleep for a few minutes. He was being a nuisance."

"Like something an Indian might do," the sheriff noted. "You learn that from Indians?"

"I learned it from a French Creole gambler on Bourbon Street in New Orleans."

Kingman shook his head. "Well, I've got to say you did me a service. Tim Sullivan runs the cotton gin over at Tightwad. And most everything else over there. He's a brawler and a troublemaker, and the rest that were with him are no better. Tightwad's a den of thieves and I'd clean it out if it wasn't for the damn commissioners . . . Anyway, there's been bad blood between Half Moon Cross and some of the Tightwad bunch for a long time. I've been afraid Cap's funeral would turn into a brawl . . . or worse."

"Folks could have been hurt," Byron agreed. "Anyway, you said you wanted to talk to me. Do you want a written statement on the shooting of Doctor Cathcart?"

"Of course I do. But first I want to know what you know about Roy Pye."

"Only what I told you. I saw him shoot Frederick James Cathcart, in the back, from a second-floor window of the Regents' Hotel in Ennis. And I heard him try to place the blame on me. I have my own ideas why. I think Roy Pye has been in contact with a man named Peter Lewellyn Dawes, who controls the Double D Ranch out of Mobeetie. I think Dawes got word that I was in Ennis, and sent a wire to Pye. I don't know what the wire said, but I think Pye saw a chance to set me up for Dawes, and took it." He sighed, shifting to ease the ache of many wounds. "That's what I think, but aside from what I saw and heard, it's all conjecture."

"Pretty far-fetched conjecture, on the face of it," the sheriff said.

"Not really. I know the kind of man Dawes is, and why he'd be out to get me . . ."

"You haven't told me that."

"No, I haven't. I also saw your reaction to what I said about Roy Pye. It's my opinion that you know some things about him yourself, along the same lines."

"What's your personal interest in Roy Pye?"

"Nothing. I never saw the man before. But he had some connection with Dawes, and I do have a personal interest in staying alive."

"It seems to me, from all I've heard about Byron Stillwell, that you're pretty good at staying alive. How come this Dawes has you spooked?"

"He's a wealthy and powerful man, Sheriff. And a vindictive one. I suppose you've heard the name Goldie Locke?"

"*Locke?*" The sheriff's eyes widened, then went slitted with speculation. He sat forward, leaning his arms on his desk. "Go on."

Stillwell smiled tiredly and shook his head. "No, I don't know anything useful about Goldie Locke. I don't know where he is, or even what he looks like. The only thing I know about him—aside from a guess at the number of people he has killed . . ."

"Assassinated," Kingman interrupted. "Goldie Locke—whoever he is—is no ordinary hired killer. He's an assassin."

Stillwell nodded. "All I know about him is that he was connected with Peter Lewellyn Dawes in some way, as recently as a year ago. He was in Kansas—or at

91

least in No Man's Land—not more than three months ago, and there's a chance that he's looking for me."

"You still haven't said why."

"No. I haven't."

There was a hesitant rap at the ornate door, then it opened just far enough for John Henry Taylor to stick his head in. "Pardon me, Sheriff, but we got folks stackin' up out here, wantin' to see you. There's Judge Knox an' my Uncle Waldo an' Stoke Winburn an' . . ." the head disappeared, then reappeared. ". . . an' the town marshal from Ennis. He says there's been a doctor murdered yonder, an' that his deputy got run over by a train."

Kingman stared at him. "His deputy? Roy Pye?"

"Yes, sir. That's what he said."

The sheriff was on his feet then, coming around his desk. "Get Marshal Raney in here, Deputy. Tell the others I'll be with them as soon as I can." He turned to Stillwell. "I'll need that account of the Cathcart murder. There's a clerk outside who'll take your statement, and get it notarized. Also, I'll need a notarized affidavit about the doings up at Mullinsville. And don't leave out anything this time. Deputy Taylor will take you to the clerk."

Stillwell stood and put on his hat. Things had abruptly become very busy around here. As he left the office, a worried-looking older man passed him, going in. The town marshal from Ennis, Roy Pye's erstwhile boss.

Deputy Taylor stepped up beside him, started to reach for his arm, then backed off at something he saw in Stillwell's eyes. With a look, the newcomer taught him a thing that seemed important: don't grab a man's gun-arm unless you're ready for trouble. At the moment, John Henry Taylor wanted no trouble with Byron Stillwell. He stepped back and grinned an apology.

"Just follow me, sir. The clerk is over yonder."

There was more of a crowd in the outside office than there had been. People working at desks, people milling around . . . and people waiting to see the sheriff. Halfway across the room Judge Arthur Knox appeared, stepping in front of Stillwell.

"I hoped we'd have a chance to talk," he said. "But things seem a bit hectic. Will you be around later?"

"I don't think so, sir," Stillwell said, "the sheriff wants a statement from me, about Doc Cathcart's death, then I'll move on, I expect."

"Cathcart, yes. I just heard about that. He was a decent man. Were you a witness?"

"I saw Roy Pye kill him."

"Pye?"

"I've told Sheriff Kingman all I know about it, Judge."

"But if you were a witness, you'll have to testify . . ."

"There won't be a trial. There's no one to try. Pye is dead, too."

The judge looked up at him, his lips thinning. "I only just now heard about that, Mr. Stillwell. How did you . . . ?"

"I heard it from this deputy about a minute ago." He eased past the old man, then turned back. "It is a pleasure to have met you, Judge Knox. And I won't forget . . . well, that you were my father's friend." He shook the old man's hand quickly, then strode away. Knox watched him go, then headed for the sheriff's office. He didn't want to wait any more to find out what was going on.

It was a sullen and silent dozen riders that stepped down in front of the Trail House Saloon on the main street of Tightwad. Bleak as the low clouds and the

93

spattering drops of rain, they looped their leads at a pair of hitchrails, glanced at the four horses already tied there, and trooped inside to sprawl at three of the place's four scarred tables.

"Drinkin' whiskey, Mac!" one called to the aproned man at the keg-and-plank bar. "Set it up an' keep it comin'."

Some of them ran sullen eyes over the four individuals seated at the remaining table, then ignored them. Kids. Guntoughs, maybe, but no more than kids.

Generally, the newcomers kept their attention on the large, beefy man who had led them in. He was angry. Hot-eyed mad, and letting it steam up inside him. And he kept rubbing his shoulder, gingerly as though he had a boil there, just inches from the base of his bull neck.

"You still ailin', Tim?" one of them asked. "You act tender."

"It hurts like hell," the big man rumbled. Hard eyes went from one to another of them. "That son of a bitch like to tore out my collar bone, an' not a one of you jackasses saw what he used on me?"

Several of them lowered their eyes and shook their heads. One shrugged and said, "We already told you, Tim. We didn't see anything. It just looked like he put his hand on your shoulder, then you sort of sagged and it looked like the jasper was tryin' to keep you from fallin' down. That's all."

"He did *somethin'*," the big man hissed. "I felt like I was dyin'. Why didn't any of you do somethin'?"

"We didn't know what was happenin', Tim. It was all that quick."

"You're gonna do somethin' about him, aren't you?" another asked.

"I'll kill the son of a bitch, if I can find him. Why in hell didn't anybody at least find out who he was?"

"Because we didn't know, Tim. Like we all told you,

we didn't know nobody had hurt you 'til you come around. It just seemed like you fainted."

The big man tossed back a second shot of whiskey, rubbed his aching collar again and scowled. "I'd have had that damn Injun's hide, if that hadn't happened. I'd have knocked his damn head off. Throwin' dirt on a white man's coffin like that!"

"Yeah," another mused, "I had my eye on that spooky kid. If he'd drawed on you I'd have put a bullet in him."

The big man looked around, seeing the four young gunnies at the next table for the first time. He glared at them, and the red-haired one grinned back at him, good-naturedly, then turned away. Tim leaned aside to mutter to the man next to him, "Anybody know them four?"

Again some of them glanced at the youngsters. "They ain't anybody," one of them told Tim, quietly. "Young hooraws. I seen one or two of 'em around, mebbe yonder around Ennis."

Tim turned toward the kids again. "You," he said. "Get on out of here. Do your drinkin' some place else."

A couple of the kids looked fit to bristle, but the redhead just grinned and got to his feet. "Yes, sir," he said, "we was fixin' to leave anyhow. Don't bother yourself about us."

Slowly the other three stood, scowling and unhappy, but they kept their notions to themselves and followed the redhead out the door.

On the slick street outside, Jude turned on Coby Shanks. "If you ain't the easy one!" he spat. "How come you to put up with that?"

"With what?"

"That bastid orderin' us out that way! I don't intend to stand for that."

"You don't have to stand for it, Jude. But let's go

easy until he's worth killin', all right?"

"What does that mean?"

"It means if you'd shut up an' listen more, you'd maybe remember why we came over here in the first place. That fella is Tim Sullivan. He's the one that's got the gin here, that's got to go in to Waxahachie to bring back the crop money. Sometimes I think you ain't got a brain in your head, Jude. Ever since you set eyes on that whorehouse woman in Waxahachie, you can't stick to a notion long enough to see it out, even when it was your own notion to start with."

Inside the Trail House, Tim Sullivan nursed his aching shoulder and told his crew, "I don't think I'll wait for Tuesday to go in to the bank. I can do it tomorrow just as easy, an' maybe that drifter will still be around. I do dearly want his hide hangin' on my fence. Bill, you an' Joe be ready to ride in with me, as usual. The rest of you might just drift up to Waxahachie separately an' look around. Try to find out who that son of a bitch is, an' where he is."

"You gonna take him on right there in town, Tim? Awful lot of law yonder."

"Just help me find him," Sullivan snapped. "Then I'll cipher out what to do about him."

Chapter Nine

The clerk had a little desk over in one corner of the records office, near a railed enclosure where several young women with starched blouses and done-up hair sat at little tables, using Remington typewriting machines. The clatter of the contraptions was like sleet on a windowpane. Byron removed his hat and nodded toward the women. Some of them returned the nod, curious eyes looking him over from behind lowered lashes. A couple of them blushed. There was a scent of perfume in the air.

John Henry Taylor grinned, forgetting his awe of the gunfighter momentarily in the presence of attractive females. "Howdy, Miss Jolene," he said. "Miss Clara . . . Miss Sadie . . . fine afternoon, Missus Sutton." He turned to Stillwell, reached for his arm and then withdrew his hand quickly, remembering. "Ladies, this here is Mr. Byron Stillwell. Mr. Stillwell, these ladies here are typewriters."

"Ladies," Stillwell nodded again, then let his glance roam around the large room. Altogether, there were at least forty people in sight, maybe half of them county employees—people working at desks, people at the slide-out drawers of big, ornate file cabinets, taking papers out, putting others in, people singly and in groups, some moving around the open central floor, some in

97

railed cubicles—as always, without being conscious of it, he surveyed the crowd the way a hunter surveys a landscape, seeing everything and missing nothing.

Nearby, a bell jangled, once and then again. Stillwell watched curiously as a man at a polished desk stood, crossed to an outside wall and lifted a brass cone from a wooden box there, to hold it against his ear. Ellis County was going all out to be up-to-date, it seemed. Telephone systems were no longer uncommon in the larger cities, but it amused him to find such novelties as telephones in a place like Waxahachie. A local system, he decided. He had seen no lines outside of town except the ubiquitous telegraph wire running along the railroad right-of-way.

A few feet away the transcript clerk looked around from his roll-top desk and frowned at the happy young deputy engaging his typewriters in light conversation. "Do you want something, Deputy?" he asked.

John Henry turned. "Oh. Yeah, the sheriff said to . . . uh . . . Mister Rice, this here is Mister Stillwell. He's supposed to give you a statement for the sheriff."

The clerk barely glanced at Stillwell. "Our typewriters are paid by the day, Deputy. And they are paid to typewrite, not to keep you amused."

"Yes, sir." John Henry cast one last, longing look at the typewriters, especially the one he had introduced as Jolene, and brought himself to attention, facing the clerk. "Sheriff needs this affidavy right away, he said."

"Affidavit," the clerk corrected, sourly.

"Sir?"

"The word is *affidavit*, Deputy. Not affidavy. *Vit! Vit!*"

"Yes, sir. *Vit*. Anyhow, the sheriff needs this . . ."

A sunburned man in starched collar and top hat pushed through a gate and confronted the deputy. "John Henry, what is going on here?"

"Hi, Uncle Waldo," the youth grinned. "Mister Stillwell, this is my Uncle Waldo. He's a county commissioner."

Uncle Waldo glanced at Stillwell. "How do." Then he took his nephew by the arm and pulled him aside. "I've been waiting since two o'clock to see the sheriff about that grading affidavy. Didn't you tell him I was out here?"

"I told him, Uncle Waldo, but he's a little bit busy right . . ."

Stillwell let the voices trail away and pulled up a chair beside the clerk's desk. He turned the chair backward and straddled it, noting the startled look on Rice's face. "Are you ready to take my statement?"

"What . . . oh, yes. You're to give me an affidavy . . . affidavit for the sheriff. Ah, your name again, sir?"

"Stillwell," he said evenly. "Byron Stillwell."

Beyond the clerk, the other young deputy had come in from tending horses and was leaning on the rail of the typewriters' cubicle, happily passing the time with pretty ladies.

There was a fair crowd now in the sheriff's office. With two senior sheriff's deputies and the chief deputy present, as well as Marshal Jack Raney from Ennis, Waxahachie Chief Constable Zeke Albert, Judge Amos Fein, Visiting Judge Arthur Knox and the high sheriff himself, the room was much smaller than it usually seemed.

"I want the man out of my town," Zeke Albert was saying. "You've seen the file on him, Sheriff. He's a drifter and a troublemaker. And worse, he's a known killer. You know yourself that he killed three men at Mullinsville not a week ago. And there have been

99

others. Byron Stillwell is a *gunfighter*. If he stays, there'll be trouble."

"That hardly sounds like the same young man I met today," Arthur Knox said, quietly. "He was polite, rather reminded me of his father, whom I knew to be a fine man."

"Stillwell's a violent man!" Albert insisted. "We all saw what he did out there at the cemetery. To Mister Sullivan."

"*Mister* Sullivan was looking for trouble, Zeke," Matt Kingman pointed out. "Seems to me that Stillwell simply kept the peace."

"By rendering a citizen of this county unconscious! Is that 'keeping the peace'?"

"I've done similar a time or two, when it was necessary," the sheriff said blandly. Beside the closed door, Senior Deputy Jim Logan grinned. It had been his pleasure on several occasions to lock up limp citizens with the marks of Sheriff Kingman's gunbarrel alongside their skulls.

"You're the law," Albert pointed out. "Stillwell's no better than an outlaw. He's a footloose drifter with a record of violence. And Tim Sullivan is a respected businessman . . ."

"In Tightwad," someone muttered.

". . . who does business with my brother-in-law's bank!"

Amos Fein raised his hand and the voices tailed off to silence. As chief district judge for Ellis County, his was the ultimate position of law. "I'd like to hear a few facts here," he said. "First, what crimes has this . . . ah . . . Stillwell allegedly committed?"

"None that I can find," Kingman said. "At least not in Texas."

"Is he wanted in any state or territory?"

"He isn't wanted anywhere," Albert said, testily.

100

"People die when he's around."

"Stillwell has become known, rather widely," the sheriff said, ignoring the constable. "As you know, Your Honor, we've developed a pretty fair advisory system among law enforcement professionals in the past few years. The Rangers coordinate it in Texas, the Association of Counties in some other states, and we're beginning to coordinate with federal . . ."

"I know all that. Get to the point."

"The point is, this man's name shows up a lot. Texas, Arizona, Kansas, Arkansas, Louisiana . . . and Zeke's right on one point, Stillwell has done some violences. But he isn't an outlaw . . . or if he is, nobody has ever pinned anything on him. He's been in jail a time or two, but never convicted of anything. He *has* been involved in killings, but in every case of record there was absolute mitigation. Usually open-and-shut self defense. I even know some lawmen who would hire him on in a minute if he wanted to wear a badge. Zeke calls him a gunfighter. I suppose I call him that, too, for lack of a better word. He *is* a very dangerous man. But not an outlaw. And not a hired gun. He's worked as a cowpuncher, a guard, a spotter for gaming houses . . . even as a prizefighter, according to one report. But he doesn't hire out his gun."

"This is a nice, quiet town," Zeke Albert muttered.

"But not always a nice, quiet *county*." Jack Raney sighed. "I've got a dead doctor and a dead deputy at Ennis."

"And you believe the deputy murdered the doctor and then threw himself under a train?"

"I believe the deputy murdered the doctor," Raney said. "After that, I don't know what happened."

"And Stillwell *was* involved," Albert pointed out.

"Stillwell was a witness to the shooting, so he says," Kingman corrected. "He's giving a voluntary

101

statement right now, outside."

"Good," Albert said. "Then let him go on his way, and good riddance."

"Do you have any charges against him?" Fein asked the sheriff.

"I do not."

"Well, then, let's get to the point. Why do you want to keep him in Waxahachie?"

Kingman took a deep breath and reached into a drawer of his desk. He pulled out a thick, yellowed folder and opened it. On top was a clipping from the Fort Worth *Herald*. He handed it to the judge. "You remember this, I expect."

"I remember," Fein nodded. "The murdered ranger."

"The ranger?" Raney leaned aside to look at the clipping the judge held. "The one who was shot here in town?"

"The same," Kingman nodded. "Ranger Lieutenant William T. Sparling, senior investigator, Company C of the Frontier Battalion, out of Waco. Shot to death by an unknown assailant at three o'clock in the afternoon, June third, 1889, right out there on Franklin Street in *nice, quiet* Waxahachie, Texas." He said the words slowly, his gaze holding Zeke Albert. "A Texas Ranger murdered, and not even a pursuable lead as to who did the shooting. Three years past, and we don't know who or where the murderer is. We don't even know what he looks like!"

"You think Stillwell had something to . . ."

"No, I don't. But I know who Bill Sparling was after. A hired killer. A professional assassin called Goldie Locke. Now Byron Stillwell shows up, with reason to think that Goldie Locke is after him. That's why I want to *keep* him. I want a chance at the murderer who killed Bill Sparling, right here in your *nice, quiet* town, Zeke. Right here in my county."

102

For a long minute no one spoke. They just looked at one another, each man thinking his own thoughts. Then old Arthur Knox murmured, "I knew Ranger Sparling. I had a high regard for him."

Albert shook his head. "I understand that you want to set a trap for Sparling's murderer, and use this Stillwell for bait. I also understand that you are likely going to turn Waxahachie into a shooting gallery, if you do. I call that reckless endangerment, Sheriff. I don't like it."

"It doesn't have to happen in town," Kingman pointed out. "We can plan it our way, if Stillwell is agreeable. And I expect the Rangers will give us their support."

"How do you propose to keep Stillwell here, if he wants to leave?" Judge Fein asked the sheriff.

"I thought maybe you could give me a hold order, Your Honor."

"Material witness?" Raney suggested.

"Maybe you'd like to deputize him," Zeke Albert said, sourly. "The more I hear of this, the less I like it, Sheriff."

Chief Deputy Jim Logan grinned. "You want that jasper to stick around, Sheriff, just say the word. We can tend to that."

Judge Arthur Knox spread thin old hands, gazing at the sheriff with shrewd, bright eyes in a wizened face. "Why don't you simply ask him to stay?"

After a moment's silence, Kingman grinned. "I guess that ought to be the first approach. Jim, would you go out and ask Mr. Stillwell to see me before he leaves the building, please?"

"Sure. Where'd you send him? To Rice's desk?"

"Yeah."

"He'll be here when you want him." The chief deputy stepped out and closed the door behind him.

"What we need right now," Kingman told the rest, "is an agreement. Judge?"

"I agree," Fein said. "Subject to having a plan that will not jeopardize innocent people."

Kingman turned to Zeke Albert. "Would you agree on those terms, Zeke?"

"The only way not to endanger innocent people is to get that gunfighter out of town and let him be bait somewhere else. Outside my jurisdiction."

Kingman sighed. "Will you cooperate with surveillance, *provided* we can spring the trap outside of town, then? We don't know anything about the killer, Zeke. We can't control where he might go. The best we can do is control where he might find Stillwell."

Albert sat frowning for a moment, then shrugged. "I've had my say. It's on your head, Sheriff. Not mine. Besides, I doubt if Goldie Locke is within a thousand miles of here. Or will be. All you've got is that gunslingin' drifter's word."

"Maybe you're right," Kingman said. He turned to Fein. "I expect the Rangers could help. They've had an ongoing investigation for at least three years. What there is to know about Goldie Locke, they know."

"Would you like for me to contact Waco?" Fein asked.

The sheriff nodded. "I also think that no one outside this room needs to know about any of this, except Stillwell, and I'll fill him in. If he agrees to stay."

Logan entered, looking worried. "He isn't here, Sheriff. Rice has his statement, but after he finished it, he left. I sent Buck to head him off at the stalls, and John Henry to check the hotels and eateries. They should be . . ."

A quick knock sounded at the door and Logan opened it a crack, then wider to let a breathless Buck Mabry enter. "Did you see him?"

"He's gone, sir," the young deputy panted. "Got his horse, saddled up and left. Him and that cat. Stabler don't even know which way he went."

Outside, thunder rolled in a darkening sky and occasional raindrops became a steady drizzle.

West of Courthouse Square and past the narrow band of saloons, hotels and stablery yards which surrounded it were mills, marshalling yards, a rail depot and spur tracks, then warehouses and cotton gins for processing what had become Texas' largest cash crop. The road crossed a wooden bridge over a shallow creek, and became a street again, an avenue of markets and emporiums, shops and music halls with residences beyond.

Byron Stillwell glanced at the lowering sky and reined in at a general merchandise sign. As he looped the paint's reins, thunder rolled and the spattering of rain increased. He stepped to the horse's head and patted its cheek, running his hand along its muzzle in a fond caress. "No restin' here, boy," he murmured. "Folks in a town like this don't need the likes of us hanging around. We'll stock up and move on."

He lifted a saddlebag flap, lifted out a folded feed sack and held the flap high as the yellow cat flowed from saddleskirt to saddlebag and vanished inside, out of the rain. Stillwell shook his head. "For a varmint, you sure have all the instincts of a grubliner," he muttered.

In the store he picked out tinned meats and vegetables, flour in a waxed wrap, coffee . . . the staples of a far traveler, including a fresh box of .45 caliber loads for the Peacemaker.

The clerk glanced at the gun on his hip as he set out the cartridges. "Don't see so many big irons these days," he said. "Mostly around here it's pocket pistols.

Thirty-twos and the like. You a drover?"

"Have been from time to time," Byron nodded, looking around the store. "I'm out of a slicker. Do you have . . . ?" His eyes lit on a stack of folded goods on a shelf. He stepped across and lifted the top one. A serape, hand-woven in the stepped-V design of the high mesa tribes. "You ship these in from the Territories?"

The clerk grinned. "Naw, we did a while back, but some of the Tonks from over on the river saw 'em and went into the business. Old Buckeye John brings 'em in to sell. He says anything a 'Pache can make, a Tonkawa can make better. Those are all carded wool. Shed water like duck feathers."

"Then forget the slicker," By said. "I'll make do with this." He removed his hat, slipped the serape over his head, squared it on his shoulders and put his hat back on his head. "This will do just fine."

He settled up, went out into a light, steady rain, and slung the feed sack with its burdens from a saddle ring. The street was almost deserted at the moment—just a couple of damp riders dismounting in front of a covered porchway, a few people standing in shelter here and there, rain-wet horses head-down at a few hitchrails and in the distance, westward, a closed carriage at a deserted intersection.

He retrieved his reins, swung into the paint's saddle and reined toward mid-street, aiming westward. Something scampered past the paint's hooves and out ahead, then turned to stare back with angry yellow eyes.

"I thought you were in the saddlebag," Stillwell muttered. "What are you . . . ?"

The cat was wet and in a surly mood. As the horse stopped it scurried toward it, bunched its haunches and sprang for the saddle. Forepaws gripped the saddlehorn as rear claws skidded on wet leather, scrabbling for purchase. A raking paw dug talons into the paint's shoulder and the horse neighed and reared, starting to paw the air as Byron clung to the saddle.

The horse reared, pawed and abruptly lurched to one side, a violent tremor going up its mane. For an instant it hung there, tall on hind legs, then it collapsed and fell. Stillwell threw himself clear of the saddle, rolling to escape flailing hooves. He felt a hot pain in his side, rolled again and sought cover. The horse lay where it had fallen. It shuddered, tried to raise its head, and blood sprayed from a gaping hole in its neck. It trembled again, and died, as a hard, distant crack echoed along the rain-emptied street. The distinctive thump of a heavy rifle, its sound trailing behind the bullet it had sent.

Even before the shot was heard, Stillwell was bellied down behind the dead paint, peering over the mud-splattered rim of his saddle. Eyes that missed nothing scanned the street to the west and everything along it. But there was nothing there to see. A cotton wagon rolled into the street from a cross-street, blocking the view, and he sprinted across to the cover of a doorway. The wagon passed, and still there was no sign of the shooter. Nor would there be, now. People were coming out to look up and down the street, drawn by the sound of gunfire.

Stillwell put away his Colt and let his shoulders sag. A knowledge colder than the rain crept along his spine and he sighed, easing the hard tension in his shoulders.

A heavy rifle. A hunter's rifle. Sharps or one of the 45-90's, he guessed. A long-range rifle probably mounted with a telescope sight. A killer's gun, precise and methodical. A gun to deliver sudden death, unexpected and unseen.

An assassin's weapon.

Goldie Locke had found him, and had opened the match.

Shielded now by spectators on the scene, he stepped out into the rain-slick street and looked down at the dead paint horse. At his feet the yellow cat stared at the fallen animal for a moment, then turned to hiss angrily at people approaching.

A paint horse. An Indian horse. Chako's horse, now gone to join Chako in whatever heaven Comanche warriors and their horses chose to share.

A paint horse, dead from a bullet intended for its rider.

There were people all around him then, some afoot, some of them on horseback. Dimly he heard a familiar voice, among the other voices.

Sheriff Matt Kingman clenched hard jaws, then turned to the panting, wool-vested man beside him. "You still think Goldie Locke is a thousand miles from here, Zeke? Well, I don't think so."

"Get him out of my town, Kingman," the constable hissed through clenched teeth. "I want him out, *now!*"

Two young deputies on horseback stared down at the fallen horse and the bleak man standing over it, then spurred their mounts through a growing crowd, spreading to patrol both sides of the avenue, westward.

"Call 'em back, Jim," Kingman said gruffly. "They aren't going to find anybody."

Stillwell ignored them. The tight tension of moments before had drained away, and in its place was a brooding, melancholy fatigue—as though all the wounds from all the conflicts . . . through all the years . . . had reopened in one agonizing instant. He felt tired. Bone-deep tired. But beneath even that terrible fatigue was something else—a hot, abiding anger that fed itself from memories and grew. Slowly and inexorably, it grew.

He knelt beside the dead horse and fumbled at the

saddle cinch. His hands ached and trembled. Then someone else was there, other fingers pushing his aside to slip the cinch free. He raised his eyes. Unreadable dark eyes in a wide, dark face looked back at him.

"I'll lend you a hand with this," Willie Birdsong said. "Man can't do everything by himself."

Chapter Ten

It seemed he had been in the bed of a wagon, cushioned by bales and covered over with rough wool blankets that had the scent of honest sweat upon them. It seemed there had been cool rain upon his face, and something small and furry there, pushing against his cheek, warning others away.

Luck, he thought—or seemed to remember thinking. Just my luck.

It seemed time had passed, and he had slept. A troubled sleep, full of faces and places, confused thoughts and snatches of conversation . . . people saying things that seemed to make sense, but just didn't quite add up, somehow. And he couldn't find the parts that didn't add up.

Someone was leaning over him. He reached for his gun, fingers searching for the comfortable bulk of its wood and metal grip. Someone touched him, then jerked away as a voice warned, "Watch it! Don't grab his gun arm!"

He blinked awake. A narrow bed in a beam-ceilinged room, slanting sunlight through frayed lace curtains. The face nearest had gray whiskers, protruding teeth and wire-rimmed glasses. Startled eyes peered at him, magnified by the lenses.

"Sorry, Doc," the same voice said. "He don't like for

folks to do that. He's a . . . a gunfighter, you see."
Deputy Sheriff John Henry Taylor sat on a peg stool a
few feet away, gazing at him curiously. "You awake yet,
Mr. Stillwell?"

"He's awake," the eyeglasses said. Then to him, "How
do you feel? Ready to sit up and take nourishment?"
The words had an odd rhythm to them, as though the
man had known another language before he knew English.

Stillwell rubbed his eyes and looked around. Over by
the door, the Comanche wrangler squatted on his heels,
infinitely patient. One other was there, leaning casually
against a wall, and after a moment the name came to
him. Stoke Winburn. Ramrod of Half Moon Cross.

He raised the sheet, looking down at himself. He was
stripped to his drawers, and had fresh bandaging
around his chest. "What happened?" he managed.

"Somebody shot your horse," John Henry said.

"I know that. I mean, to me."

Eyeglasses shook his head. "Not too much, this time.
Spent bullet slapped you across the shortribs. But you
were lucky. It went through your horse first, then that
tight-weave serape of yours stopped it. No sig-
nificant damage, beyond a deep bruise that'll need
watching for possible abcess. That's about the extent of
it, *this time.*"

"Then how come I passed out?"

The medic removed his eyeglasses and polished them
on his sleeve. Without them, he looked like a wrinkled
squirrel. "Best I can tell, this wound might have set off
a delayed reaction from several others that you sus-
tained earlier. It's called latent amneopathic shock,
among other things. What it means is, your system's
been about at its limit trying to recover from previous
traumas, and when one thing more happened to you, it
just put you over the edge. In short, your recuperative

111

system shut you down so that it could have some time to mend you."

"I never seen so many different kinds of scars," John Henry said, with awe. "You look like you went to war an' lost. How'd you get all those?"

"One at a time, mostly." Stillwell sat up, feeling slightly dizzy. "Where's my gun?"

"Right there behind you, hangin' on the bedpost. How many times have you been shot, anyway? Seven? Eight? Wonder you're still breathin'."

The man lounging near the door shot a warning glare at the deputy. "John Henry, didn't anybody ever teach you good manners?" To Stillwell he said, "You're at Half Moon Cross Ranch, Mr. Stillwell. This is the main house. You can rest here for a while, and welcome. My name is Winburn. I'm strawbossin' here 'til the bank and the lawyers get Mr. Freeman's affairs settled."

The deputy fidgeted a minute, then put in, "Sheriff had to put you *someplace,* 'cause Constable Albert has been raisin' so much hell about you bein' in town. He says you're a lightnin' rod."

"Willie's idea, bringin' you here." Winburn tilted his head toward the stolid Indian squatting at the door. "He figured we owe you for keeping ol' Cap's layaway peaceful."

"Biggest problem gettin' you here was that damn cat," John Henry chatted. "Critter wouldn't let hardly anybody get near you. Nobody but the Inj . . . uh, Mr. Birdsong there. Critter gets mean as a yard dog. How'd you teach it to do that, Mister? I never knew a body could teach a *cat* anything."

"I didn't teach him," Stillwell breathed, reaching around to lift his gunbelt from the bedpost. He drew the Peacemaker, checked its loads and its oiled action, then put it away. "And it's not my cat. Where's my clothes? I need to . . ."

112

"You need to stay in that bed for a while," Doc said, sternly. "Your cat may have nine lives, but you don't. Not any more. You've used up about eight of them."

"Nobody knows you're out here," John Henry said, cheerfully. "Sheriff an' Logan an' these gents, they slicked you out of town so fast, nobody else knows you're gone. If some shooter's lookin' for you, he won't even know where to start."

Stillwell looked around at the youth, feeling both irritation and a kind of sympathy. The bland assurance of innocence, he thought. And so much to learn, if he's to survive. He pushed the medic's restraining hand away and sat full upright, feet on the polished floor, gunbelt on his lap. His hat rested on a bedstand, and he picked it up and put it on his head. John Henry's eyes narrowed, and he grinned. Somehow, with every movement Stillwell made, his gun seemed always to be within inches of his hand.

At the door, the Indian came to his feet, a sardonic smile on his dark face. "The man knows better than that, Deputy," he rumbled. "Goldie Locke doesn't get fooled that easy. Better give the man his clothes, Stoke."

Stillwell gazed at the Indian. "You know Goldie Locke?"

"That's who's after you, isn't it? Nobody knows him. Nobody *livin'*. Heard of him, though. Up in the Nations they talk about him."

"What do they say?"

"They say he kills for money . . . killed fifty, maybe a hundred men so far. They say he gets top dollar, and guarantees his work. And never misses. They say he's like a ghost. Goes where he pleases, kills who he aims to kill, makes a lot of money an' nobody can find him. Nobody knows who he is or where he comes from, or where he goes between jobs."

Stillwell nodded. He had heard all that. "Anything else?"

"They say maybe he holes up somewhere in the Strip. Otherwise somebody would have found him by now. Nobody's invisible."

Stoke Winburn had gone outside. He returned now with Stillwell's clean flannels, shirt, stockings, pants and boots. "The rest of your gear is on the porch," the ramrod said.

Stillwell nodded and began getting dressed. He felt weak, and sore all over, but standing seemed to clear away the dizziness. "I've thought about that. I was up in the Strip, when I got the idea he might be after me. For money."

"Only reason he kills, they say. For money or to protect himself. You got some fresh burn scars," the Indian said, casually. "Like from a prairie fire, maybe. Big fire up in No Man's Land a few weeks back. Like to burned out the whole Strip."

"Fires happen."

"Sure," the Comanche nodded. " 'Specially when somebody sets 'em."

Stillwell buttoned his shirt, stuffed it into his britches and buckled his gun rig around his hips. "That mean something?"

"Rumors travel," Willie shrugged. "Cheyenne kid up on the Canadian, he's got some horses a Comanche left with him. Wild Kwahadi named Chako. Kid says he ran with a white man sometimes. Man with a Peacemaker an' a grudge against one of the Panhandle spreads. Chako had a grudge, too, kid says. Then there's a fire, an' the big spread's whole venture herd is wiped out. Kid says Chako never came back."

Stillwell simply held the Indian's eyes. "You hear a lot, don't you." The rest were listening intently.

"Cheyenne kid talks to a Pawnee drifter," Willie

shrugged. "Pawnee shares biscuits with a couple of Kiowa fur-hunters, they trade with Tonkawas on the Brazos . . . ," he shrugged again. "Rumors get around."

Stillwell held his gaze a moment longer, then lowered his eyes. "Chako's dead," he said quietly. "My horse—the paint horse that killer shot—that was Chako's horse. I found him, later."

Willie Birdsong nodded. "That grudge the Kwahadi had . . . did he settle it?"

"He settled his grudge," Stillwell murmured, remembering. "He walks the sunset now, with eagle feathers trailing to his heels."

Willie Birdsong tipped his head. "You know of such things?"

Stillwell pulled on his boots, not responding.

John Henry's eyes were as wide as dollars. "You *set a prairie fire?*" he croaked, stunned and appalled. The idea was inconceivable to him. What kind of man would deliberately set a prairie fire?

As though reading the youngster's mind, Willie Birdsong said, "*Indian* might do somethin' like that, if he had reason enough."

The medic was packing tools, salves and rolled linen into a valise. He closed and strapped it, then turned. "It's obvious that you aren't going to take good advice, like confining yourself to bed rest until you're properly healed. But consider it given, anyway."

Stillwell nodded. "What do I owe you?"

"Nothing. It's paid."

"Who? The county?"

The doctor shook his head. "My name is Rosenthal. Julian Rosenthal. Does that name mean anything to you?"

"Not that I recall. Should it?"

"You were in St. Louis, Missouri, six years ago. Fourth day of May, eighteen eighty-six. You were on

115

your way by cab to the Lipton Theater, and you saw a disturbance in an alley."

"I was in St. Louis. I don't know if I . . ."

"A lot of people were passing by, and saw the disturbance, but there are always disturbances and people don't like to be involved. No one stopped, except you."

"I remember. Some toughs, roughing up a foreigner. It was nothing much."

"Nothing much," Rosenthal said, shaking his head slowly. He seemed truly puzzled. "Five hoodlums with knives and clubs . . . that's nothing much? Oi!"

"Well, it wasn't something I cared to see."

"Nor I," the doctor said. "The *foreigner* was my brother. He would have died in that alley if you hadn't come along."

"Oh." Stillwell turned away, tossing it off. "I never heard his name."

"I don't suppose you did. Barak didn't yet know English. He tried to thank you, but he could speak only in Hebrew. Or Yiddish."

Stillwell turned back, remembering. "Barak? *Barak Rosenthal?*"

"Yes." The doctor smiled, his whiskers twitching. "The endowment . . . for the Baltimore Conservatory of Music. He couldn't thank you, but he did inquire about you. And thanked your mother, in his own way."

"Mattie's never mentioned . . ."

"Oh, no. Barak wouldn't say anything about you, of course. How would one tell so gentle a lady about the sort of mayhem her son committed on five St. Louis criminals? What you did to them . . . one doesn't discuss such things with ladies. But Barak has done well in Baltimore, and he appreciates good music."

"And you're here in Texas."

"A friend of your mother's helped me to set up my practice. Doctor Cathcart. A fine man, may God cher-

116

ish his soul." Rosenthal picked up his bags. "And, I suppose, the soul of his murderer." Eyes magnified by lenses held Stillwell for a moment, as though trying to see into his mind. "It is very messy, what iron wheels can do to a body. Iron wheels. But first, seven inches of stiletto between the ribs."

He turned away and strode out, Stoke Winburn following him. Willie Birdsong's teeth glinted in a half-smile.

"Kind of a small world, isn't it?" the Indian noted.

"I just can't believe a man would *set* a prairie fire," John Henry muttered. Then he stood quickly, as Byron started for the door. "Ah . . . we'll have supper directly, Mr. Stillwell. And you're not supposed to go anywhere, 'til the sheriff gets back. He told me to make sure you stay here."

"For how long?"

"I don't know. But he should be back this evenin'. He just went up to Ten Mile Tank to meet a train."

In the summer of 1842, when a man named Lowe was setting survey stakes in the blackland strip of Milam Municipality, in what would later become Ellis County, Texas, he and his party camped on a hill with a band of roving Kiowa hunters. In the evening, after making gifts and exchanging courtesies, Lowe pointed to the north, where a wooded stream meandered. "What place is that?" he asked.

His Tonkawa interpreter repeated the question in Kiowa, and the hunt leader spread his hands in an eloquent shrug.

"Wa'csa-hatsi," the Indian said.

Translation being an imprecise art, the question the Kiowa heard was, "What is that thing?" It was probably the stupidest question he had heard lately, but it

117

would have been impolite to say so. Therefore, he simply answered the question. "Wa'csa-hatsi," he said. *"It is a creek."* Lowe recorded the name of the place as Waxahachie, and named the stream for its location, Waxahachie Creek. When a town grew there, the name continued.

Thus it was on the wooded bank of a creek called creek, that Coby Shanks and his followers reassembled after a day of prowling through the town called creek.

"Sullivan's still in town," Jude reported. "He's took a room at a hotel, an' stayin' over. He ain't been to the bank yet to draw his money."

"Seen several of them that was in Tightwad," Ollie Chadwick told them. "They're lookin' for that stranger they talked about, an' it's the same gent we seen at Ennis. The jasper with the paint pony an' the cat."

"Well, he ain't got any paint pony any more," Tandy O'Neill grinned. "Somebody shot that horse out from under him, right out on the street."

"I already heard about that," Coby frowned. "First I thought maybe Sullivan did it, but I don't think so now. Feller in town said it was a long shot, with a rifle. I don't recall seein' any of that bunch with rifles."

"So what do we do?"

"I say we hang around that bank in town 'til Sullivan shows up and gets his money, then we take it away from him," Jude Meece said.

"Right there in town?" Coby sneered. "If you had a brain, Jude, you'd haul it out an' play with it."

"I'm gettin' a little tired of your mouth, Coby," Jude said slowly.

"Any time you think you're up to shuttin' it, you just go ahead and try," Coby purred, his hand an inch from his gun. "What we do is wait. Sullivan will be headin' for home, and that's time enough to brace him."

Jude backed off, but a sullen anger burned deep

within him. "Cautious," he muttered. "Too damn cautious for my taste. May be time for a change soon."

Only Tandy O'Neill heard him.

At Half Moon Cross, a yellow cat wandered through an open door and stared at the people in a bunkhouse room. One was an injured man, lying on a cot. The other was the Indian wrangler, Willie Birdsong.

At sight of the cat, the injured man raised himself on one elbow and squinted, then turned to the Indian. "Is that the one? The cat that saved that feller's bacon?"

"That's the one, Frenchy." Birdsong squatted and held out an inviting hand.

The cat stared at him with slitted eyes, then padded toward him. As it passed the bunk, Frenchy reached out to stroke its fur—then yelled and jerked away. He had claw marks on two fingers. The cat went serenely on, to rub itself against the Indian's knee while he scratched its ears.

"How come he'll go to you and not to me?" Frenchy demanded.

Willie glanced around, his face stolid. "Cats are natural-born judges of character, Frenchy. This critter knows who's reliable here and who isn't."

Chapter Eleven

The highball liner called Midlands Express didn't usually stop at places like Ten Mile Tank. The Express was a shuttle train on a tight schedule, making a nine-day run every ten days with a twenty-four hour turn-around at the Wharton yards. In spring and summer it shuttled timber and rails to the Panhandle railheads and backhauled hides, hulls and quarrystone for switching to Houston. In the fall and winter it carried cotton.

This time, though, it pulled in at Ten Mile Tank with its whistle wailing and clouds of steam hiding its drive wheels. One man stepped down from the last passenger coach, late sun highlighting the dark creases of his long coat, brightening the gray-streaked hair below his dark hat. A porter handed down his valise and a pair of wear-slicked saddlebags, while attendants two cars back rolled out a ramp from a stock-gate and led down a tall, saddled sorrel horse.

The new arrival glanced once at those waiting for him, then took the reins of the sorrel and walked toward them, not looking back. Behind him the ramp was rolled in, the gate slammed and the Midlands Express made steam to resume its run toward Waxahachie, Ennis and points beyond.

Deputy Sheriff Buck Mabry had never seen a captain

of Rangers before, and studied him with bright-eyed curiosity as he approached ... a tall, quiet-seeming man with a face like a cloudy day.

Sheriff Matt Kingman stepped out to meet the newcomer, not extending a hand to shake, but simply nodding to him. "Glad to see you, Captain," he said. "It's been a while."

"Three years," the ranger said. "Who's this?"

Kingman turned toward Buck, who was a few steps back. "One of my deputies. Buck Mabry. He's learning the ropes. Buck, this is Captain Walter Mitchell, Texas Rangers."

The ranger looked him over, and Buck had the feeling that the teeth in his mouth had just been counted. "Howdy," he said.

Buck nodded, flustered. "Howdy."

"Surprised you didn't come up from Waco," Kingman said. "Been on field work?"

"Nosed around Mobeetie for a time." Mitchell stepped around the sorrel and tied his valise up behind the saddle. "You heard about the Double D drive, few weeks ago?"

"Heard it didn't make it to Kansas," Kingman said. "Fire wiped it out, up in the strip."

"Lot of questions about all that," Mitchell nodded. "Adjutant General's kind of curious about why Dawes would have put that many cows across the state line, when he knew there was a quarantine ahead of him, at the Kansas boundary. Some ways of thinkin', that doesn't make good sense."

"Is there any way it does?"

"Maybe. Politics bein' what they are these days, maybe so." The ranger checked out his saddle gear, snugged his cinch and stepped aboard. "Still a lot of who-owns-what that isn't rightly settled up that way.

121

Ever hear of a gunslinger named King Minter?"

"Who hasn't? They say he's the fastest man alive these days with a handgun. Up in Colorado, I hear."

"Not any more," the ranger drew his rifle, checked its action and loads, and returned it to its saddle-sheath. "Funny thing. King Minter is the new ramrod at Double D. Ready to go?"

"Bring up the horses, Buck."

"Yes, sir." Reluctantly, Buck hurried off to the shade of the old water tank where their mounts were tied. He hated to miss any of what might be said, though he hadn't understood much of it so far.

"New recruit?" the ranger asked, when the deputy was beyond earshot.

"Green as grass," Kingman nodded. "Got a couple of them I'm breaking in. They'll turn out all right, if they last."

"Your judge said you had yourself an interesting situation here. What's it all about?"

"I've got Byron Stillwell. You know about him?"

"Heard about him. What did he do?"

"Here? He witnessed a murder at Ennis, then got shot at in Waxahachie, and I think it was Goldie Locke that shot at him."

The ranger looked down at him, his eyes narrowed. "Stillwell dead?"

"Pure luck he isn't. His horse reared and took the bullet. Stillwell was just grazed. But *if* it was Locke, and I have reason to think it was, he'll try again. I want Goldie Locke, Walter. I want him real bad."

"You and a hundred others," Mitchell said, drily. "How sure are you that he's around here?"

"Stillwell thinks he's after him, and I believe him."

"He say *why* a killer like that might be after him?"

A trace of a smile dented the sheriff's cheeks.

"Stillwell started that fire up in the strip, Walter. Maybe he'll tell you so and maybe not. Texas law won't apply. But he did. Now Peter Lewellyn Dawes wants him dead."

"And Goldie Locke is on the streets of Waxahachie again, just like three years ago."

"I want him," Kingman said, quietly. "This time let's get that son of a bitch, Walter."

Mabry returned with the horses, and Kingman mounted. "Buck, you go on back to town now, and report to Chief Logan. And remember, you're not to say anything to anybody about Byron Stillwell, or about Ranger Mitchell being here. Anybody that's got any business knowin' any of this, already does. Understand?"

"Yes, sir. Ah, is Deputy Taylor going to be out for a while, Sheriff?"

"I'll probably send him in when I get to Half Moon Cross. Why?"

"Oh, no reason." Mabry swung aboard his horse and put heels to it, heading east along the tracks.

"Buttons," Kingman breathed.

Mitchell glanced at him, curious.

"Him and John Henry Taylor," the sheriff explained. "They're trying to beat each other's time with some of the typewriters at the courthouse. Especially a little sweet thing named Jolene." He shook his head in disapproval. "I know it's the latest thing, teaching women to operate telegraphs and typewriting machines and telephone centrals, and I'm not old-fashioned about such things. But I do believe it's a serious mistake, letting women work in public places. No good can come of it."

* * *

123

By most any standards in Texas, Half Moon Cross was a small ranch. Sprawling in the rough, stony hills northwest of Tightwad, spanning the west boundary of Ellis County, Half Moon Cross held little more than 3,000 acres in deed and lease. About five sections of land. But under Cap Freeman's management it had become a widely respected brand.

Freeman had started out, they said, as a brush-popper down in the coastal plains, fighting heat, flies, mosquitoes and Indians to chouse wild mosshorns out of the thickets and move them north along the trails. But where some had failed to change with the times, old Cap had been innovative. In the terrible postwar years, Cap had begun buying land in Ellis and Johnson Counties—bits and parcels where he could find them, in the hill ranges east of the Brazos. He bought, he traded and he consolidated. And as Half Moon Cross grew he brought in cattle. Tough, wild Spanish stock from the southern ranges, and a choice few breed bulls imported from Scotland and the Shetland Islands.

Most folks back then thought Cap Freeman was crazy. Later, they changed their opinions.

Longhorns and brush-busters still came up the Chisholm in season, herds of two or three thousand critters heading for Fort Worth and the stockyards. But they were not the same breed now as those cattle that grazed Half Moon Cross.

Cap Freeman's stock did not go to the mass markets for meat. Half Moon Cross now was a rancher's ranch, and most of its produce went to the northern spreads for breed stock.

Cap Freeman's animals didn't sell for six dollars a head. Generally, they sold for six hundred or more.

Stoke Winburn showed Byron Stillwell around headquarters while John Henry Taylor tagged along, worrying. The sheriff had ordered him to keep Stillwell out of sight . . . but how does one keep a man out of sight if the man doesn't want to stay that way? How does one give orders to a gunfighter who still has his gun?

"You notice the ear tags?" Winburn said proudly as they strolled past grading pens and chutes where cattle were being separated into holding pastures. "First place I known of to go to ear tags to verify the brand. But Cap was a believer that jinglebobs and notches are for trail critters, not for breedin' stock. He used to say, 'Who's gonna believe a damn cow is worth fifty times what any cow ought to be worth, if somebody's been whittlin' on its ears?' Then he'd say, 'Boys, these breed critters we sell, they ain't just beef. What they are is *progress*. An' the folks that buy 'em ain't buyin' beef. They're *buyin' investment*. This devil-spawned mess of trouble-on-the-hoof is by God *breed stock,* an' by God it's gonna *look* like breed stock.' "

"Smart cattleman," Stillwell noted. "Smarter than a lot I've met, including some I've worked for."

"What brands have you worked?" Winburn asked—a civil enough question, among cowhands. It wasn't always polite to ask a man his name or where he'd been, but comparing brands was shop talk. If a man didn't want to say what brands he had answered to, then he just didn't mention cows at all.

"I knocked around some," Stillwell said. "I rode for Lazy K for a while, up in the Mesillas, and did a stint at trail-bossing for Diamond Tie . . ."

"I learned the trade on Diamond Tie," Stoke nodded. "The south spread. Did you know Earl Hayes?"

"Answered to him. And played stud poker with him and the line crew a time or two."

"Lost your stake, I reckon."

"No, as a matter of fact I won a good horse and a Wyoming saddle from him."

"From *Earl Hayes?*" Stoke squinted at him. "He always cheated at stud poker."

"I know. Gave me a real advantage. I'd played with better cheats."

"I declare," Winburn breathed. "You ever have dealin's with any of the Shanghai Pearce bunch?"

Stillwell smiled, a tight, distant smile. "Once. But I never rode for the brand."

"Any others?"

"K-Bar, once. And an outfit called Four Star out of Tucson."

"You been around," Winburn nodded.

"A little." Stillwell rubbed his mustache, noticing that he needed to shave his other whiskers. "Right now you're wondering whether I ever drew gun wages. The answer is no. This," he touched the butt of the Peacemaker at his side, "cost me thirty dollars. I paid for it. It's mine, and nobody else's."

"I never asked," Winburn pointed out.

They wandered past the remuda pens. Beyond were horses grazing on good pasture. Byron stopped to look. "I'm short a horse," he said. "Might dicker with you about that."

"I'm in charge until the bank or the lawyers say otherwise," Winburn admitted. "Sure, I can sell a horse. See one you like?"

He looked them over, his eyes going thoughtful. "Nice paint over yonder. The liver-and-white. Fifteen hands, would you say?"

"That's my best day horse you're lookin' at," the strawboss said.

"Most horses have a price."

"I'll think about it."

They completed their circuit of the headquarters grounds, and Byron turned to take it all in. Sad, he thought, how so much of a man goes into building a spread like this that when the man is gone, it's like he was still here. Everything about the place had the flavor of a man he had never met. But he felt as though he knew him. Cap Freeman.

"What happens to the spread now that Mr. Freeman is gone?"

Winburn shrugged. "Banks and lawyers. Cap had some kin back east someplace, but they never came out here so I suppose they'll auction the spread. Bust it up or have new management, one."

"Where does that leave you and the outfit?"

"Out, I reckon." Stoke scuffed his toe at a patch of devil's claw. "Most of the boys can find work, I expect. They're all top hands, and anybody knows it. Cap didn't hire on greenhorns. Be harder for the Injun, I guess. Not many spreads in Texas will take on a Comanche, no matter how good a stock hand he is. An' Frenchy Boudreau yonder in the bunkhouse . . . he's still busted up from that bull. He tried to draw it away from Cap, and it stomped him, too. Then there's the kid. I don't know what he'll do." The strawboss gazed into distance for a moment, a worried frown on his weathered face. Then he shrugged. "Every man winds up on his own eventually."

From the hayloft a man called, "Riders comin' in, Stoke!"

There were two of them, just coming around the far fence and heading for the main gate. Even at the distance, Stillwell recognized one of them as Sheriff Matt Kingman. The man with him was a big, slope-shouldered silhouette in the evening light. A tall, dark man on a tall, dark horse. He rode easily, as one who spends plenty of his days traveling far places.

"How much for that dark paint?" Stillwell asked Winburn.

"You serious?" the strawboss tilted his head. "Plenty of other horses around that will get a man where he wants to go. That paint is . . ."

"I know what he is. I have eyes, and I won't argue. That's the best piece of horseflesh on this spread. How much?"

"Let me think about it."

"No, now. Name a price and I'll give you a bank draft. You can verify it with Western Union in Ennis, but I want to buy that horse now."

"Anything to do with the sheriff bein' here?"

"Yes."

"You on the run, Stillwell?"

"Not from the law. But a man who owns a horse has more choices than a man who doesn't."

Winburn gazed at him quizzically.

Stillwell shrugged. "What if the sheriff were to tell you not to let me have a horse, Stoke?"

"Then I guess I wouldn't let you have one."

"Has the sheriff told you anything like that?"

"No, he hasn't."

"Then sell me that horse, here and now."

Night breezes wafted through the long, low porch of Half Moon Cross' main house—breezes sweet with the scents of fresh clover and distant rain. Supper was over, the crew had dispersed—some to night guard, the rest to their bunks—and now only three men sat on the porch, sipping coffee and gazing into the night.

Three men, and a yellow cat that slept atop the

stack of gear they had brought out with Byron Stillwell.

"I won't promise to stay around here, Sheriff," Stillwell said for about the third time. "I expect there are ways you can keep me here, but not willingly. Your 'trap' is so full of holes a longhorn steer could walk through it, and all it's going to do is get people killed."

"Locke can't get to you if *nobody* can get to you," Kingman argued. "You'll be safe enough here, with Winburn's crew on the lookout. All we need to do is watch, and see who *tries* to get within range of you. Then we'll have our man. I already have a stakeout in town, where I hope everybody *thinks* you are."

"You'll have dead people," Stillwell muttered. "You think a professional like Goldie Locke is going to walk into a setup deal like that? Who's going to guard the guards, Sheriff? All Locke has to do is start picking off innocent people, and how long do you think your trap will last? What you're talking about isn't a trap. It's a shooting gallery."

The Texas Ranger sipped at his coffee and shook his head. "The man's right, Matt. It won't work. Locke isn't going to walk into a setup. It's been tried before."

The sheriff sighed angrily. "So it isn't perfect! What do you want to do instead, Stillwell, just ride out and take your chances? And yes, I know you bought a horse. Knew what I had in mind, huh?"

"I had a notion."

"So you just head out. You'll die if you do. Locke can come at you any time, from any direction, and you'll never even know it 'cause you don't know who he is. Hell, the son of a bitch could be *anybody!*"

"All I can do is take it a step at a time," Stillwell said. He turned to the ranger. "One thing I haven't heard: how does somebody who wants to hire Locke get in touch?"

"Oh, that's simple," Mitchell shrugged. "Locke advertises."

Kingman's head jerked up. "He *advertises?* I didn't know about that."

"Sure." The ranger sounded tired. "We didn't know it at first, but we do now. He runs advertisements in newspapers. We've gone back, built a whole file of clippings. Clear back to a box in the Denver *Post* five years ago. Things like, 'Professional exterminator . . . satisfaction assured . . . wire for rates Wednesdays . . . Goldie Locke . . . Dallas General.' Word gets out, people who might hire killers understand the meaning."

"But if you have a 'wire for rates' address, then why don't you . . . ?"

"Private telegraph keys. Anybody with a key and two clamps, and a little education, can intercept a message anywhere on the line," Mitchell explained. "The advertisement I quoted happened to be in the Nacogdoches newspaper, a year or so back. It was mailed in, along with the printing fee. We saw it, and had law waiting in Dallas. But there's no Goldie Locke in Dallas. Locke simply tapped the wire someplace between—on a Wednesday—and made direct contact. He probably has tap-points all over the country. Then again, if he carries the equipment, he can stop most anyplace and tap a line."

"So there *was* a contact?"

"There was. A week later a state senator was found murdered just outside of Austin. A senator from Nacogdoches."

"No question it was Locke?"

"There's never any question. The bastard advertises his kills, too. Things like, 'Barringer eliminated . . .

130

courtesy Goldie Locke.' He always does it. That's why we have a fair record of his kills."

"How is payment made?" Stillwell asked.

"They pay in advance. Cash up front, and the victim's name, left someplace like an old barn or under a certain tree ... and yes, we've tried that angle, too. Got us nowhere. Nobody collects if there's surveillance, and Locke knows. Somehow he always knows."

"Then the person hiring him never knows who he's hired, and there's no trail."

"Not so much as a track. Ever. It's clean and simple."

Kingman shivered. "It's like trying to find a ghost." He turned to Stillwell, his voice stubborn. "A few days, at least? I'd still like to give it a try."

"There's something else to talk about," the ranger said. "Whatever you do, Stillwell, I want some say in it. You're going to have to have some authority ..."

"I have all the authority I need," Byron said quietly. "It's called self defense."

"Not if you get tired of fooling with ghosts and decide to go after the person who paid for your assassination."

Stillwell turned to stare at the man, his eyes trying to pierce the darkness. "Second-guessing me, Ranger?"

"It's something I'd think about, if I was in your boots."

From the barn, they heard a shout. "Hey, the house! Somebody comin', in a hurry!"

A moment later they heard hoofbeats, and within a minute or so a puffing horse skidded to a halt beyond the porch, its rider peering into the shadows. "Sheriff?" a young voice called. "You there?"

"I'm here, Buck. What's the matter?"

"Chief Logan sent me, Sheriff. There's been another killin' over at Ennis, and word just come. Feller named Michaelson's dead. He was a telegraph operator over there."

Chapter Twelve

"Coby ain't gonna like this, Jude," Tandy O'Neill wiped his nose with the sleeve of his coat and sniffed, loudly. "He told us to wait out yonder."

"I'm tired of waitin' " Jude snarled, not taking his eyes off the lamplit entrance of the Liberty Bell Saloon across the street. "Sullivan's got the money, ain't he?"

"Yeah, I saw him get it, at the bank. But if he was startin' back to Tightwad he'd already have set out. It's late."

"Then we take it off him here, when he comes out. That damn Coby acts like an old woman."

"He just doesn't like to pull jobs in town," Ollie Chadwick offered. "He says it's chancy."

"Just like a damned old woman," Jude repeated.

They had been here, in the shadows on Courthouse Square, for more than two hours, waiting. Twice Jude had slipped across to look into the Liberty Bell's paned window, to make sure that Tim Sullivan was still inside. Sullivan was still there, sitting at a table with two of his cronies, putting down occasional shots of rotgut and seeming to be in no hurry.

The three watchers weren't sure where Coby Shanks was. He had left them by the creek at the edge of town, and gone in to look around.

But Jude had made up his mind. He was tired of

waiting and watching—two whole days now of doing nothing else—and fed up with taking orders from Coby Shanks.

"Won't be long now," he muttered. "Evenin' crowd's clearin' out."

By twos and threes, habitués of the Liberty Bell were leaving, stepping out onto the dim street to go their various ways. Jude shifted position to ease his cramped legs, and glanced around the area. The square was dark except for post lamps at the corners and near the entry steps, and he half expected to see a sheriff's deputy or two making the rounds. But none were in sight. The only law they had seen all evening were the town constable and one of his patrollers, and them only once.

Ollie was noticing the same thing. "This town's usually so full of badges a man can't spit without bein' noticed," he whispered. "Where do you reckon they all are?"

Jude hadn't the slightest idea, and cared less. The absence of visible law only reassured him that his choice was correct, and that reassurance grew now into a certainty that the time had come for him to take charge.

"I don't want to hear any more about Coby Shanks," he told the other two. "From now on we do things my-way."

Tandy O'Neill's eyes narrowed. "You takin' over, Jude?"

"Yeah." Jude grinned, his teeth glinting in the darkness. "Yeah, I guess I am. Ain't that somethin'?"

"You think you can outshoot Coby, if it comes to that?"

"Maybe I can, boys. But I won't have to. You know why? Because I know damned well the three of us can take him, and that's how it'll be if he don't like me callin' the shots."

"Why?"

"Why what?"

Ollie took a deep breath. "Why do you think we're gonna back your play, Jude?"

Jude turned slowly, gazing at him. "Because if you don't, and I put him down, then the next people I kill will be y'all. That's why. An' I'll tell you somethin' else, too. With me runnin' this outfit, we won't spend our time waitin' around an' actin' like cautious old women. We'll get ourselves some real money, an' keep on gettin' it."

They didn't answer, and he knew he had made his point.

Across the dim street, the Liberty Bell's doors fluttered again and two men stepped out.

"How about that!" Jude hissed. "Them's ol' Sullivan's buddies. That means he's all by hisself now."

The two Tightwadders stood for a moment, looking up and down the empty street, then one of them said something to the other and they both walked away, heading north toward the next street lights a block away.

"Well, they ain't leavin' town tonight," Jude decided. "So when Sullivan comes out he'll likely be goin' back to that hotel." He pointed westward, where the fronting street darkened for a block, a deserted area fronting a cotton warehouse on one side and some stables on the other. Beyond were the dim windows of one of Waxahachie's five travelers' hotels. "You boys head on down there about halfway an' get out of sight. When Sullivan comes out, I'll slip in behind him. We'll take his money when he gets to where it's nice an' dark."

Ollie hesitated. "Are we gonna shoot him, Jude?"

"I don't know. We might. Now get goin'!"

They went, and Jude fingered the butt of his gun, his eyes fixed on the door of the Liberty Bell.

* * *

135

Coby Shanks was ready to spit nails. He had returned to the creek after a careful scout of Waxahachie's thirsty areas to find his "gang" departed, and he knew what that meant. "Damn you, Jude," he muttered, guiding his horse along night-quiet streets. "Just had to take charge, didn't you? Now you're gonna get yourself killed, an' I ought to just stand and watch." Stupid, he thought. Walk right into a nest of rattlers just for lack of good sense.

He had learned what he had gone to see about. Tim Sullivan didn't have just two men with him in town. He had eight or ten, maybe more. It was what Coby had worried about. Sullivan was so set on getting even with some drifter that he had his toughs out in force. The trip to the bank was just an excuse. The Tightwadders were prowling the town, looking for Byron Stillwell.

He had learned something else, too. Something was going on in town, something that had the law all stirred up. The sheriff had every deputy available on the lookout for somebody, and they were all downtown, just sitting tight and waiting. Even some reserves were out. And not where they could be seen, they were in dark windows and on shadowed walks, watching. Coby didn't know what it was all about, but it was no time to be robbing cotton money.

Of all the times for Jude to finally get some sand in his craw . . .

Lamplight washed a corner where two saloons stood gaudy and bright on diagonal sides, both facing the dark bulk of the courthouse across the way. He eased his horse to midstreet, staying mostly out of the light, and turned left. If Jude and the others *were* here, they would be watching the Liberty Bell, where Tim Sullivan was. A block away. Behind him, two men entered the Irish Palace and came out a moment later, followed by

several more. They untied reins at the hitchrails and began mounting, while others came from the saloon
across the corner, the Prairie Rose.

Coby glanced around at them and went on. "Jesus,"
he breathed. He squinted into the darkness to his right,
wondering where Jude and the others might be. Ought
to just back off and leave them, he thought. Serve
them right if I did. Dimwits.

Ahead of him, the Liberty Bell's batwings fluttered
and a man stepped out. A bull of a man, with a slouch
hat. Coby's eyes narrowed. It was Tim Sullivan. The
man turned away and walked westward, into darkness.
When he was gone a shadow separated itself from the
shrubbery around the courthouse and ran, angling
across the intersection. Even in the poor light, he knew
who it was. "Jude!" he muttered. "You dumb son of a
. . ." He spurred the horse to a run and heard surprised
shouts behind him, up the street.

"Jude!" he shouted. "Wait! Don't . . ." But it was too
late. Gunfire flashed on the dark street beyond the intersection, and the thunders of it crashed and echoed
from the walls of buildings. Too many guns. Far too
many. Coby hauled on his reins, edging the horse to the
right, trying to see what was happening ahead. Another
gunshot, then two more, and a confusion of voices:
"Did you get him?" "There was more than one. Three,
looked like." "Who's down over there?" "Who was that
they braced? Stillwell?" "I don't think so. Joe! Bring a
light!"

Coby brought his mount almost to a halt, realizing
that he had his sixgun in his hand and the lights from
the Liberty Bell were on him. Behind him, fifty yards
back, he heard more shouts and the beat of hooves.

"Here's another one!" someone roared. "Get him!"

Guns cracked and Coby felt something tug at his
shoulder . . . something that made his arm go numb.

137

He started to bring his gun around, and heard bullets frying the air around him. They sounded like angry hornets. With a curse he put his gun away, leaned low and raked his horse with stinging spurs.

"Hold that fire!" someone ahead shouted. "Who in hell is that?"

Coby clung and ran, seeing men dart aside, shadows in the looming dark as he went through them. He dodged, swerved and spurred again and lighted windows flicked past. Then he was in darkness again. At a dim sidestreet he pounded around the corner, turned again at the next one and let the horse stretch out and gallop.

When finally the animal slowed, most of the town was behind him. He kept moving, heading west.

"I don't give a damn where the sheriff is!" Zeke Albert pounded the wood rail with a white knuckled fist and glared at the stolid face of Chief Deputy Jim Logan. "I don't care if he's halfway to hell, I want you to send someone to find him and get him back here! I want to see him now!"

The south wing of the courthouse was ablaze with lamps and astew with people—men with badges and men with guns, men fully dressed and men with nightshirts falling out of hastily-donned pants, men with prisoners and men in custody, and in the clerk's corner two wide-eyed young women clattering away at typewriting machines while men lined up beyond the railing gate, waiting to dictate charges, reports and statements. One of the typewriters had long, combed hair falling below a lace-trimmed sleeping cap, and a smear of drying soap on one cheek.

The clerk himself, Edwin J. Rice, wore no shirt under his buttoned coat, and had woolen slippers on his feet.

"I keep telling you, he'll be back soon," Logan assured the angry municipal constable. "Deputy Mabry already went to get him, because of that telegrapher at Ennis."

"Telegrapher at Ennis!" Albert snorted. "I got four dead men right here in Waxahachie, and three others hurt, and it's Matt Kingman's fault."

"I don't see how it could be his fault," Logan said soothingly. "He's not even in town . . . John Henry! Get the hell away from them typewriters! Haven't you got something to do?"

"Yes, sir." The deputy gave the girls a final adoring gaze, then vaulted the rail and sprinted to the main entrance to head off a Tightwad citizen escaping in the confusion.

In a far corner a man's voice rose in frustration. "I know who it was! It was that Stillwell! The one that attacked Mr. Sullivan without no reason t'other day at the ol' man's funeral!"

The duty deputy trying to question the man waved him down. "Why do you think it was Stillwell, sir? Did you see him?"

"Hell, no! But I heard somebody out there say his name, an' I know he knows we're lookin' for him."

"You see?" Zeke Albert thrust his face an inch from Logan's. "I told the sheriff the man was nothing but trouble! I told him so, and now look!"

"Stillwell isn't even in town, Zeke," Logan tried again. "How could he have anything to do with this?"

Another deputy arrived at Logan's side, cutting off the constable's response. He handed Logan a sheaf of papers, indicating the top one. "This is how it looks so far, Chief. Tim Sullivan had a gang of Tightwad boys in town lookin' for one Byron Stillwell, for reasons not yet specified—the ones we have aren't real sure whether Sullivan meant to beat him up or kill him, or what.

139

But Sullivan was carryin' a large amount of cash, and somebody jumped him to rob him of it, and some of our spotters misapprehended the situation. Word's out there might be a hired killer runnin' loose, and some of the boys figured either Mr. Sullivan or some of the robbers might be him." The deputy shrugged helplessly. "Damndest thing I ever seen to happen around here."

"Where is Sullivan?"

"Don't know. They think he grabbed a horse an' lit out, with some of his bunch. We have his money, though. Took it off one of the deceased. About five thousand dollars. Mr. Rice has it to count and record, and we'll get a verification from the bank tomorrow."

"Have the deceased been identified?"

"Yes, sir. Two of the robbers, a couple of rowdies named Tandy O'Neill and somebody Chadwick. They been seen around Ennis. Mr. Sullivan appears to have shot one of 'em, and I guess our fellers maybe shot the other one. Then there's Junior Travis, the day bartender at Liberty Bell, and Fred Calder, who was workin' as a reserve deputy. Mr. Sullivan may have shot him, too, but we ain't sure. Pretty dark out there."

"It's that Stillwell," Zeke Albert put in. "He's behind all of this, I'm telling you."

"He's not behind anything," Logan snapped, running out of patience. "I told you, he isn't even in town."

"I know better than that. The sheriff's got him hid someplace . . ."

"He's hid, all right, but *not here!* I told you that, damn it, Zeke. He's out at Half . . . he isn't anywhere near your precious town. Now get out of here. We have work to do . . . John Henry! Damn it, get away from them typewriters!"

With a final glare at the chief deputy, Albert stamped out of the noisy room and out of the courthouse, almost colliding with Judge Fein coming in. The judge was wearing a maroon robe and no hat. His hair stuck out in wisps.

Outside, Zeke Albert looked at the again-quiet town around him, thinking about what the county lawman had almost said. Half Moon Cross. Yes, it made sense. That redskin wrangler had been there when Stillwell's horse was shot, and then Matt Kingman had spirited the gunman away so fast that nobody seemed to know where he had gone.

He suspected the sheriff had gotten the man out of Waxahachie, though it had been made to seem that he was hiding in town somewhere. And he knew Matt Kingman wouldn't give up easily once he had a plan for bringing Goldie Locke out in the open.

"Want to hang the killer that made your county look bad, huh, Sheriff?" he murmured. "Think you can outfox Goldie Locke, do you? Think ol' Goldie is right here among us, stalking Byron Stillwell? You could have a point about that, Kingman. But I surely don't think you're going to be the one to put down Goldie Locke. Chances are, it could be the other way around."

Byron Stillwell was at Half Moon Cross. How many people knew that, right now? A few, obviously.

He turned north, walked a block and stopped when a closed carriage rounded the lamplit corner ahead and pulled up, its driver peering at him. Albert touched his hat. "Evening, Mayor. On your way to the courthouse?"

"Is that you, Constable?" The man squinted. "Thought it was. What's going on down here? They said there was shooting."

"Sure was, but it's over now. I don't think there'll be any more for a while, at least not in town."

"What was it about?"

Albert stepped out to the carriage and leaned on its fender. Lamplight glinted on its polished surfaces and gleaming brass trim. "It's kind of complicated, and the sheriff's office isn't saying much, Mayor. But some of their people were involved, I understand. Them, and some trigger-happy hooligans from Ennis. Several of them tried to rob Tim Sullivan of his crop money. Did you happen to pass Miz Walcott's house on the way down?"

The mayor's nose wrinkled in distaste. "I did."

"Any lights on there?"

"I certainly didn't notice. Why?"

"Oh, I just wanted to ask the lady a question."

"Lady!" The mayor snorted. "I don't know as I'd call the owner of the biggest whorehouse on the hill a *lady,* Constable. You'd be well advised not to be seen in that woman's presence, if you want my advice."

"Yes, sir, I appreciate that. But I have my duties to attend to. Speaking of which, I'll need an emergency order from you—or from the Council if that's what it takes. Starting tomorrow I want to post a ban on the carrying of firearms within city limits."

"Now, Zeke, you know how some of our . . . ah . . . citizens are going to take that."

"Then tone it down a little, but get me an ordinance, Mayor. I may have to be gone a few days, and I want to post it before I leave."

"If you'd stay around town more, Constable, and tend to your duties . . ."

"I do my job," Albert glared at him. "And where I go on my own time is my business. Just get me that ordinance. And if you want to know about the trouble this evening, ask them at the courthouse. It was their party, not mine."

Albert touched his hatbrim and stepped away. "Good evenin' to you, Mayor. I need to be on my way."

Chapter Thirteen

Neighbors still referred to it as the McIntyre House, stubbornly refusing to admit that it had changed hands three years before and adamantly refusing to have anything to do with the new owner. A scarlet woman, they whispered, outraged that Waxahachie's finest neighborhood housed such a creature. There were those among them who would never forgive Tobias McIntyre for dying and leaving his house up for bids.

It was a handsome house, tall and elaborately trimmed, maintained outside by a deaf and dumb caretaker and inside by a Chinese woman who spoke only enough English to do the marketing and answer the door. Neither was of any use to the lively curiosity of indignant neighbors.

Lamplight shone from downstairs windows as Zeke Albert climbed the steps and rang the doorbell. After a moment the Chinese woman opened the door a crack and looked up at him. "Yes, please?"

"Here to see Miz Walcott," he said, and pushed past her into the wide foyer. He didn't remove his hat.

From an open doorway in the hall, he heard, "Who is it, Ling? I . . ." Then the voice trailed off and she stood in the interior doorway, looking at him. She was fully dressed—either just going out, he thought, or just coming in. "Oh, it's you," she said, her nose wrinkling in distaste. "What do you want at this hour?"

"Evening, Daisy." Albert met her hostile stare with a cold gaze. "Seein' a lot of each other these days, aren't we?"

"Taffy said you'd been hanging around the Hill on a regular basis, *Mr.* Albert. But I don't relish having you visit my home. What do you want?"

"Just information, Daisy. That little show you put on the other morning . . . I gather you've known that drifter, Byron Stillwell, for a long while. Is that right?"

"Who I know and who I don't isn't any of your . . ."

"I can make it my business, Daisy. If I have to. How long have you known Stillwell? And how *well* do you know him?"

"I don't really know him at all. We met once, maybe five years ago. I haven't seen him since until the other day."

"Kind of strange a man like him would wait five years, then come to see you, isn't it? And at your whorehouse, too! My, my, Daisy . . ."

"He didn't come to see me. He just happened by. What are you getting at, Constable?"

"Well now, I don't know exactly. But Byron Stillwell seems to be a pretty important man these days. To *somebody*. Important enough maybe to be worth some real money, don't you think?"

"I don't know anything about it. If you're trying to find him, you've come to the wrong place. How would I know where he is?"

"Oh, I know where he is," Albert smiled, thinly. "The sheriff has him hid out at Half Moon Cross. What I want to know is where he might go from there."

"How should I know that?"

"Maybe he told you."

"He didn't tell me anything, Constable, and that's the truth and if you don't like it you just go ahead and try

144

making trouble for me. You might run into some surprises if you do."

He gazed at her, shaking his head. A handsome woman, tall and red-amber blonde. A striking woman, in her evening dress of imported silk. A wealthy woman, they said. Wealthy, but still only a whore. "Don't go threatening me, Daisy," he purred. "I don't like it."

"Get out of my house." she rasped. "Get out or I'll have the sheriff up here to put you out." She glanced toward the foyer wall where a brass and walnut telephone set hung between leaded-pane windows.

He sighed and half-turned. "You ought to choose your friends better, Daisy. Even a damned whore might improve herself, I suppose, but she could get hurt pretty bad, mixing with a fast-gun troublemaker with a price on his head."

Her eyes had gone intensely cold, hatred blazing there like winter ice. "Get out."

He stared at her for a moment longer, then turned to the door. "You just think about it, Daisy. Maybe you'll remember where Stillwell was going before somebody shot his horse. And when you remember, you tell me. I mean it."

"Out!"

He left, not looking back. He hadn't learned anything, really, but there would be other chances. The whore knew more than she was saying, he was certain of that.

Daisy Walcott came to the parlor window to watch him walking away, down the street. She watched until he was out of sight, then let the curtain drop closed. Large, wide-set eyes in a sculpted face were as cold as winter night.

"Bastard," she muttered.

* * *

145

With salve and time, the pains had begun to ease. The fresh, deep bruise along his ribs ached unmercifully, but the earlier bullet-wounds were healing and even the burn-tissue on his hands, legs and cheeks was slewing away, leaving healthy skin in its place.

"You are a remarkably fast healer," a doctor had told him once . . . where? In troubled half-sleep, the images were confusing. Features and faces of Julian Rosenthal, Frederick Cathcart, a sawbones up in the Nations, a medic in Kansas—they all blended one into another and it was hard to tell who was saying what had been said to him, once. "It's a good thing you heal rapidly," the dream voice continued. "The day you take the time to heal properly will probably be the day you're dead."

Tumbling dreams, images and sequences crowding around, vying for attention. I'm doing fine, Mattie . . . just having the time of my life. Hope you are the same. Dark eyes, knowing eyes that contained and accepted the worry they held . . . then other eyes, bright and alluring, eyes with a promise that they made no attempt to conceal. I'll be back to you, Patty. Back with you when I can, when the dangers are all gone and nothing lurks there that might harm you.

Eyes. And other eyes. Wide-set, inquisitive eyes that saw into him and said, "There's a woman, isn't there." Eyes he had almost forgotten, from out of the past.

Curious eyes. Curious circumstance. What was it that just didn't seem to fit?

A dead paint horse lying on a rain-soaked street, and somewhere a killer with a long-range rifle. Somewhere . . . so close, ready to shoot again. But where?

There had been a closed carriage . . . where? On the street? Or in the dark railyard where a lawman gone bad had fallen under iron wheels . . . fallen? No. Left there with a knife hole in him, because he was in somebody's way.

Shadowed eyes . . . hard, shrewd eyes below a dark brim. A Texas Ranger . . . and there had been another Texas Ranger, they said. Three years before. Dead on the street, like a paint horse dead on the street . . . why? That ranger had been on a trail. The trail of a killer with no face. And the trail had brought him to Waxahachie. Why?

Vague pains and tumbling dreams, vivid fire-and-darkness dreams set to a background of leaping flames and searing lead. Thunders and guns and the music of death, and eyes. Implacable eyes of a municipal constable, looking at him, wanting him gone. Gone? Or maybe dead?

Why was that dead ranger in Waxahachie, three years ago? Three years. *Three* years . . .

"You sleep like a man fighting snakes," a voice said.

Stillwell came awake in an instant, bolt upright on the low cot, Peacemaker drawn and cocked. Willie Birdsong's mouth dropped open, and he raised a hand, palm outward. "Easy! Easy, *'Chito*. Whoo! Do you always wake up like that?"

Stillwell lowered the gun and let its hammer down. "Sorry. You startled me."

"Remind me not to do any more rude awakenings," the Comanche said. *"Tsa'seyi!* I didn't even see you draw that thing! How'd you learn to do that?"

"The hard way, mostly. You could have knocked."

"Sure, and got shot through the door." He stepped to the bed table, moving carefully, and set a steaming mug on its marble surface. "Here, coffee's on and I brought you some. This was full a minute ago. Most of it's right there on the floor now. *Tsa'seyi,* but you're a wormy one!"

"I guess I was asleep." Stillwell put the Peacemaker away and stretched, noting where each ache and pain resided, cataloguing them as he always did so as never

147

to be surprised or slowed by them. A sudden, unexpected pang at the wrong instant could kill a man in certain situations.

He swung long legs off the cot, found his boots and shook them out, taking stock of the morning. He pulled on his boots, britches and shirt, and strapped on his gun. Then he picked up the coffee and sniffed it.

"You want me to sample it?" the Indian asked, wryly. "I saw Cook boil it, and I brought it over, and if either one of us is the varmint tryin' to kill you we've both had better chances."

"Sorry," Stillwell sighed. "I'm goosey, is all." He gulped back a good draw of hot coffee. "What's going on?"

"What isn't?" Willie pulled a chair around and straddled it. "Some doin's in town last night, an' come light this mornin' there was a process server at the range gate with paper for Stoke . . ."

"What was it?"

"He hasn't said. But he's called in the whole crew, so I guess I know. It's our driftin' papers."

Stillwell finished the coffee and put on his hat.

"An' there's a message for you," the Indian continued. "Louie found it tacked to the hinge-post when he went to see who the process server was. Don't know who left it." The agate eyes in the dark face went distant. "Yeah, I know what it says, but maybe you better see for yourself. Stoke's got it. He's out on the porch."

Stillwell felt a chill up his spine that had nothing to do with the weather. The shreds of recent jumbled dreams hung at the edges of his mind, tauntingly. Intuition like icy winds whispered to him, and he remembered what they had said about the telegraph operator at Ennis being killed.

Goldie Locke had no patience with the sheriff's games, or any others. Goldie Locke was ready for

Byron Stillwell to die, now.

Stillwell picked up his serape and hat, strode through the beamed parlor of what had been Cap Freeman's home and stepped out onto the porch. Several men were there—Stoke Winburn, looking bleak, the ranger, Mitchell, and a haggard-looking Matt Kingman among them.

"We're out of luck, Stillwell," the sheriff said. "I'm sorry. I thought we had a chance, but we don't."

"What happened?"

"Two little pieces of paper," Kingman shrugged. "That document in Stoke's hand there is a legal order for immediate possession of this ranch, filed by the executors of Cap Freeman's estate. I heard about it last night, from Judge Fein. It's legal and final, and there wasn't anything he could do about it. By six o'clock this evening, all persons 'residing on, occupying or currently present upon or within any portion, segment, structural improvement or domicile contained within or appurtenant to the lands known collectively as Half Moon Cross Ranch are hereby ordered to absent themselves therefrom under penalty of trespass.' " He completed the recital and sighed in disgust. "It means everybody that's here has to leave. Today."

Stillwell scowled in thought. "Locke?"

"Could be. I don't know how, but maybe so. Sure-fire way of getting you out of here, legally. I suppose we could find another hidey-hole, but . . ." he pulled a folded and wrinkled paper from his coat. "Well, there's this. It was on the hinge-post little bit ago." He handed it over for Stillwell to read.

The note was typewritten and unsigned. It read, "To Byron Stillwell . . . You cannot run or hide . . . Come out."

Beneath were two names and addresses:

"Mrs. Mattie Stillwell, c/o Rosenthal Trust, Baltimore

149

Conservatory of Music, Baltimore, Maryland.

"Mrs. Patricia Mills, c/o Silas Rutledge, Fargo Springs, Kansas."

And a final line: "You . . . or them. Come out."

Kingman looked at him with real sympathy. "I've seen some mean things, By. But I believe that's about the meanest."

"Bastard isn't even subtle about it, is he?" Captain Walter Mitchell growled, narrowed eyes searching the horizon.

"Maybe Goldie Locke had something to do with the eviction order, and maybe not," Kingman said. "But there sure isn't much doubt about this, is there?"

Stillwell started to fold the note, then handed it back to the sheriff. It was evidence. "Who found the note?"

"Louie Patton. He was ridin' guard when the process server showed up. The note was already there. I've already talked to him," he added.

"I went and looked, too," Willie Birdsong said. "No tracks that anybody could pick out. Nothin'."

Stillwell nodded. "Who filed the eviction notice?"

"The bank," Kingman shrugged. "Planters' Bank and Trust, who else. They're the executor."

"Banks aren't executors," Stillwell said, quietly. "People are. Who filed it?"

"Well, the banker did, of course. Selby Phillips. He's . . ." he stopped, in thought. "Oh."

"Oh?" Mitchell cocked an eyebrow.

"Phillips. He's Zeke Albert's brother-in-law. So I guess that explains that." He shook his head. "The son of a bitch."

Stillwell nodded, "He sure doesn't want me in his jurisdiction, does he?"

"Or anywhere near, I guess."

Stoke Winburn sat apart from the rest, half-straddling a porch rail, gazing off into the distance. "The

150

boys have pay comin'," he said, as though to himself. "We all do."

"You won't lose your pay," the sheriff assured him. "It's owed and it has to be paid. You still have the accounts, don't you? Then just figure what everybody has coming and issue bank drafts. Phillips will honor them. He has to."

· Nobody said anything for a while. Then Stillwell stood and started restacking his gear, which was still on the porch. The others watched him, and Winburn motioned to Willie Birdsong. "Man there owns that liver-and-white paint out in the corral. You want to go get it for him?"

The Comanche nodded. "Nice horse. Had my own eye on the gray that Frenchie favors for day work. Wonder what it's worth."

"About what's owed you, I guess," Winburn said.

The Indian went off around the house, the ramrod following him.

"Mobeetie's quite a ways from here," the ranger muttered, making it clear that he was talking to no one but himself. "Three, maybe four days, even by train. But ridin' on a train makes a man pretty vulnerable, seems to me. Then, there's all that nice scenery you miss, too."

Kingman gaped at him. "Mobeetie? What in hell's Mobeetie got to do with anything?"

"Never said it had anything to do with anything," Mitchell shrugged. He turned to gaze at Stillwell, squatted by his piled gear. "You say you never wore a badge, young feller?"

"Never had a reason."

"There's reasons and reasons. I'd have to come down pretty hard on anybody that took the law into his own hands in Texas, maybe like was done up in the Neutral Strip. No law there, of course, but *in Texas* there is."

151

Stillwell hoisted his saddle over the porch rail, and hung his saddlebags on it.

"I'm authorized to appoint Special Rangers," Mitchell said. "Generally that's somebody workin' for a range association, that might have need of a badge—even after the fact—due to the nature of his duties."

Stillwell shook out his saddle blanket, and picked up his bridle gear.

"I'm *not* authorized to offer any pay to a Special Ranger," Mitchell said. "Either somebody private pays them or they serve for free. But they've got the same authority—and the same responsibility—that a regular ranger has."

Stillwell put on his serape and hat. "You got some new kind of badge these days, Captain? Something that will stop bullets?" For a moment some private wall within him seemed to crack, and Mitchell saw in his dark eyes a feral glint, almost like the eyes of a hounded wolf at the instant it stops running and turns to fight. The look was gone as quickly as it had come. "Swear me in, then," Stillwell said. "But I don't take orders." He turned to Kingman. "Some questions I'd be thinking about, if I were you, Sheriff. Like, that ranger who was murdered in Waxahachie, why was he in Waxahachie? And like, just supposing somebody who lives here, *in your jurisdiction,* happened to be in the murder business, what sort of person could come closest to being invisible, and still be in position to know everything that's going on?"

"Do you have an idea?"

"No. Just questions. Like, why is that ranger's murder the only one within a hundred miles of this county that's attributed to Goldie Locke?"

While Mitchell was taking Stillwell's oath, Willie Birdsong came around the house, leading two horses. The gray was saddled and packed. He led the paint to the porch rail and handed the lead to Stillwell. Some paces away, another rider sat his saddle, waiting silently. The pale-haired kid that Stillwell had first seen at the funeral. Stillwell walked around the paint, stroking its glossy coat. He ran a firm hand along its neck, patted its cheeks, stroked its muzzle and got it to turn its nose to him, curiously. When it did, he breathed into its nostrils.

Willie grinned, watching. "You learn that from a Comanche?"

Stillwell rubbed the paint's ears while it rested its chin on his shoulder. "Learned it from a man named Sean O'Keefe," he said. "He used to train thoroughbreds for August Belmont in New York. Claimed he learned horse-talk from the Prince of Wales. This horse is mine, now."

"Been yours since you bought it," Kingman frowned.

Stillwell glanced around. "I've *owned* it since I bought it. Now it's *my horse.*"

He saddled, packed his gear and climbed aboard. "Thanks for trying, anyway," he said to Kingman.

The yellow cat appeared suddenly at an open door, glared out at him and came bounding across the yard. Stillwell shook his head, then leaned down, lowered a feed sack and the cat climbed to the saddle while the paint looked back, white-eyed and skittish. "Get used to it," Stillwell muttered, tightening the reins.

He reined around, headed westward, and looked back as hooves scuffed the ground behind him.

"We don't have anyplace special to go," Willie Birdsong said. "Maybe we'll tag along with you a ways." Behind the Indian, the pale-haired kid sat his saddle, waiting.

"Go where you want," Stillwell said. "But not with me. I don't need company."

The Indian gazed across at him for a moment, then

153

shrugged and turned away, aiming his horse north of west. The kid followed after him, saying nothing. A kid like others the gunfighter had seen, a kid who could be most anywhere and never be noticed.

Always around, but just sort of invisible . . . unless a man had call to notice him.

Running around with a white-educated Comanche, of course, folks would take note of him. But by himself, they wouldn't.

Chapter Fourteen

Twice Coby Shanks had stopped, once to bind the bullet-nick on his arm, and once because he and his horse needed an hour's rest. Both times, he was tempted just to turn around and circle back to Ennis, to hole up there and let things blow over. The railroad town had been a haven for him before, when things had turned hot.

But not this time. Both times when he stopped in the night his instincts told him to keep moving, to get as many miles behind him as he could. Because there were men back there who intended to find him, and by now they knew his trace if not his name.

That Jude, he told himself. That stupid damned Jude. Always itching to use his gun, always looking for a shortcut where there wasn't one, always pushing for position, testing the waters, waiting for the opportunity to be what somebody else had earned the right to be, even if it was just leader of a penny-ante hooraw gang.

Jude might be dead by now. *Somebody* was. Coby had seen at least one of them fall when the guns opened up. Maybe all three of them were dead. If so, it served them right. But each time he thought about that he wound up hoping that Jude was still alive. "We have unfinished business," he muttered to himself as the tired steeldust picked its way up a draw somewhere south—at least he *thought* he was somewhere south—of the Half Moon Cross headquarters . . . somewhere near the Johnson County line.

He didn't know who was behind him, but he knew someone was. Twice in the night he had seen lantern-light on his back trail. Someone was behind him, and not far back. A few miles at most. If that someone was Ellis County law, he needed the county line behind him. Nobody could possibly be sure just what had happened back there at Waxahachie. It had all been too fast, too chaotic. If those were county law back there, chances were they wouldn't give chase too far into another county.

If they *weren't* law . . . well, he would just have to wait and see. One thing was sure. They weren't friendly.

The steeldust was weary, and he was weary. With first light he began picking his path, angling a little north. He had in mind that he might try to make it up to Fort Worth, or maybe up into the Nations . . . someplace to lay over and hole up. Someplace to let things pass him by, while he thought about what to do next.

From a rise he looked back, trying to see distances against the light of growing morning. He saw nothing, but he knew they were there. Back there somewhere, and now with light they would be faster on the trail. He studied terrain to the west and north, looking for a northward angle, then hissed through buck teeth as a tiny plume of smoke moved, far to the north. The rail-road was up there! If there were more on his trail than those behind him, they could drop a line of eyes along the cleared right of way, and have him in a box.

The grin that spread across his impish face had no

humor in it. Damn you, Jude, he thought. Damn your stupid soul straight to hell!

Two hundred miles away, in caprock hills west of the deadline that was the west boundary of the Indian Nations lands and north of the forks of the Brazos, a rider headed north from Mobeetie by first light. Near midmorning he trotted his rangy mount into the central compound of the Double D Ranch headquarters and dismounted, slipping off his saddlebags and draping them over his shoulder.

He walked across the compound to the main house and rapped at the front door. A burly, sun-weathered man with a silvered Colt at his side opened it and the rider handed over the saddlebags. "Mail's in, Minter," he said, holding the other's eyes in silent challenge. "Some kind of package for the old man, too, that came plain freight."

King Minter weighed the saddlepockets, bouncing their heft in a large, gentle-seeming hand. "Took your time about it, Cole," he said. His voice was barely more than a whisper, yet it carried—the way far-off thunder carries, or the warning purr of a cougar.

"The package," Cole eased back a step, keeping his gaze challenging. "They had to run it through the mail depot before they'd hand it over."

"That's all right, Cole," the purr assured him. "We live and learn . . . if we live." Quietly the door closed and Cole Sanders turned away, clenching his jaws.

He was getting damn tired of dealing with King Minter. The new ramrod was like a rattlesnake—always coiled and twitchy, like he was just itching to strike out at whoever made a wrong move.

"All a damn bluff," Cole muttered to himself. If it weren't for the gun wages the old man paid . . .

Things had been different at Double D, before the big drive. Sure, there had been some snaky jaspers then, too. Like Ed Johnson and Pony Bidell—Cole felt a shiver as he recalled the flat-eyed gunman with the fancy draw—and Morgan had been the ramrod then. Morgan, tough and mean as any jasper Cole had run across, but a man generally knew where Morgan stood. A hard crew, but mostly gone now. The big herd had pushed northward, heading for Kansas where old Dawes and his cronies had two or three counties just set to topple and go under when the quarantine was broken.

But it had all gone wrong up there, somehow. Only a few of the drovers had come back, and none of the gunhands. And the herd was gone. Some crazy drifter had set fire to No Man's Land, they said. And the law in Kansas had got wind of Dawes' plan and closed the border. Most of Double D just never came back. Even Davy Dawes, the old man's power-hungry grandson, was gone. Probably dead, just as most of them were probably dead, though a few might just have gone their own ways and not looked back.

Just like I ought to do, Cole told himself. Or maybe just put the new ramrod under. But that would mean giving up the wages the old man pays.

Peter Lewellyn Dawes hired top guns, and paid top wages, and Cole had been satisfied, mostly. But not now. Not since the old man brought in King Minter. It rubbed him raw that some whispering show-off from who-knew-where was in charge, and he kept thinking about showing the man what a fast draw looked like from the spitting end—just for the pure murderous sport of it.

Cole led his mount around to the haybarn and shucked his saddle. Shag Newton wandered over from the well-house and leaned on the fence nearby. "Heard some of that," he said, laconically. "How long you gonna take that stuff, Cole?"

"What's it to you?" Cole glanced at him. There were people around who were afraid of Shag Newton, and for good reason. But Cole Sanders wasn't one of them.

"Nothin' to me," Newton drawled. "Any news from Mobeetie?"

"If you mean do I have any idea what the old man's gonna do next, no. I don't. I guess we'll know when he tells us."

Shag gazed at him. "Or when Minter does." He grinned. "Minter's pushin' you pretty hard, ain't he?"

"He'll know when it's too hard."

"That so? How?"

"I'll kill him."

In the main house, Peter Lewellyn Dawes sat in a wingback leather chair, at the head of a polished oak table sixteen feet in length. His was the only chair at the table, though there were others scattered around the big, low-ceilinged room.

The old man—at first glance—seemed frail and shrunken, eroded away by time until what was left seemed little more than a skeleton. His slumped shoulders in the high, wide-back chair, the folded quilt covering his lap, the very stillness of him as he gazed at the things on the table before him, all contributed to the impression of great age and frailty . . . until he looked up, turning toward the big, belted man standing a few steps away. Then the impression collapsed.

The sunken eyes in the aged face blazed with such an intense, malevolent hatred and radiated such power that no one who saw them could have considered him frail.

"Ennis," he rasped. *"Shipped* from Ennis? Not mailed?"

"What the stamp says," King Minter turned a large, elegant hand to indicate the wrap of the package. "Somebody delivered it after hours. It didn't get a stamp on it 'til Mobeetie."

"Read the letter," Dawes husked. "Read it aloud."

Minter picked up the folded paper that had been in the package. " 'You paid for this badge,' " he read. " 'It's right that you should have it.' " He put it back on the table. "That's all it says. Not even signed."

Dawes stared at the distorted, flattened bit of copper the package had contained. It might once have been a lawman's shield, but no longer. It was crushed thin, curved at the edges and the width of the crown of a locomotive wheel — or the rail beneath it. Dark stains speckled the metal, stains like dried blood.

"Do you know whose it is?" Minter purred.

"A nobody," the old man breathed. "A deputy town marshal at Ennis. I forget his name . . . ah, no. Pye. Roy Pye. A flunky. I asked him to watch for a man. Apparently he found him, and apparently he did something stupid. But it confirms that the man I inquired about — who should be dead by now — obviously is not." He spread other opened mail across the polished tabletop with a skeletal hand, picked up a handwritten Western Union message and held it out to Minter. "Read it."

" 'General notice,' " Minter read. " 'Stillwell no longer this county. Bound west. Seek elsewhere. A friend.' " He replaced it on the table. "Who's that from?"

"It doesn't matter," Dawes took a long, shallow breath. "What matters is that this message was sent 'general notice' to at least twenty destinations. Someone wants it known that the man is no longer in Ellis

160

County, and willing to pay to get that information out. No," he waved Minter back. "It doesn't say that, but the fee paid tally at the bottom of it does. And it indicates that what I assumed was an excellent, ah . . . professional . . . has failed. Byron Stillwell is alive. I want him dead, Minter."

"Yes, sir. Is this why you brought me to Double D?"

"No. But this takes precedent, now. The rest can wait. Bring me those range and route maps, Minter. There in the chart cabinet." As Minter pulled rolled paper maps from their compartments in the big cabinet beside the hearth, Dawes watched. "That one, yes. And that one, and the next one to the west . . . and our own range charts. Yes. Now spread them out here, in order."

When Minter had the charts spread, their corners weighted with bits of cedar kindling, Dawes studied them. He lifted his walking stick to use as a pointer. "Ellis County is there," he said. "There is Ennis, and there is Waxahachie just northwest of it. At the time that wire was sent, it seems Byron Stillwell was somewhere west of this line here, and bound westward. Here are rail lines, here and here. And these are public roads . . . do you know this country, Minter? Between there and here?"

"I know it," Minter smiled. "I can count the graveyards."

"How many men would you need, to find one man in that much area?"

"Depends on what I wanted to find him for."

"To kill him."

A dark glow grew in King Minter's eyes. "Not many, if I pick them . . . and if I have a free hand in makin' them understand what I expect."

"How many?"

"Five."

"I'll pay well, Minter. Very well, indeed."

"Oh, I know you will," Minter nodded, smiling slightly.

"The man's name is Byron Stillwell," Dawes said. "I have never seen him, but he has been described as six feet plus in stature, about thirty years old, dark hair . . . go to the cabinet and open the first drawer on the right. Do you see a framed picture there?"

Minter found it and studied it. An old, yellowed likeness of a man and a woman, posing in the stiff, expressionless manner of people counting seconds while a lens exposes sensitized glass. Two young people, the man tall and muscular, with the flowing sideburns of an earlier time, the woman blonde and tiny, fragile-looking beside him.

"This is an old picture," Minter said. "Might be twenty, twenty-five years old."

"Something like that," Dawes shrugged. "But look at the man closely. His name was Samuel Dance. I understand that Byron Stillwell is his son. There may be a resemblance."

Minter studied the features of the man in the picture, then returned it to the drawer. "I'll remember," he said. "Who was the woman?"

"My daughter," Dawes said, distantly. "When can you start, Minter?"

"Any time. Do I have my pick of your gunmen . . . and my terms?"

"You have. And a bit of advice, as well. The man you're after should already be dead. But he isn't. It seems that Goldie Locke has failed."

"Locke?" For the first time, Minter's voice was other than a rumbling purr. *"Goldie Locke . . . missed?"*

"So it would seem," Dawes pulled his quilt tighter about him, impervious to the fire in the hearth and the heat of the big room. "It's something you should consider. Key Begley set out to kill Byron Stillwell. They found Begley in a frozen coffin up in Kansas. Wiley Dobbins tried, and died. At Beer City in the Strip. Morgan Hayes . . . he was your own predecessor here. I'm sure you've heard of him? He said he had killed Stillwell, six months ago. Said he shot him down. Morgan Hayes is dead now, and Stillwell is alive. And there was Pony Bidell . . ."

"Bidell?" Minter stared through narrowed eyes.

"He's dead, I suppose. At least he never came back. And Ed Johnson, and Sturdevant . . ."

"Sturdevant . . . the man with the big rifle?"

"They found him up in a tree in the Neutral Strip. What the birds had left of him. Shot to death at close range, with spent rifle cartridges all around him. That's what I'm telling you, Minter. Make no mistakes. Those others did."

"I don't make mistakes," Minter whispered.

Dawes looked at him, old eyes in an old face, ablaze with hatred and an absolute intent. "Neither does Goldie Locke, I'm told. But that drifter is still alive."

When the midday meal was finished, Minter sent ranch hands to pack provisions, snag out saddle stock and fill canteens, then he washed his hands carefully, dried and powdered them and stepped out into the compound. Morning sun glistened on the silvered pistol at his hip. He looked from one to another of the nine gunhands—all that remained of Double D's army of shooters. Hard men, every one. Renegades from the territories, fugitives from murder warrants in various places, survivors of Piney Woods feuds, border gunmen and fast-draw artists. He let his eyes rove over them, coming to rest on Cole Sanders.

Of them all, Sanders had the meanest reputation—

both as a gun artist and as an outright killer. He saw the resentment there, that Dawes had brought in an outsider to be ramrod. Cole Sanders would have expected, by right of pecking order, to be given that job and the pay that went with it.

Minter smiled slightly. "We have work to do,". he said, his purr carrying easily to all of them. "A man to kill. I'll take five of you with me."

"Six of us for one man?" Sanders smirked. "Why not just go tackle him yourself, Minter? You're some kind of hotshot, ain't you?"

Minter's tone didn't alter. "We have to find him, first. So six of us will go. I need you, Newton," he pointed. "And Bodine, Trask, Billings, Caine . . . and Sanders. The rest of you can tend to things here until we get back. I've already ordered up six saddle-mounts and some packs. We leave when they're brought around.

Cole Sanders frowned, stepping away from the porch. "You said five to go with you, Minter. You called off six names."

"So I did," Minter smiled. "Well, Cole, I guess I don't need you, do I?"

Sanders stopped, turning a little aside. He sensed what was coming, and crouched slightly. "You don't *need* me?"

"Not at all," Minter purred. "I never did."

"You son of a . . . !" Cole's hand dived for the gun in his oiled holster, lightning-fast, and drew . . . or tried to. Something was wrong, he realized numbly. Minter had a gun in his hand, and there was fire at the muzzle of it. A bright blossom, like a flaming, flaring rose. And he couldn't make his arm finish its movement . . . couldn't seem to breathe . . . couldn't . . .

It had happened in an instant, and it was over before Cole Sanders' limp legs collapsed and dumped him on the hard ground. King Minter thumbed a spent cartridge from his smoking .45 and slipped in a fresh one, then put the gun away.

He looked around at the rest of them. "So you'll know," he purred. "Any questions . . . about anything?"

None of them had questions.

The horses were brought around and they mounted. Shag Newton glanced down at the still body of Cole Sanders. His lip twitched as he clicked his tongue in acceptance. Minter had made it real plain who was boss.

Chapter Fifteen

Someone has threatened you, Mother. And Patty. Someone who doesn't miss has missed, and now is threatening you to get at me. Unthinkable? I could see that the sheriff thought so. But it isn't unthinkable. Uncondonable, but not unthinkable. Someone ruthless and very logical has seen directly to the heart of me, unerring as though he knew me personally. He has offered what I can't refuse, to bring me out into the open. Come out where he can find me, and he won't go after you. Is it a bluff? It may be, but I can't chance that.

Ahead of him, the land became more hilly, more forested as it stepped down and away toward the Brazos valley. He had set a course that lay through the rough country, away from the rails and away from roads, away from the farmed fields of the blacklands, down through the miles of breaks and washes beyond which lay the forks of the Brazos.

Since leaving Half Moon Cross' back range, he had seen no one. There was just the land, himself and the paint horse.

And a cat, he reminded himself, bleak creases forming momentarily on his cheeks. All this, and a cat.

For the moment, no one was watching him, no one fine-sighting a heavy rifle or waiting in brush for him to come into range. Instincts fine-tuned by the habits of a lifetime told him that. Instincts born of the back streets of Philadelphia, the St. Louis waterfront and the unforgiving isolations of the west. Instincts born of backstage intrigues where the lights were bright, gaming-table face-downs where the lights were smoky and sullen, instincts honed by years of familiarity with the uncertainty of life, the abruptness of death.

Instincts . . . and the senses of a man who had been both hunter and prey, and sometimes both at once. *But he is out there somewhere,* he thought. *He controls the game now, and he knows it.*

Is there just one of him, or more than one? Are there assassins on their way right now, to find two innocent women, to keep them in their gunsights until this is done? Maybe someone even now, making train connections from somewhere to Maryland . . . from somewhere to Kansas, to back the play for Goldie Locke? To kill you, Patty . . . to kill you, Mattie . . . if I don't step willingly into the killer's net?

The paint climbed a long rise, moving easily with the sure-footed pace of a horse born for distances. Near the top Stillwell reined in for a moment, giving himself a long look at what lay beyond. A faint pall hung along a crest a mile ahead and to the left, as though riders had passed that way—or were converging toward his path. He saw no movement, and the trace of dust was gone almost as he saw it, swept away by prairie breeze. Someone was ahead, there. He went on.

I don't think there are others, he told the images in his mind. *I think there is only one. Come out, the message said. Just . . . come out. Not come to me and die. No, he didn't quite have the hand to play dead showdown. I wouldn't have had so much room left to me, if the threat to you were immediately enforceable.*

I will gamble that far, my ladies. The images looked

167

back at him—two pretty faces, both caring for him, both trusting to his judgment. *I have to believe that Goldie Locke is only one person—as his elusiveness says he is—and that he is here somewhere, setting a trap for me. It is the only edge I have, that he cannot be two places at once, and that he cannot threaten you as long as he is busy seeking me. He has used you as pawns to force me to play his game. And the only edge I have is to play it my way if I can.*

As the sun climbed behind him, he crossed a wide, tangled area of gullies and draws where scrub cedars stood above little sandstone shelves. Beyond was another rise, and beyond that was where the haze of dust had been. As he neared the crest, he heard distant popping sounds and knew what they were. All his life, it seemed, he had known the sound of gunfire. He walked the paint to the crest of a wooded ridge slanting beyond the main rise, and stepped down.

The yellow cat roused itself from a nap behind the saddle, stretched luxuriously and looked around, then jumped to the ground and stalked off into the brush, not looking back.

Stillwell led the paint into good cover and tied its reins low, allowing it to graze on the tall, clumpy grass among the cedars. From his saddlebag he drew a small, brass telescope and opened it, then crept to the far side of the thicket where a stone slope dropped away, and squatted on his heels with his back to a cedar stump. Braced there, he raised the glass and scanned the distances beyond.

At first he didn't see them, then two more gunshots sounded, thin on the breeze, and he homed on the sound. On a flood-carved slope where stone-bed washes meandered toward a sun-hazed stream, a battle was taking place. A dead gray horse lay head-down in a little gully, a black horse dragging its reins stood skittish and alert beside a willow copse and a man lay sprawled nearby, his arms outflung, his face to the sun. Just beyond, maybe fifty yards farther down the slope, men on foot were spreading and moving, using what cover they could, making for a bend in the gully beyond.

As he watched, someone in that gully stood, fired and ducked aside as shots answered him. One of the attackers went to his knees, then pitched forward.

"Fine shot for a handgun," Stillwell muttered. He scanned the terrain again, studying the men, their placements and their movements. It was a lop-sided encounter, whatever its cause. There were at least five attackers—seven, counting the two on the ground—and only one man returning their fire.

Bracing the glass, he saw a face clearly and clicked his tongue. Sullivan. Tim Sullivan, the trouble-maker he had silenced at Cap Freeman's funeral.

Sullivan and some of his crowd, and they were after somebody. One of the cowboys from Half Moon Cross? The crew was evicted, broken up and some were drifting. The lone man out there could be one of them. Possibly even the loquacious Comanche, Willie Birdsong, or the pale-eyed kid who rode with him.

"None of my business," Stillwell muttered. "Doesn't matter who that is, it's none of my business. But then, things hardly ever are." He folded his glass, ducked back into the cedars and went for his horse.

Coby Shanks had three cartridges left. He hugged the shoulder of the little draw where he had taken cover, spun the cylinder of his Colt and grinned—a grin that held no mirth, but only a kind of stubborn fury. Jude, you stupid son of a bitch, he thought, I hope you're dead because it looks like I'm fixing to be . . . thanks to you.

The breeze shifted and he heard rustlings in the brush, on the slope above the draw. They were closing in on him, spreading to flank him, to maybe get him in a crossfire. He knew who they were now. He had seen Tim Sullivan in the instant when his gray horse went down. The big man had been behind a stump, firing a lever carbine, but he had seen his face. And others.

He didn't know how many were left. He knew that two of them were down. He had placed those shots and knew they hadn't missed. But how many were left, coming down on him?

The humorless grin widened on his leprechaun face. More than three. He knew that.

He glanced back along the draw, toward where his horse lay dead. It was out of sight and out of reach, and his coat with it—the coat with the bullets in the side pocket. All he had was the bullets in his gun, and three of them were spent. Even if he could get back there, it would do no good. The coat was under the horse. It would take digging to retrieve it.

I should have gone into another line of work, he chided himself as a bullet clipped shrubbery just above his head. He eased a foot to the side, raised himself a few inches and tried to see where the attackers were. At first they hadn't been so cautious. They'd figured that one lone man couldn't stand up to them. There were two less now, though, and now they were being careful.

He reached aside, rustled a little clump of dry salt-cedar and bullets sang past as he dropped into cover again. They seemed to come from everywhere, and they sounded like stirred-up hornets, whining and ricocheting for an instant before the crash of gunfire drowned them out.

Definitely more than three, he assured himself. Five, maybe. All fanned out and closer than they had been.

He eased out from the shoulder, looking one way and

then the other, up and down the draw. It curved here and he could only see a few yards each way. He let himself down farther, sliding backward, and a bullet kicked up gravel an inch from his bootheel.

"Jesus!" he whispered. The Tightwadders were everywhere, and they had him pinned like a rabbit in a soapweed stand. Desperately he scanned around him, looking for a way out.

Three shots left. Of course, they didn't know that. *Maybe* they didn't. He needed a way to move, and somewhere to move to. Somewhere where he could see something to shoot at, a chance to slow them down, to make them reconsider . . .

He peeled off his shirt, looked at it thoughtfully for a moment, then selected a fist-sized rock and shoved it into one of the sleeves, at the shoulder. The rock slid down the sleeve, caught for an instant at the cuff, then fell through. At the sound of it, three more shots crashed and bullets sang over him. Somewhere nearby a gruff voice called, "Quit that poppin', damn it! Let's get where we can see the bastard, *then* shoot him!"

Coby found a bigger rock. This one slid into the shirtsleeve but stopped at the narrower cuff. He wadded the shirt around it, gritting his teeth. "Not a chance in hell this is gonna do any good," he breathed. "*Nobody's* trigger-happy enough to . . ." He stopped thinking about it. With a deep breath in his lungs and his gun in his left hand, he threw the bundle of fabric as hard as he could. The missile sailed across the draw and over the brush on the other side, not straight across but at an angle. Stained linen unfurled behind the stone, fluttering in arching flight, and guns roared and crashed.

Even as they sounded, Coby was over the shoulder of the wash and racing uphill, crouching and weaving, switching his Colt to his right hand. He heard shouts, and bullets clipped twigs behind him. He burst through a stand of brush and a man was there, holding a pistol in both hands, extended . . . but pointed the wrong way. A surprised face turned toward him and he put a bullet through it, then swerved and dived for the next cover. He crashed through, hit and rolled and ran again, zig-zagging up the slope.

"You dumbasses!" someone shouted, off to one side. "He ain't over there, he's right . . ." Coby's bullet took the man in the gizzard as another shot from somewhere else scored a red-spray gouge along Coby's thigh. He stumbled, fell and rolled, and found himself in open ground, yards from any cover.

"I got him!" someone shouted. "Come on, he's down!"

Coby tried to get his legs under him, but the right one collapsed, numb from the shock of the hit. He fell again and a bullet sang past his ear.

"Now kill him!" Sullivan's voice roared.

Coby looked up, into the muzzles of guns. The faces behind them were gloating, excited faces. Two, then three as Tim Sullivan shouldered through scrub cedar to join them.

"By God," the big man sneered. "It's one of them kids from the saloon. Where's that drifter? This ain't him."

The voice that responded came from up the slope. "Will I do? Drop those guns!"

The three men looked up, beyond Coby, and their faces went blank. Then Tim Sullivan roared, "It's him! It's that no-good . . ." He raised his gun and stopped, seeming suddenly frozen in place as a shot boomed above, behind Coby. Sullivan looked around in dull surprise, then looked down at his own chest, where blood was spurting. "I . . ." he said.

Again the unseen man behind Coby said, "Drop

172

them!"

Tim Sullivan fell to his knees, still staring at the hole in his chest. The two with him gawked at him, stunned. Then abruptly, they came alive. As one they whipped their guns up, and as one they were thrown backward as Coby's bullet and another one from somewhere behind him flew together.

Tim Sullivan's gun fell from his grip, and he stared at the blood pumping from him. Then he toppled forward and lay still.

Coby felt sick. He had killed men before today. Four times, that he knew of. And three of those had been shooting at him when he did. But there was something about this that shook him. For a moment he didn't know what it was, then he did. It was the way the man's voice sounded — the voice behind him, up the slope. It was a voice as flat and calm as pond ice . . . and every bit as cold.

He raised himself, sat upright and turned, his bleeding leg thrust out behind him.

The man there wore an Indian-looking serape, and his hatbrim shaded his eyes. His gun was not in his hand, but rode ready at his hip and somehow Coby knew that was where it had been when the others raised their weapons to fire at him.

"You, too," the icewater voice said. "Just drop it on the ground there."

Coby dropped his gun, eased away from it and stood, favoring his sore leg. The grin that twitched at the corners of his mouth spread slowly outward, and this time there was humor in it.

"At least you're smarter than they were," the newcomer said. "They should have dropped theirs, too."

"Wouldn't have done me any good if I'd kept it," Coby said. "I'm flat out of bullets. They had me dead to rights."

173

"Seems to me you did your share of the festivities," the man nodded. "What was this all about?"

"Serious lack of common sense," Coby grinned. "Me an' them, both. You still got that cat?"

In the wardroom in Ellis County Courthouse, Sheriff Matt Kingman stuck his head out his office door and motioned to his chief deputy. When they were inside, Kingman produced a sheaf of papers—handwritten lists, notations and instructions. He handed them across. "Here's where we begin," he said. "The items at the top are the open procedure. Let's have men visible on these items. Don't make any secret of what we're doing."

Logan nodded. "And the others?"

"You and I know about these," Kingman said. "Nobody else needs to. Any word on Zeke Albert yet?"

"Confirmation from the station agent. He left on the 8:05 this morning, bound for Paducah Crossing. Mayor says that's where he usually goes when he's away. Relatives there, or somethin'."

"Westbound," Kingman said, and nodded. "Who else was on that train?"

"Can't get a list," the chief shrugged. "It's a general run. Open fare anywhere along the line, clear to Santa Fe. No passenger manifest. But the agent says there were several passengers that boarded here. More than usual, maybe. Some of the hands from Half Moon Cross, headin' out to look for work. Pair of yard bosses from Ennis, laid over here for a few days and then went on. Couple of women, a young feller with a satchel . . . that's about all I could find out."

"All right," Kingman nodded. "Break out the top list and get everybody busy on it. Byron Stillwell has given us the best chance we'll ever have to smoke out Goldie Locke, by leading him away while we work on it.

174

Stillwell's probably going to die for his troubles, but I'd sure like to make his misfortune pay off."

"You think Locke headquarters around here, don't you?"

"I think there's a good likelihood. So do the Rangers. And what Stillwell had to say just makes it seem more likely. We'll play it that way and see what we can find."

Logan read through the bottom list again, shaking his head. "Lordy, I never would have considered all these possibilities. Mitchell's ideas?"

"His and others'. The Rangers have never let up on that investigation. They've given it a lot of thought, the past three years. We're just taking what they've come up with and applying it here."

Logan grinned at him. "This makes me wonder why you're lettin' me in on this, Sheriff. Like you said, Goldie Locke could be damn near *anybody.* How do you know I'm not him?"

"You remember where you were when the ranger was killed out there three years ago, Jim? Ranger Sparling?"

"Well, yeah. I was here in this office, with you and Judge Fein, going over some depositions. Rice was here, too."

"That's why," Kingman said. "There are four people—*only* four people—in this county that I'm absolutely sure are not Goldie Locke. You and me and those other two."

"Reminds me," Logan said, reading through the lists again, "Rice is raisin' hell about the affidavits and reports from that shoot-up out there. Says there's no way he can get everything filed like you an' the judge want. He says he's short-handed because one of his typewriters has disappeared."

Chapter Sixteen

Stillwell bypassed Mineral Wells in late afternoon, cutting south around the little town to avoid the railroad that went through there. The greatest danger now, this close to Ellis County, was to be spotted from the rails. He had no doubt that Goldie Locke had figured out his direction by now, and the killer probably had even guessed where he was headed. Locke was no fool. He knew who had hired him, and would know that Stillwell knew that, too.

He would be searching westward. And how better for a lone killer to seek out a man heading west than with a map and a train schedule? Locke could travel by train, measure distances and drop off at any point he wanted to, ahead of his prey. And wait. It might not work the first time, maybe not even the second or third. But sooner or later—the killer must assume— Byron Stillwell would pass by, heading north of west. And when he did, the killer would strike.

Locke would figure that out, and he'd be right. He had left his victim no other options.

Beyond Mineral Wells, he looked for high ground for a last look around while good light lingered. All day, the land had become rougher and hillier, broad scrubranges dotted with mazes of draws and little canyons, the hills rising in ridges above them. Forks of the Brazos country, the old-timers called it, this thirsty, lonely expanse between the agricultural blacklands that he had left behind him and the towering Scarp—still a hundred miles ahead—where the caprock lands began, and beyond that the Llano Estacado. The staked plains.

No more messages for a while, Mother, he thought bleakly. Or for you, either, Patty. Not here and not now. Not until all this is done . . . one way or another. Whichever way it ends, after it's done you'll both be safe.

Keep the ladies safe. That's what civilization is all about, he mused. Men don't need civilization, not for themselves. Without civilization, without law, men would just kill one another off and what would be the difference . . . if only men were involved. But the women must be kept apart from that.

He had seen it even in the lawless lands of the Neutral Strip, a place where no jurisdiction extended and the only law was the law of the quick and the dead. Even there, even when men fought and died, there was a code that must be followed. Keep the women out of it. Few men, even the worst of those in the worst of places, would willingly hurt, threaten or even embarrass any female. It simply was not tolerated. A man who broke that code was the lowest form of life in the west, and likely to be hunted down and put to death by everybody else around—friend and foe alike.

The lowest form of life. Goldie Locke had broken the code, by threatening Mattie Stillwell and Patricia Mills.

But who was Goldie Locke? *Where* was he?

After me, Stillwell told himself. That's where he is. He's after me. And he won't be evaded very long.

From the top of a hill, Stillwell looked back the way he had come, and muttered a curse under his breath. That redhaired kid was still back there, still following.

"Stupid," Stillwell breathed. "Stubborn and stupid."

177

He had left Coby Shanks where he found him, after helping him strip his gear from the dead gray. The redhead was lucky to be alive, and Stillwell had told him so in no uncertain terms—then left him there to rearrange his values and go his own way. But all through the afternoon the young hoodlum had been back there, just following along, dogging his trail. It was becoming a real irritation.

"Stupid kid," he muttered again. "What do you think you're going to do, try me out? Maybe get yourself a fine reputation for the price of a bullet?"

It was a thing that lived in him always, the memory of four graves he himself had dug. Four sad, unmarked graves . . . two in Arizona Territory, one in New Mexico and one just a few miles from El Paso. Four graves that nobody but him would ever remember. Graves that would no longer even be visible—the land healed its scars in just a season. Each grave contained the body of a young man who had gone in search of Byron Stillwell, and found him, and learned too late that even the fastest gun will find a better gun, if he goes looking for it.

He would never forget those graves, and he didn't want to ever dig another one. If the damned guntoughs were determined to get themselves killed, then let them find another way.

"Stupid," he muttered. Stupid and very sad, he thought.

But he was going to have to do something about Coby Shanks.

Coby Shanks was pleased with the horse he had found, a short-coupled chestnut with stockings and a blaze. It reminded him of another horse that he had wanted but never had. The man who had it had been

178

too stubborn to give it up and too frightened to give him reason to draw and fire. It was the kind of stand-off he hated. To get the horse, he would have had to simply kill the jasper hanging onto its reins. In cold blood.

An embarrassing situation. He had finally robbed the man of eighteen dollars and a silver-cased watch, and gone away. He hoped nobody had ever heard about that . . . about Coby Shanks backing away from a sweating, trembling weak-knees who just wouldn't hand over his horse to save his life. To this day, he couldn't see how any horse could be worth that.

Now he had a blaze chestnut, though, and there wouldn't be any argument about it. It had been wandering loose after Sullivan's bunch was dead.

In last light of evening, with high clouds in the west throwing down the final glow of a long-since-gone sun, he topped out on a swell and saw a twinkle ahead, low down in the shadow of a limestone bluff. Firelight . . . and on the wafting breeze the scent of coffee boiling in a pot. He licked his lips and grinned. He had begun to wonder whether the big man on the paint ever intended to get down and rest.

"Yonder he is," he said, happily. "I hope the coffee's strong."

He eased his six-gun in its holster, drew his new rifle from its boot and checked the loads. "Man can't be too careful," he muttered.

A hundred yards from the fire he got down, tested the air and went ahead on foot, leading the chestnut.

"Just like comin' home, ain't it?" he whispered, glancing back. Then he shook his head. "I must be gettin' light-headed," he decided. "Here I am, talkin' to critters again."

It was just a hatful of fire, built careful and small, right down in the rocks under a thirty-foot ledge where anybody passing by in any other direction would never have seen it. Cautious soul, Coby thought. Man's been on the dodge before, for sure.

He squinted in the near-darkness. There was a pot on the fire, and the smell of coffee hung in the air. Near it lay a saddle and some bags, and a rolled bed. To one side, almost invisible, a figure sat slumped as though in sleep. Coby looped his reins on a stump and crept forward, rifle in his left hand, his right free and poised above his Colt. The figure in shadows didn't move. Coby crept near, peered into the darkness, satisfied himself that no one else was around, then set his rifle aside and squatted by the fire. There was a tin cup behind the steaming pot, and he filled it half-full of coffee and blew on it to cool it.

"Go on an' get your sleep," he muttered. "I ain't goin' any place."

The voice behind him froze him where he sat. "If you'd pointed a gun at that serape there, you wouldn't have gone anywhere ever again. What do you want?"

Slowly he set down the coffee cup, then came to his feet and turned. Byron Stillwell stood ten feet away.

"I haven't got anywhere to go," Coby shrugged. "Seemed like you did, so I thought I'd tag along."

"And get yourself killed walking in on a night camp? I don't want you tagging along. I thought I made that clear."

"Oh, you did," Coby nodded. "Real clear. But you see . . ."

In the night shadows fifty feet away Coby's chestnut skitted nervously and a small shadow dropped from its saddle to the ground, disappeared, then reappeared trotting toward the fire.

"You see," Coby shrugged, "I didn't have much choice about it. You went off an' left your cat back yonder. So I brought it to you."

* * *

"That isn't my cat," Byron Stillwell said for the third or fourth time, his voice thin with irritation. "I don't have a cat."

"Well, that cat thinks you do," Coby grinned, pointing.

The yellow cat had circled the little camp a few times, then curled up on Stillwell's dropped saddle. It was asleep.

Coby finished his coffee and sprawled back against his own saddle, grinning contentedly at the veiled stars overhead. "How come that jasper's out to gun you, anyway?"

"Who?"

"Whoever it is that's out to gun you. You said the best thing for me to do would be to stay as far away from you as possible, so I figgered somebody's gunnin' for you."

"It's none of your business. And I meant what I said."

"Oh, I know you did. Thing is, though, I don't hardly ever take good advice. Prob'ly why I got into the outlaw business in the first place. But I owe you a favor, seems to me. And I'm a pretty fair hand with a gun, if I do say so myself."

"Not good enough," Stillwell rumbled, chewing a piece of jerky. "You're way out of your depth here, son. Take my word for it."

"I heard a little about you, Stillwell. While I was nosin' around Waxahachie. They say you're greased lightnin' with that Peacemaker there. One ol' boy back yonder said he allows you're the fastest man alive in a draw-an'-shoot. Is that right?"

"People are likely to say most anything."

"Yeah. They are, for a fact. But just say I was

181

to take a notion to find out for myself, what would you do?"

Stillwell sat in silence, ignoring him. After a time Coby said, "Well?"

"You asked me that question once before." The shadowed face turned toward him. Coby couldn't see the older man's eyes, but he could feel them boring into him. "The answer hasn't changed."

"You sayin' you'd kill me? Are you that sure you could?"

"I'm sure. I'd kill you if you tried, because I know you're good with a gun and I couldn't take the chance of trying to wing you or teach you a lesson in good manners. I'd kill you, then I'd bury you because I'd feel a little sorry that another damn fool kid had died of sheer stupidity. And it would be the fifth time I've had to do that."

Coby gawked at him. "You've killed four men? They said back there in town it was twenty or thirty . . ."

"I didn't say four men. I said four damn fool kids who didn't have sense enough to quit while they were ahead. They're the ones I buried."

"How come you ain't in jail or hung?"

Stillwell shook his head, got to his feet and went to have a look around.

Coby tagged after him, intrigued. "You ain't the least bit afraid of me, are you?" he asked, genuinely puzzled.

"No, I'm not. Now shut up."

"Then how about the jasper that's gunnin' for you? You act like you *are* afraid of him."

Stillwell turned, so abruptly that Coby backed off a step, his hand going to his gun. Then he moved the hand away, realizing somehow that what the man said was true. He might start the draw, but he would never finish it.

"Yes," Stillwell grated, his voice thin and cold. "Yes, I am afraid of Goldie Locke. Like I've never been afraid of anybody before. And that's why if you have any sense at all you'll get away from me first thing in the morning . . . get as far away as you can and never look back. You think it's something, being a fast gun? You think I'm something, because of that? You don't know the first thing about killers, boy, and Goldie Locke is the worst kind of killer there is. You get in his way, you'll never know it. You'll never even see where that bullet or that knife came from, and you won't even have time to know you're dead. Now get away from me, and stay away! I don't want your company and I don't need your help."

Puzzled and disheartened, Coby went back to the fire. The cat was awake, nosing around the packs. When he came into the light it backed away, glaring at him with big, feral eyes that were like gold rings around pieces of night.

"You're about as spooky as that Stillwell is," he told it. He dug out a piece of jerky and cut it into little cubes, laid them on Stillwell's saddleskirt and then backed off to squat again by the fire.

With a warning glare, the cat nosed the jerky, then relaxed a bit and began to eat.

"Goldie Locke," Coby muttered. He didn't recall ever hearing the name, though when he turned it over in his mind it did sound slightly familiar. As though he had heard it somewhere, but it meant something altogether different. Not about gunfighters or killers, not about anything that would explain why a man like Byron Stillwell would be afraid. Something altogether different from any of that . . . if he had really ever heard it at all. But the more he thought about it, the more he was sure he *had* heard a name like that . . . somewhere.

After a while he rolled into a blanket and went to

sleep.

Stillwell prowled the area for an hour, not really scouting—he knew exactly how the land lay, and he knew there was no one around for miles except himself and Coby Shanks—but just thinking. The night air was sweet with the messages carried on the western breeze— hints of tangy sage greening toward summer, of distant clover in a meadow where deep loam contained good moisture, the night-scents of milkweed and spring this- tle, and the cool sweetness of rain on dry ground some- where to the west where little lightnings danced under banked clouds. Night birds wheeled overhead, weaving patterns among the stars. Somewhere a coyote sang its melancholy song, and another took up the chorus.

Scents and sounds of the land, so attuned to their surroundings that a man sometimes forgot to notice them, yet so lovely that it was hard to imagine how they could be ignored. Music for the senses, he mused. Every chord a proper chord and every note in place.

And every scent was earth's very finest perfume, deli- cate and delicious. Like the subtle rosewater scent of Patty Mills, when she was dressed for the day. Like the fine cachet that was as much a part of Mattie Stillwell as her silver hair and the white lace at her collar. Like Daisy's perfume, that morning on Gingerbread Hill.

He frowned slightly, wondering. Why did Daisy have perfume on, that morning? It seemed oddly out of con- text, and as he thought about it some other things did, too. Why had she been there like that . . . clad only in a thin shift and appearing at an upstairs window, like a girl who worked the place? She *owned* the house, she said. She had come into some money. Nothing said she couldn't work there, too, but he doubted that she did. It just didn't seem likely. Supposing she did, though . . . did a girl smell of fine perfume first thing in the morning, before she bathed and dressed? Not stale per-

184

fume, or the strong tang of perfume freshly applied moments before. But like a lady set to meet a gentleman.

Who had she been there to meet?

And he had smelled the same perfume another time, in Waxahachie. When he gave his deposition to the sheriff's clerk . . . Rice? Yes, his name was Rice. The same scent had been there then. He recalled noticing it, thinking that one of the typewriters was wearing it.

A half moon was rising when he started back toward the sheltered camp, a light in the east to give substance to the rising clouds that covered the western sky. Half moon, like Half Moon Cross. He had felt a comfort there, among those cowboys. A sort of oneness, as of men who had all tasted the dust of the drive, smelled the scorch of branding camp and had supper standing around a chuckwagon. He knew them as a breed, and as individuals . . . most of them.

But he found himself thinking again about the pale-haired kid among them. A kid like so many wild kids of the time, a kid with no name and no background. A kid whose big gun showed signs of wear, and whose presence in any crowd might never be noticed.

"Neither is someone driving a carriage," he muttered. There had been a carriage there when the Comanche horse was shot. He had noticed a carriage at the raily-ard at Ennis, the night Roy Pye died. But there were always carriages around. Unbidden, the memory came of the carriage he had seen earlier, at Ennis—a carriage in the distance, stopping where he had stopped.

I'm afraid, he told himself. I'm more afraid than I have ever been. Afraid of the unknown and jumping at shadows. Where is Goldie Locke? *Who* is Goldie Locke?

Does Taffy Bates really have scrambled brains? Nobody ever notices the feeble-minded. Or expects

185

a real threat from someone who fumes and blusters . . . the way Zeke Albert does.

Hard intuition told him that he had been close to Goldie Locke within the few days before the Comanche paint was killed. Very close. Something said he had been close enough to touch—or had actually touched—the killer who was after him.

A hunch. The kind of hunch he had learned to trust a long time ago.

A long way off, he heard a train whistle, and it sounded as sad as last goodbyes.

A long day's ride to the east, in Waxahachie, Probationary Deputy Buck Mabry was doing one of the hardest things he had ever been called on to do. In a weedy back lot behind the railroad station, he knelt in the light of hand-held lanterns and drew back the corner of a dirty blanket to look at the face beneath. His breath caught in his throat and he trembled violently, fighting to regain control over his nerves. Finally he stood and turned away.

"I know her, Chief," he said. "It's Jolene Todd. She's one of Mister Rice's typewriters. What . . . what happened to her, anyway?"

Chief Deputy Jim Logan laid a large and sympathetic hand on the young man's shoulder. "Somebody stabbed her, Buck. Last night or early this morning, it looks like. Nobody found her 'til the night clerk came out a little bit ago and saw a couple of dogs nosin' around over here."

"But why? Why Jolene? Who'd kill . . . Jolene?"

Grim-faced, Logan raised his lantern and pointed. Nearby was a small, wooden box with no lid. A few sheets of paper were scattered around it. "Offhand, I'd say it was whoever she was meeting here at the station.

186

Whoever she was bringing that stuff to."

Buck looked at the litter, not comprehending.

"That's a clerical file, son," Logan said. "Miss Jolene came here to give what was in it to somebody. And what was in it was confidential files from the sheriff's record cabinets."

Chapter Seventeen

"We don't know who she was, then?" Matt Kingman let his shoulders slump in a deep, tired sigh and handed the telegraph message back to the bleak-eyed ranger who sat across the desk from him. The other three men in the room looked as haggard as the sheriff, Edwin Rice even more so. The dead typewriter had been his direct employee.

Ranger Walter Mitchell spat unerringly into the bell of the corner cuspidor. "We know her name has been Jolene Todd for the past five years," he rumbled. "She's been here a little more than three years, on the county payroll, and before that she was a student at Bryan Business College. She studied typewriting and telegraph operation. Her name there was Jolene Todd, and she listed her residence as Fort Worth. But there wasn't any Jolene Todd from Fort Worth, and no such family as she listed as her parents."

"We know something else, too," Judge Fein said. "The coroner says she wasn't twenty-two—as her employment record indicates. He estimates she was approximately thirty years of age. And she was no *girl*, gentlemen. Our 'Miss Todd' was a woman of . . . ah . . . experience, physically. He suggests she was treated sometime in the past for a social disease."

"My God." Edwin Rice dropped his face into his

188

hands. "She roomed with us—with Mrs. Rice and myself, and the children—for nearly a year when she first came to work here. Until she found lodging of her own, at the Crest House."

"Them two youngsters are takin' it hard," Jim Logan noted. "Buck an' John Henry. They never seen a murdered woman before."

"Doc says she was killed by a professional," the judge continued. "Stiletto-type weapon, double-edged, maybe seven inches of blade. A single stab wound, upward from a point of entry just left of the sternum, then the knife was pivoted to the right and downward before being withdrawn. Very little external bleeding, but she bled to death inside. Doc says she died within seconds, from a wound like that. And it was just like the knife wound he found in Roy Pye over at Ennis."

"The same person killed them both," the ranger nodded. "And that person was Goldie Locke. It's a favorite method of his."

"But how?" Rice looked up, shaking his head. "People don't just let somebody walk up and . . . and *stab* them, for God's sake!"

"Somebody they both recognized," Kingman said. "Somebody they knew, and weren't afraid of. Somebody they trusted, maybe. Certainly somebody they didn't see as a threat." He looked at the ranger. "You're certain it was Locke?"

"Sure as I can be. He's killed that way before, several times. Neat trick, for a man who knows how. Probably never even got his hands bloody. He knows several little tricks like that, all with the same result: the victim dies within seconds, without any outcry or struggle, and it's all real tidy."

"But that shot he took at Stillwell . . ."

"Neat and tidy," the ranger shrugged. "Long-range rifle, probably with a telescope. No mess, no bother, no

189

witnesses. Just like Ranger Sparling, three years back. And we know now how Locke knew what Sparling was doing here, don't we?"

"Yes," Kingman hissed through clenched teeth. "He identified himself to me, and to the judge. It was in my case files."

"And Miss Todd had access then, just like . . ." Edwin Rice had his face in his hands again.

"She's been reporting to Locke all this time," the judge nodded. "I wonder how many others there are."

"How about the Bryan Business College?" the sheriff asked.

"That will take time," Mitchell said. "But if there's a lead there we'll find it. It may not tell us much, though. Goldie Locke doesn't leave loose ends lying around."

"What about Stillwell? You still plan to broadcast that notice on him?"

"Tomorrow. As planned. He'll be in range of Buffalo Wells by then, if he's still alive."

"Yeah." Kingman's mustache twisted in a grimace, as though he had a foul taste in his mouth. "If he makes it that far. But I wouldn't bet on him getting any farther. That broadside ought to just about guarantee that Byron Stillwell will die out there."

"Twenty years ago this was buffalo range," Byron Stillwell said, looking out across the miles of mesa-and-meadow land that formed the rising tongue between the Clear and Salt Forks of the Brazos. Morning sun slanted from behind, making long, distorted banners of the shadows that rode ahead of them. "I wish I'd been here to see it like it was. The great southern herd would be up here this time of year, maybe hundreds of thousands of them, spreading clear across everything you see out there. And fifty kinds of people spread out around them. Kiowas coming down from the northeast, Cheyenne from the northwest, maybe a few Apaches dodging around way off there to the west, Tonkawas to the south if they could stay out of the way of the Lipans there . . ."

"Cow country," Coby Shanks spat. "Better for cow country. Damn buffalo just attracted redskins, is all."

"Cow country now," Stillwell shrugged. "Good cow country. But I'd like to have seen how it was before."

"I wouldn't," the redhead said flatly. "Listen, you don't have a little whiskey or somethin', do you?"

"No. I don't. Why?"

"This here leg hurts like hell," Coby scowled. "I think it's swellin' up, too."

"Infected," Stillwell nodded. "I told you to keep it clean."

"How am I supposed to do that? Way out here, I mean."

"Your choice, to be way out here." The older man glanced aside at him, then reined in the paint, circled behind the chestnut and came up on the kid's right side. "I told you to stay away from me, but here you are, still here." He leaned to have a better look at the redhead's gashed thigh, pulling back linen bandaging.

Shanks winced and gritted his teeth. "I told you I don't usually take good advice."

The leg was swollen and inflamed around the gouge the Tightwadder's bullet had left. Stillwell hauled up, looked around and pointed ahead and to the left. "There ought to be water over there, where the willows are." He headed that way and Coby followed along. Half a mile down a sage-dotted slope was a limestone gully, where recent rains had left pools of water in the dips. They coaxed the horses to the bottom and reined in.

Stillwell dismounted. "Get down and shuck your britches," he said. From a saddle pocket he drew a chunk of yellow soap wrapped in wax cloth. "Strip down, go sit in that water and wash that cut with this until all the crust is gone."

"It hurts bad enough now, without aggravatin' it," Coby muttered. But he got down and began shucking his clothes. He glanced around. "What are you doing?"

Stillwell was a few yards away, using his belt knife to cut a leaf off a prickly pear. He ignored the question.

Coby limped to the nearest shallow pool, waded in and sat down. Reluctantly, carefully, he began washing his wound, gritting his teeth and hissing as the harsh soap went to work on raw flesh. "This hurts like hell!" he shouted.

Stillwell stood and came to the pond, squatting on his heels. "No, it doesn't," he said flatly. "It hurts like a bullet sear that hasn't been treated right. Thing you need to learn about in your line of work, son. Haven't you ever been shot before?"

"Hell, no, I never been shot! Nobody ever managed, 'til now."

"Well, you better learn how to deal with it, because it won't be the last time. Of course, maybe you'll get lucky and just be shot to death, then you won't have to worry about things like soap and herbs." He held the cactus leaf up and started picking off the spines.

"That's no herb," Coby frowned. "That's cactus."

"It's medicine if you use it right. Get that wound clean this time. Scrub harder."

"I scrubbed enough. What are you . . . ?" His voice trailed off to a squeak, though his mouth remained open. There was a gun in Stillwell's hand and it was pointed at him. He had been looking directly at the man, and wasn't rightly sure he had seen him draw, but the gun was there and the echoes of its drawn hammer

192

still clicked among the limestone rises.

"Scrub," Stillwell said.

Coby scrubbed. When Stillwell was satisfied with the cleaning he let the redhead come out of the water and handed him a half-peeled prickly pear. "Lay the pulp side of this over the wound and wrap it good," he said. "And next time you get shot try to keep it clean."

Coby glared at him. "You talk so damn much about bein' shot! Wait'll it happens to you and see how *you* like . . ."

Clattering erupted in the brush behind Stillwell and Coby gawked. Even as the sound was registering on him, Stillwell spun, crouched and leveled his Peacemaker. Again, Coby had not quite seen him draw the gun.

". . . it," the redhead finished as a brace of bobwhites burst from the brush and raced away, low and urgent. "Jesus Christ," he muttered.

A moment later Stillwell straightened and put away his .45. The cat appeared at the edge of the thicket, head high, carrying a fluttering quail in its teeth. Ignoring the men, it marched grandly to a bit of open ground near the pool and began shredding and eating its meal.

Stillwell clicked his tongue and shook his head. "I'm spooky as a colt in bear country," he chided himself. "Be shooting at shadows before long." He turned to Coby. "Wrap that good, then leave it alone. You'll be all right. This time."

"How in hell do you do that?" the kid demanded.

"Do what?"

"Draw a gun that fast! Jesus, I never seen anything like that."

"I thought you said you were a hand with a gun," Stillwell gazed at him. "Seems to me, you've thought a time or two about showing me what a *real* gun-artist can do."

Coby shook his head. "No, I don't want to draw against you. You think I'm crazy?"

"Not crazy," Stillwell said. "You're just like a lot I've run into. Pretty fair hand with a gun, and too young to know it takes more than that to get by in this world. You've been lucky so far, but luck doesn't last long by itself, son. You keep going the way you are, somebody better and faster is bound to put you in the ground."

"Teach me how you do that."

"No."

The redhead glared at him, then lowered his eyes. "Well, I found out one thing, anyway. Those jaspers in that town are right. You *are* the best there is."

"No, I'm not," Stillwell shrugged and turned away. "I'm not the best gun around and I'm sure not the fastest. You ever hear of Pony Bidell? Or Ed Johnson? They were faster than me. And Morgan Hayes . . . twice as sudden with a handgun as any man I ever saw. Believe me, I know."

"How do you know? I mean, how do you know those fellers are faster than you? There's only one way to . . ."

"I know because I killed them. That's how I know about being shot, too. They were all faster than me. And there are plenty of others. Cal Farrington, for one. He's a sheriff now, up in Nebraska. And Wooly Hinds, and Joseph P. Morley, and . . ."

"I never heard of no Morley. Who's he?"

"He runs a shipping dock at Savannah, Georgia. One of the best men with a handgun I ever met. He taught me most of what I know about guns, including when not to use one."

"Who's the fastest, then?"

"I don't know. Lot of folks say a fellow named King Minter, up in Colorado, is the most dangerous man with a gun alive today. Maybe that means he's fastest, I don't know." He watched Coby lash up his sore leg, then walked to the paint and adjusted its cinch.

"That's where I'm from," Coby said. "Colorado. But I lit out from there when I was just a kid. You know," his leprechaun face went thoughtful, "I think that's where I heard that name Goldie Locke before. Seems like . . . hey! Where you goin'?"

Stillwell had already mounted and was heading away, up the sloping limestone toward the top of the draw. He glanced back. "Same place I was going before. And alone. So you just go someplace else, and try to stay out of trouble. And think about what I told you. You're in the wrong line of work, Coby. You're not a first-rate shooter, and you're not cut out to be an outlaw."

He was at the top of the rim, and looked around for an instant, then touched heels to the paint.

Coby shouted, "Hey, you forgot your cat!"

The words came back from over the rise. "I don't have a cat!"

Coby stood, looking where the gunfighter had gone, then he stomped into his boots, cursing. "Try to do the decent thing an' see what it gets you! Hell, all I did was try to help out. Son of a bitch saved my life, I guess, but will he stand to be backed? Crap! Don't he know I owe him? Cold-eyed bastard prob'ly wouldn't let a man hand him a chicken-leg if he was starvin' to death. Thinks I wouldn't be any good to him in a showdown because I'm too damn slow! That's what he thinks, all right. Damn him to hell . . . *I owe him!*"

Boiling mad and trying not to think about what Stillwell had said, Coby limped to his horse and swung aboard . . . so full of righteous indignation that for the moment he didn't even notice the pain of his bullet wound. "Lucky, he says! 'Luck doesn't last,' he says. 'Luck runs out,' he says! Hell, he's prob'ly run out on more luck than ever run out on him. Serve him right to go off an' get killed by that Goldie Locke! I could of told him somethin' about that name, but no! Off he goes!" He took a deep breath and shook his head. "Prob'ly don't mean anything, though. That Goldie Locke sure as hell ain't this one."

He lifted his reins, then hesitated and turned. "Luck ain't all that jasper runs out on," he muttered. Then he shouted, "You, cat! You comin' or not?"

The animal wiped a few feathers from its cheeks, stood and stretched lazily, then sauntered toward him. Coby watched it come, taking its own sweet time, and a grin split his face. "Luck," he muttered. "Ain't anybody else around here claimin' that name, so maybe it's yours. Get on up here, Luck. Let's see us some more country."

From where he left the redhead, Stillwell angled north of west, making good time. The unerring map in his mind told him exactly where he was, and he knew where he was going. It was another eighty miles to the desolate little place called Buffalo Wells—nothing more than a couple of abandoned station buildings and a few barns and sheds sitting on bald prairie above the Salt Fork of the Brazos, but a place carefully chosen by himself and Ranger Mitchell. A place where he could bait Goldie Locke, maybe even bring the killer out in the open . . . though he realized the chance of that was slim.

Still, slim chance was better than none, and it was— he hoped desperately—a way to keep Locke occupied with him, to keep the assassin on his trail, rather than taking the chance that Locke might make good on his threat to go after Patty Mills . . . or even after his mother.

What kind of man is that? The question played tag with itself in his mind. A professional killer, the most successful he had ever heard of. A killer that every lawman in half a continent had hunted for years, yet to this day almost nothing was known about him. An invisible killer, whom no one had ever seen . . . or seen and knew of it . . . or lived to identify.

A killer who advertised in newspapers, and took public credit for his kills. A killer who was absolutely professional and absolutely ruthless and didn't hesitate to threaten—or, he was sure, actually attack—women if it served his purpose. A killer hired by Peter Lewellyn Dawes, to find and kill Byron Stillwell. A killer who probably lived in or near the pretty, progressive little town of Waxahachie—probably was known by a hundred people there, as someone else—maybe tipped his hat to the ladies along Sherman Street, maybe visited the barber shop across from the courthouse, maybe even went to church there every Sunday.

What kind of man?

Someone who drove a carriage. And who could fire a long-range rifle down a daylight street there and never be seen doing it. Someone who so far had killed a crooked lawman and a harmless telegrapher . . . and Chako's painted pony. And how many more, just in process of closing in on him?

He had kept out of sight of the rails so far, but he would see the tracks soon enough. At Buffalo Wells, he would watch the trains go by.

And just maybe, with a lot of luck, he might see who was watching him.

Chapter Eighteen

Near evening, a rider on a head-down, limping horse made his way out of the breaks of Cane Creek and shaded his eyes, looking carefully around. A mile ahead, the graded bed of a rail line ran along a low ridge and diminished into distances to left and right. The steel rails were visible only where the late sun gilded them, tiny twin threads of amber heading northwest. To the east were tended fields of cotton interspersed here and there with smaller areas of corn, soft wheat and bean-vines. To the west and north were rougher lands where the terrain began its long, lonesome slope toward the multiple valleys of the Forks of the Brazos.

Brief rains had darkened the earth and cleared the air, and he could see for long miles every direction but east, where the gray pall of rain still lingered. Out there somewhere, east and south a half-day's ride—or two days on a crippled horse like his—was Waxahachie. Beyond was Ennis, another twenty miles distant.

For two days, Jude Meese had dodged, run and hidden, jumping at every distant movement, trembling through the dark hours, afraid of being found. Afraid of being overtaken, without knowing even who might be looking for him. He had no idea what had happened in Waxahachie. One minute he and the others

198

were closing in on Tim Sullivan on a dark street. The next, people had been shooting—gunfire all around, like rolling thunder with bees zinging through it. He had seen Tandy fall, and supposed that they were both dead though he didn't wait around to make sure. He had been bowled over by a running horse, almost trampled by another, then found one dragging its reins and managed to swing aboard. Low in the saddle he had run, blind to everything around him. As far and as fast as the horse would run he had gone, not knowing where he was or where he was going, just getting away.

Now he was tired, hungry and jumpy, and the horse was about done in. He had spent most of the latest day making a wide circle around the Half Moon Cross spread, thinking dimly that he might try to get back to Ennis. He remembered what Coby Shanks had said there: Ennis is a nice town to come back to. It hadn't meant anything to him then, but now it meant shelter and security, and he clung to the thought until a better one came along.

A simple, direct idea. Get to the railroad, wait for a train and get aboard somehow. It didn't matter which way it was going. He could jump a freight car maybe, or find a place where a train might stop and crawl up on the frame-rods under one of the cars. Then go as far away from here as he could, and start over somewhere else.

He didn't puzzle over what had actually happened at Waxahachie. He was only vaguely curious now. Whatever it was, he had escaped. Now his only desire was to be away . . . until the next better idea came along.

As he looked across the empty mile or so toward the rails, though, that next idea presented itself. Over there was a landmark he recognized. They called it Ten Mile Tank, and he remembered passing there more than once, helling around the country.

It had been a manned station at one time, but now it was only a deserted siding where parallel tracks ran along for a few miles with switches at the two ends. A place where trains could pass, and midway along the deserted station where trains might stop if they had a reason to. The water tank was still there, and a falling-down barn that once had held switch gear and crew stock.

He didn't know when a train might come by. He wasn't even sure what day it was, though he thought it might be Wednesday. But then, he didn't know the train schedules anyway. Sooner or later, though, a train would come along here. And when one did, this would be the place to get on it. If he could break the lock on a siding switch, and shift the rails, the train would have to stop.

And if he could find some food and a place to hide—maybe in the old barn—he could even choose his train. He could go east—maybe get off at Ennis and go to ground there for a while, or maybe just keep going right on down to Houston or someplace—or maybe he would decide to go west. Maybe all the way to Santa Fe.

Pummeling the limping, exhausted horse with his heels, Jude headed for Ten Mile Tank.

He looked the place over carefully as he approached, wary of any sign that someone might be there or some-where around. But it seemed deserted, just a lonely, isolated little station abandoned in the name of progress and nothing more. The only things about the place that didn't look older than time were the bright rails running past it and the bright wire of the telegraph line following them, looped from pole to pole on shiny glass insulators. Just above the little station house, bright copper clips were fastened to the wires, other wires draping down from them, entering the shuttered window on the side of the building.

No sign of anyone, as far as Jude could see. He walked the limping horse across the double set of rails, then stepped down from it, stripped off his saddle and headgear, and carried them around back to the slant-roofed old barn.

At its open door he stopped, drew a quick breath, then dropped his gear and drew his gun. Carefully, he eased himself around the sill and into the shadowed interior. There was a horse in the first stall. A sleek, heavy-shouldered draft horse, wearing a feedbag. It turned to look at him, then resumed its feeding, the crunching of fresh-fed grain a steady rhythm in the silence.

Jude flattened himself against the side of the stall, his gun up and ready, then eased around and looked beyond. In the shadows stood a covered carriage, its lacquered panels gleaming softly in the dim light. A fine rig. An expensive rig, designed for comfort and stability. And, he realized abruptly, it was clean. Not a trace of dust lay on its dark fabric top. There was drying mud on its spokes and a few splashes on its fenders, but no dust.

He became aware of the contented munching of the horse in the stall, realizing what the sound meant. The horse had been fed within the past few minutes. Somebody had been here, even while Jude was approaching.

Someone was here now!

Wide-eyed and breathing rapidly, Jude made a circle around the barn's interior, then stepped back to the open sill and looked at the boarded-up station house fifty feet away. Someone was in that building! Someone who might be waiting for him there, who had surely seen him coming, probably heard him unsaddling the crippled horse . . . someone who knew he was here.

The two small windows on the back of the building were securely boarded up, but he saw now that the boards across the door had been loosened, pulled aside just far enough for someone to go through. The door behind them was closed.

Taking a deep breath, Jude ducked and sprinted across the open space and flattened his shoulders against the wall beside the door. "Who's in there?" he called. When there was no response he shouted, "I've got a gun in my hand an' I know how to use it!"

No sound came from the building. After a moment, Jude spun around the frame, hit the door with his shoulder and followed it inward, crouching, pointing his gun ahead of him with both hands, trying to see while his eyes adjusted to the gloom of a boarded-up cubicle where the only light was a small oil lamp. He saw the telegraph key on the plank table, an open pad beside it . . . and the person who had been using it.

"Well I'll be damned," he breathed. He straightened slowly, glancing around, then put his gun away. "I will just be damned," he said. "I thought this place was deserted. What in the world are *you* doin' in a place like this?"

Curiously he approached the plank table, gaping at the bright telegraph key there, the pad of paper, the sheaf of typewritten files, the steel pen lying beside an ornate brass inkwell. He stepped close . . . and stopped, his eyes bulging as a strong hand gripped his shoulder and another hand drove furies into his chest.

Jude Meese didn't see the knife that slipped between his ribs, opened his lungs and severed the arteries above his heart. He made no sound . . . there was no means now to force air across his vocal cords. He might have tried to struggle, but there was no time. Even as things shifted and collapsed inside him, he stared dumbly at the withdrawing blade, a slim, needle-pointed dagger red with his own blood. Gloved hands turned the knife and began wiping off the blood with a piece of linen cloth. Jude's mouth opened and closed in spasms of searing pain, then his knees buckled and he fell to the dusty floor. A polished boot slid away from his dimming vision and somewhere far off a telegraph key began to rattle.

Goldie Locke looked down at the young outlaw for a moment, not particularly curious about who he might have been, then turned away to listen to the language of the wires.

King Minter's plan was simple. Somewhere between Waxahachie and Mobeetie, a man was travelling westward, heading for Double D to find Peter Lewellyn Dawes. The man must be stopped, once and for all. There were two means by which the man could travel — by rail or by horse — and he wasn't on a train. At least not yet. Dawes' network of lookouts and informants was extensive, and most of them had been alerted. If Stillwell boarded a train — if he even showed his face in any of the towns on the rail — Minter would know.

On the southbound San Antonio Chief, Minter spread his maps in a parlor car and gathered his gunmen around him. With a slim, almost effeminate finger he indicated an area above the breaks of the Salt Fork of the Brazos. "He's here, somewhere. Probably just about asleep by now. At first light in the morning he'll be on the move again, angling north of west."

"How can you be so sure?" Sid Newton squinted at the chart. "Seems like he could be anywhere by now."

"I know where he's going," Minter purred. "We're here to see he doesn't get there. You, Trask. You know that Red River country. If a man is here this evening," he pointed at the area above the Brazos forks again, "and is heading for Mobeetie and doesn't much want to be seen, where will he go tomorrow?"

J.D. Trask looked at the map thoughtfully. "If it was me, I'd hang south of the rails 'til I was past Buffalo Wells, then I'd cross over and follow the old jayhawk trail west 'til I got past the Nations. Then I'd head north to Mobeetie."

"You wouldn't cut across Nations land?"

"Not right now, I wouldn't. Not that Cheyenne Strip country. Government's runnin' settlers in there ahead of the Cherokee Outlet rush—politicians an' their friends, like that—lookin' to get 'em first grab at the best lands, an' it's a good time to get shot at by just most anybody around, redskin or white. If I's headin' someplace and needed to get there, I'd figger it would save time to go around that kind of mess."

Minter nodded. "I think it's a good assumption that Stillwell will think so, too. Therefore, you boys ought to find him pretty easy, somewhere around Buffalo Wells, if you get there tomorrow and spread out."

"Us?" Hull Billings looked up. "Where you gonna be?"

Minter regarded them one by one with hooded eyes, sitting back and lacing his soft fingers together. "I'm going to lay back and let you boys have first crack at him," he purred. "I have faith in you all. Especially so, because the five of you are going to split ten thousand dollars if you kill him. Mister Dawes authorized that price, and an extra thousand for the man who actually brings Stillwell down."

Ned Bodine drew a quick breath and blew it out

through his teeth. "That's a lot of money for one man. But you still ain't said where you're gonna be."

"Waiting," Minter said softly. "At Paducah Crossing. You boys go get Stillwell, and you bring him—whatever's left of him—back there to me. Like I said, I have faith in you boys. But just in case he should get past you, well . . . he won't get past me."

The five gunmen exchanged glances. Then Riley Caine peered at the Colorado killer. "You playin' some kind of game with us, Minter? If he's where you say, there's no way he'll get past all of us. I don't care who he is, he ain't *that* good. Nobody's gonna make it past all five of us."

"I could," Minter purred, "if it were me."

None of them said anything. He had shown them what he could do. The killing of Cole Sanders was fresh in their memories.

"He's there, all right," Minter smiled coldly. "And I expect you boys will handle him just fine. But I've heard some things about Byron Stillwell, and I just believe we'll do this my way. That way we don't take any chances about it. None at all."

Hooded dark eyes watched the five as they moved away. They would find Stillwell, all right. King Minter was certain of that. And maybe they would kill him. Maybe some of them would live through it, and maybe that would be that.

Most likely, though, he himself would face Stillwell later, at Paducah Crossing. He was satisfied with that. All the money from old man Dawes would be his—he really didn't intend to share it, anyway—and they would have made his job easier.

You boys find Stillwell, he thought. Find him and kill him if you can, but even if you can't, maybe you'll wear him down some for me. Run him, tire him, bleed him . . . and whatever's left, I'll take it from there.

He spread his hands before him, gazing at them in the muted light of the parlor car's sconces. Slim, fastidious hands, well cared for and lightning fast when he needed them to be. Good hands. He didn't care to get them any dirtier than necessary, and he saw no reason to take unnecessary risk. There were plenty around who spoke of Byron Stillwell. Maybe the stories were exaggerated, maybe not.

You boys take your best shots, he thought. Whatever's left of Byron Stillwell shouldn't be so much to handle after he gets through with you.

Chapter Nineteen

For some reason the eastbound had stopped at Buffalo Wells. By lantern light, in the predawn hours, with rainclouds building to blacken the westward sky, Willie Birdsong had seen saddle mounts being led down from a stock car by men off the little train's single coach. Now the Indian squatted on his heels atop a caprock mesa just north of the dark station, waiting for dawn's light.

The kid had slept a few hours, then gone off somewhere in that way he had—coming and going with seldom a word to anybody, maybe he would show up again and maybe not. It was always that way with the kid and some found it disconcerting. To Willie, though, it was just the nature of the pale young man—no more to be questioned or fretted about than why spring storms came out of the west, or why wild goats could be trapped and held by no more than a circle of yellow paint on the ground. It was just the way they were.

And part of the way Willie Birdsong was, was curious. Maybe it was his Comanche blood, maybe the teachings of the Methodist preacher who had "adopted" him when he was no more than a waif at Fort Sill, twenty years before. Or maybe it came of a lifetime of being an outcast. A Comanche in Texas, a clanless person among Comanche, a white-educated Indian anywhere he went, Willie had found a home in only one society. He was a top-notch wrangler and therefore was readily accepted—most of the time—among cowboys . . . when he was lucky enough to find a cattleman willing to hire an Indian.

Cap Freeman had been the nearest thing to God for Willie Birdsong, for nearly fifteen years. And the Half Moon Cross crew had been the nearest thing to family. But that life was gone now, and he was in no great hurry to begin the long, hard task of finding another Cap Freeman to work for. There were things to be curious about first. Like, what sort of person could carry so many wounds as Byron Stillwell did, and still be on his feet—or on his horse? And what kind of drifter could have such a reputation for sudden death, yet seem so at home and accepted among stock hands?

Gunfighter, they said. But Willie had seen the big man's hands. They were hard and calloused, as solid as sledges and as honest as any wild-string wrangler's. Drifter, they said. But Willie had heard Stoke Winburn sizing the man up, and knew how he measured. Not a down-at-heels ne'er-do-well, but the very opposite—a day's-work man with a head on his shoulders and strength in his arms.

And a paid assassin on his trail.

Stay away from me, Stillwell had said. Leave me alone. Willie respected that, it was the man's right to be alone. But it was *Willie's* right to be curious, and he was.

And right now, he was curious about the train that had stopped down there at Buffalo Wells Station, and the armed and mounted men that had disembarked from it. They had looked as though they were going hunting, and the Indian was pretty sure they weren't out for meat and hides.

Through the growing pre-dawn he kept an eye on the tiny speck of light off to the south, a little campfire where they waited for the light. And when the light came—the first gray-pink borning of a new day—they were on the move.

The kid showed up then, climbing the caprock crest to squat beside Willie. "There's five of 'em," he said. "Mark on a couple of the horses is Double D."

Willie didn't turn toward him. He wasn't surprised that the kid had gone down for a look, any more than he would have been surprised if he hadn't. The kid did whatever suited him, generally.

"You get close?" the Indian asked.

"Close enough to listen to 'em. Heard a couple of their names. Newton an' Trask. Mean anything?"

"Trask does." Willie squinted, trying to see where the five were going. The light was still poor. "Could be J.D. Trask. He's got a bad name over in the Nations. A hangin' name, if some of the marshals up there could get their hands on him. Anything else?"

"They ain't too keen on somebody named Minter, an' the reason they're here is to kill Byron Stillwell. For pay."

"Well, well," Willie breathed. "Gets to be a small world where that feller's concerned."

"Seem to think they know just about where he is, too," the kid said. "You s'pose they really do?"

Willie shrugged. "See how they've commenced to spread out, yonder?" he pointed. "They act like folks that know where to look, don't they?"

The kid didn't answer. He was watching the tiny, shadowy figures of the hunters a mile away, and turning to look to the east of where they were. For a time they both sat and watched, eyes accustomed to distances peering in the rising morning light. After a time

209

Willie said, "uh," and pointed. South and east, several miles away, something had moved on the crest of a low hill. An instant, and it was gone. But they both knew what they had seen. A lone rider, wary and travel-wise, staying to cover where he could, exposed for a moment by the lay of the land.

"I'd guess that's him," Willie said. He kept his eyes on that distant spot, and a minute or two later saw the instant's motion again, but not in exactly the same place. "He's coming this way," he said. Then he turned, realizing that he was alone. Some distance to his left, the pale-haired kid was just disappearing over the ledge of the caprock.

Going again. It was his nature, to come and go and never a word to anybody about it. Willie shrugged and watched the drama setting itself up miles to the south—the hunters spreading to watch-points while their prey came closer, ever closer to the trap they would lay when they located him.

A few minutes passed, and Willie heard scuffing hooves on the slope below. He edged closer to the caprock ledge and looked down. The kid was below, just swinging into the saddle of his horse, already heading down the slope, southbound.

Willie squinted then, and frowned. The kid had something slung to his saddle that the Indian hadn't seen before. Some kind of rifle. In the early light it was hard to tell, but it looked like a big-bore, like the heavy, long-range rifles that some plains hunters favored.

He wondered briefly where the kid had come up with that, then turned his attention again to the barely-visible movements in the southern hills. It was like the kid, to come up with things a body didn't know he had. The kid was full of surprises. It was his nature.

210

Yet, suddenly, Willie Birdsong had a bad feeling about the kid having that big rifle . . . and heading out in Byron Stillwell's direction. The more he thought about that, the less he liked it. Rain-scented breezes drifting ahead of the building clouds in the west — and overhead now — whispered to the Comanche. They said somebody was fixing to wind up dead.

When Buffalo Wells was less than half a day ahead, Stillwell made cold camp in a narrow arroyo and spent an hour working with the paint — rubbing the horse down, inspecting its shoes by firelight, letting it crop at the rich bottom grass and interrupting every few minutes to give it a handful of meal from his stock. He owed it to the animal, he felt. Since leaving Coby Shanks at the rain tank, he had pushed the paint through the waning day and into evening, making up lost time. He had to be at Buffalo Wells ahead of the ranger's broadside message . . . ahead of Goldie Locke, wherever Locke might be. He had even ridden another ten miles by starlight after nightfall, before stopping.

The paint had held up well. A strong horse, it was well-suited to hard travel. But there was still a long way to go, assuming he lived past Buffalo Wells, and the horse must be kept in top shape. It was still a long way to Mobeetie.

Even if he could escape Goldie Locke — or best, draw him out into the open and stop him once and for all — it would not be over until Peter Lewellyn Dawes was brought to justice. Once he would have settled just to have Dawes defeated. He would have left the old man to spend his remaining time thinking about what he had sought and lost . . . and how many good men had died in the process. He hadn't intended to go after

Dawes. It could have been over . . . if Dawes had let it be.

He had wanted only to deliver Sam Dance's old badge to his old friend, and that might have been an end to it. But there was no such end now. Doc Cathcart was dead. Chako's pony was dead, and how many more would die—or maybe already had?

Dawes' dream of a Panhandle empire had gone up in smoke, along with the prairies of No Man's Land. The old man had played his hand and lost. But like a writhing viper, dying of its own causes, Peter Lewellyn Dawes had struck out once more, still seeking a target for the venom of his hatred. And now the game had to be played out to its end.

Stillwell made a cold meal of hardtack, jerky and water from the little stream that trickled along the arroyo, then tried to sleep while the ministered paint cropped contentedly nearby.

He slept, but only in fitful snatches while his bleak thoughts and troubling dreams laced themselves around and around in his mind.

Why had the Ranger, Sparling, been at Waxahachie three years ago? Looking for Goldie Locke. And he had found the killer there, and died. Goldie Locke . . . Waxahachie. A bustling, busy, pretty little town. Cotton crops and trail herds, railroad business and breed stock, Gingerbread Hill and the Strip, fine big houses with leaded-pane windows, the fanciest courthouse west of the Mississippi . . . and a saloon on every corner around it. A squabbling, confusing, tempestuous little town surrounded by other towns that kept the county law busy round the clock . . .

Waxahachie. What more perfect place for a professional assassin to have his base and never be noticed? Goldie Locke was invisible. What better place to be invisible? Anybody could be invisible in a place like Wax-ahachie.

And that was just who Goldie Locke might be.

Anybody.

The thoughts and the dreams wrapped themselves around one another, indistinguishable except in those moments when he came awake to shift his position, to ease his aches . . . to listen as he always did to the voices of the night.

Old habits. The habits of a man who could never take anything for granted. Not and stay alive.

Goldie. Goldie Locke. Not a real name, certainly. But an odd choice for a false name. Almost as though the name itself were a message . . . an insult? A taunt? Goldie Locke! It had a sound to it, a feeling, as though it were chosen to bait the very people the assassin so casually eluded. "Catch me if you can," it laughed.

Like advertising in newspapers. Like announcing the kills when they were done. "You'll never catch me," the name taunted, "but go ahead and try. Here's your first clue. Now catch me if you can."

What clue? The name itself? What did it mean?

Goldie Locke. Like a children's fable, or a folk song. Like something from a rhyme, or a pet name for a pony. Like a brand of Scotch whiskey on the show-off shelf in a New Orleans French Quarter bawdy house . . . or like a name one of the girls upstairs might use. Cute and patent and without reality.

Like Daisy, when he had first run across her in Slick's bawdy house at Leadville. He didn't know Daisy's name . . . at least not her real last name. The only name he had known for her was Daisy Delight.

Daisy had lived at Waxahachie for three years, she said. Did Daisy know Goldie Locke? Did she see him now and then, on the street or in the bank or at the market? Was he someone she would nod to, or speak to . . . someone whose real name she knew? The invisible person. Someone anybody might know . . . but only by an ordinary name.

It was a troubling thought . . . that Daisy might be casual acquaintance with — or even good friends or more with — Goldie Locke. Then again, so might Sheriff Matt Kingman. So might Judge Arthur Knox, or the state district judge, Fein. Or anyone else, for that matter.

Those young deputies the sheriff was training, they probably knew Goldie Locke. Maybe they passed him and nodded to him each morning on the street or at the courthouse. Maybe they even said, " 'Mornin', Mr. Smith," or "Fine day, Mr. Jones." Maybe that friendly telegrapher at Ennis had said the same thing, a moment before Locke killed him.

Maybe Roy Pye had walked right up to him that night at the rail yards, all unsuspecting. Probably somebody he knew. A man like Pye would have made it his business to know anybody who might matter in his county.

How do you face an invisible foe? First you have to see him. There was just the off chance that he might see him at Buffalo Wells, with the help of Captain Walter Mitchell. And *maybe* there was a chance that he would live through it.

Goldie Locke knew where Patty Mills was. And where Mattie Stillwell was. He knew, and if he decided to go after them they would die. They weren't Byron Stillwell. For them there would be *no* chance . . . no chance at all.

He awoke with a start, cramped and sore from the cold ground . . . and sweating.

He shook himself awake, checked his gun and brought in the paint for saddling. It was still dark, except for starlight, and the sky to the west held no stars. The breezes carried a smell of rain.

He was moving by first light, with a mile behind him and the bluff beyond Buffalo Wells visible in the distance. The gray dawn light was deceptive. The old station looked to be only two or three miles away, though he knew it was closer to fifteen.

Then he noticed something that brought him up short, with a tight rein on the paint. He couldn't see the abandoned station yet. Rolling terrain intervened. But atop the caprock mesa beyond, a tendril of smoke drifted on the breeze . . . then a second one, and after a moment a third. Smokes that from this distance might have all been one smoke, unless a man knew what to look for.

The way Chako had once taught him. If you see smoke over high ground, see it as a Comanche sees. It might mean something important.

Three smokes rising . . . and one of them—the one to his left as he looked at them, or on the side that indicated the trail ahead—began to puff and flutter, as though the rising tendril were a series of dots.

Danger, the smoke said. Ambush ahead.

He sat motionless for a time, thinking. Then he walked the paint to the highest ground nearby—a bare ridge-crest just ahead—and rode to the top of it. With first morning light behind him, brighter than the clouding skies above, he paused there and stood in his stirrups, scanning the land ahead. For long minutes he waited, memorizing the features of the next few miles. Every rise and dip, every bit of cover and every draw, he saw and noted. Finally he flicked the paint with rein-ends and went on, down toward lower ground.

If there was someone out there, he hadn't seen him . . . or them. But one thing he was sure of. Whoever might be out there *had* seen him. And had seen the route he took coming off the crest.

From the time they led their mounts off the train, J.D. Trask took the lead and set the pace. It was a matter of knowing the terrain. If they had been in the Piney Woods of east Texas, Ned Bodine would have led. The hulking Bodine was a product of those lands and knew the tricks and the trails. Up on the Llano Estacado, Sid Newton or Hull Billings would have called the shots.

Newton, at least. Since breaking coffee-camp in the pre-dawn darkness, Billings had been surly. Somewhere between getting off the train—he said—and saddling to head out, he had lost his pack. The rest figured he had left it on the train, and so what? He had everything he needed for the moment.

In West Texas or the border lands Riley Caine would have been the leader. But here in the hills between the Brazos Forks and the Red, Trask was the expert.

At first light he spread them, picking vantage points with the skill of a guerilla captain. And within the hour the strategy paid off. Minter had been right. Stillwell was where he had guessed, and was coming toward them.

Billings showed Trask the ridge on which Stillwell had appeared, and pointed out where he had gone.

"We got him," Trask nodded. "Hell, he's worked himself right into a trap."

From the distant ridge, Stillwell had angled downward, following a swale that led into a dry canyon. The canyon deepened westward, feeding into a wide, rock-sloped draw where a creek flowed among stands of cedar and cottonwood, its bends lined with willow thickets.

216

"Right down there," Trask pointed. "That narrow bend where the cliffs push in. He'll come through there. He has to, or skyline himself for a mile to go around. He'll come around that bend and we'll be waiting for him. Let's go."

"Be easier if I had the right hardware," Hull Billings growled. "Hell of a fine range for a turkey shoot."

"Forget it," Trask snapped. "It don't matter."

Bodine grinned, looking at the setup. All the talk about Byron Stillwell had left him edgy—how the drifter was hell on wheels in a showdown, how Morgan Hays and Pony Bidell had never come back when they went after him. But there wasn't anything smart about a man walking himself into a funnel, and Stillwell himself had set the course. The dumb bastard would never know what hit him. He wouldn't even know there was anybody around, until they cut him down.

"Easy money," Sid Newton allowed. "Easiest I seen in a long time."

In single file the five angled down the hill, out of sight of the approaching Stillwell, toward the cut below where the shallow creek ran between limestone bluffs. The high, heavy clouds drifting from the west now covered most of the sky, and a grayness hung in the morning air. As they neared the bottom, fine misting rain began to fall.

Trask led them into the streambed and turned right. The tight bend with the high walls was just ahead. He let his eyes rove the banks on each side, the cedar stands and willow growth, the patterns of the scoured limestone. Right in the bend, he decided. Right where the turn is tightest, that is where the ambush should be. A man coming around that bend will be trying to look beyond. That's where to hit him.

Bodine had pulled ahead a few yards, but Trask

217

called him back. "No hurry," he said. "Man won't be along here for another ten-fifteen minutes, at least. Let's do this easy an' do it right."

"Extra thousand for whoever brings him down," Newton scowled. "You thinkin' about settin' us so's you get first shot, Trask?"

"Be me if I had my tools," Billings grumbled.

Bodine glared at him. "Will you shut up about that?" He slapped the butt of the Winchester at his knee. "I got all the tools we need, right here."

"Minter's playin' games," Trask growled. "Forget the extra thousand. We're *all* gonna bring him down. Any objections?" He glared at the rest of them, and Newton eased off.

"That's fair," the plainsman said. "Stick to business, that way."

Bodine nodded, loosening his Winchester in its sleeve. "Fine with me."

The others nodded.

At a walk, they rode into the tight bend, little rivulets of water dripping from hatbrims as they looked up at the slopes, picking out hiding places.

"Two men on the inside slope, three out," Trask said. "We'll leave the horses back of that outcrop, then settle in. When he's dead between us, the party can start."

Bodine raised his head abruptly, tightening his reins. "What was that? You boys hear . . . ?"

Suddenly the canyon was full of noise—harsh, sharp running sounds that rattled confusing echoes off the banks. Thirty yards away a rider appeared—a tall man on a charging paint horse, low in the saddle, serape thrown aside and a big gun in his hand. The cascading sounds became thunders as the Peacemaker opened fire.

Chapter Twenty

The paint was a big, strong horse—all the horse he had known it would be when he first saw it at Half Moon Cross. And now the attention he had given it paid off. Whoever was setting an ambush for him would count on being in place and ready before he arrived.

He couldn't let that happen. From the moment he rode down from the open ridge, letting it be clear what his path would be, Stillwell gave the horse its head and the demands of his heels. The paint stretched out to a belly-down run across the gentle shoulder of the valley, putting a mile behind them and part of another before it began to lather. He eased the pace, but only a little, as the valley deepened and curved away to funnel into a descending, dry-bed canyon that he knew would lead to a draw a mile ahead.

He didn't know where they would be, but he knew the tricks of ambush and he knew that they would choose a site near enough to where they started to allow them time to get in place. He watched for blind bluffs—outcrops and thickets and places where men with guns might expect to set a surprise.

And he pressed the horse carefully, getting all the speed from it that terrain allowed . . . changing the timing of what those ahead had in mind.

You'd have loved this, Chako. The thought came uninvited and he almost grinned as canyon lands swept by. I'm sorry you can't be around now. What could you ever have relished more, than charging full-tilt into an ambush on the off chance of catching them off guard? Bloodthirsty Kwahadi, you would have bust a gut at the glory of it all.

Ahead, the canyon narrowed, funnelling toward a deeper draw where he glimpsed water. A stream, bounded by limestone banks to the left. Little raindrops hit his face and steamed on the paint's glistening coat, moisture flying back from its whipping mane as it found its second wind and lengthened its stride again.

Stillwell leaned low over his saddlehorn and let the horse run. Cowpony, he thought. Let it alone, it knows what it can do. The stream was just ahead, angling away to his left, its banks steepening where centuries of gentle flow and occasional roaring floods had etched a deep path through the limestone hills. They would be close now, somewhere just ahead. Would he see the place they would choose? Would he surprise them?

You would have loved this, Brother Wolf, he thought. Headlong and hell-for-leather . . . this is your kind of fight.

The paint cleared the canyon and its flashing hooves threw sheets of spray as it hit the creek. He reined to the left, his eyes taking in the terrain. Steep banks, steep inclines above, cedar stands clinging to the slopes, willows vying with stone along the water's course—I'd choose this place, he thought. If I were them, here's where I'd be.

The paint seemed to respond to the fierceness in him. It bunched powerful haunches and sprinted, sheeting water with each step. Stillwell whipped back his serape and drew his Colt. Just ahead—yards ahead—was a tight, blind bend to the right and he knew where they were . . . where they had to be. Wind of passage sang in his ears and a deep, soft voice seemed to sing with it. *Go, Brother Wolf.*

Its silent echo mingled with the clatter and splash reverberating from canyon walls.

The horse hit the bend and leaned into it, charging. And they were there. Five of them, four bunched together and one a few feet aside, their wide eyes stared at him, their mouths dropped open and guns came up. A bullet whistled past his ear and the Peacemaker spoke. Rolling hard thunder lashed at the rocky banks and echoed back and back, rebounding.

The nearest one, the one who had drawn and fired so fast, was smashed backward out of his saddle, flailing against the one behind as he fell. That one's mount reared and spun, throwing off its rider's aim as Stillwell's second bullet took him in the throat. The others were firing then, too, and he realized that these were seasoned men—hardcases with the skills to stay alive and the skills to kill. Double D, something told him. Like Pony Bidell and Ed Johnson . . . like Morgan Hayes . . . these were Double D gunmen.

The Peacemaker was speaking, as though of its own accord. Two had gone down in an instant and a third hardcase slumped in his saddle as Stillwell and the paint burst through them, through the gap where an instant before armed riders had been. To his right a rider ducked low, spun his terrified horse and snapped a shot from between its ears. Stillwell felt the slug as it whipped through the serape, stinging his arm. He swivelled and fired back, over the paint's fanning tail. The man seemed to come apart, and fell. His horse ran, dragging him over the stony creek bed.

Four down. Stillwell let the paint run and looked

221

back, and saw his mistake. He had charged through them. He should have closed and stayed among them to the end. The remaining rider was a big, hulking man—the one who had been off to the side. He was still where he had been, fifty . . . sixty yards back. Diminishing range for a handgun. But now he had a rifle at his shoulder, leveling it.

The shot that cracked out then, overriding the echoed thunders in the canyon, was like lightning striking a stump. The man with the rifle had been at the point of firing. But abruptly his chest exploded. Like pulp from a burst melon, red spray erupted and the man pitched forward, over the neck of his horse. The horse bolted and the rifleman hit the creekbed headfirst and limp. A red stain eddied about him, growing rapidly.

Stillwell eased back on his reins, bringing the paint down to a trot, then to a walk. He eased the horse up the nearest bank and into cedars, feeding fresh cartridges into the Peacemaker. He started back, then, gun in hand, eyes roving the canyon. When a voice came from ahead he stopped, then eased his gun down.

"All they was, was five," the shout told him. "They ain't any, now."

He had heard the voice before. The pale-haired kid from Half Moon Cross. Still, he held his cover. There had been no mistaking the sound of that last shot. A big rifle. A long-range rifle.

The same rifle he had heard on the street at Waxahachie . . . Goldie Locke's rifle? He couldn't be sure.

"Show yourself!" he shouted.

There was silence for a moment, then the scuffing of boots on stone, and the kid stepped out on a ledge seventy yards away. His rifle was cradled across his arm. Sharps .50. A buffalo gun.

The kid looked across at him for a moment, then

222

down at the carnage in the creek. "We seen these jaspers from the bluff yonder. Me an' Willie. Been watchin' 'em since they got off the train. You all right? There's blood on your shirt."

Stillwell glanced down. A red stain was spreading slowly on his left sleeve, just forward of the elbow. He took a look and shrugged. It was just a scratch. "I'm all right," he called. "Why are you here? Did Willie Birdsong send you?"

Even through seventy yards of drizzling rain, the kid looked surprised. He hesitated, then raised the Sharps over his head, showing it. "Willie didn't say one way or another," he said. "I only come 'cause I wanted to try out this here big rifle. Never shot one of these before."

"It belonged to one of them," the kid said, matter-of-factly. "I don't know which one, but he left it layin' around when they made coffee camp. All wrapped in sheepskin—this here big rifle an' some cartridges, along with his Sunday shirt an' possibles. I pitched the rest."

The kid had gone and got his horse, then helped Stillwell drag the bodies of the ambushers out of the creek. Two of them, Stillwell recognized. Sid Newton and Hull Billings had reputations up on the high plains, and he had heard they were bad men to tangle with. Newton was a fast-gun artist and Billings was a dry-gulcher from way back.

"I guess that rifle you found was his," he told the kid. "I heard he favored a range gun."

"Not no more, he doesn't," was all the kid had to say.

One of the others had carried a Winchester '73 in an oiled sheath, and Stillwell tied it on his own saddle. There was something to what the kid said, after all.

223

Now they rode northward under leaden skies that couldn't decide from one minute to the next whether it was raining or not.

"You shouldn't have told Willie to go his own way," the kid allowed after another mile of rolling country. "Willie's Comanch'. He don't do what he's told, generally."

"Can't argue about that right now," Stillwell agreed. "I guess he made the smoke up there, did he?"

"Nobody else on that bluff last time I looked."

"And I'm obliged to you for nailing that fifth one."

The kid glanced across at him, pale eyes unreadable. "Yeah, you are."

"You have a name?"

"Yeah."

An hour later Buffalo Wells was in sight, and by noon they were stepping down and nodding at Willie Birdsong, who had made himself at home in the cot shed next to the deserted station house and had a cook-fire going in the mud hearth.

"You're not dead again," the Indian grinned at Stillwell. "You want some grub? I already tasted it to make sure I didn't poison it or anything."

"Sounds fine, Willie. Why are you here?"

"Why not?" Willie took the paint's lead and started toward the stock shed. "You're here."

"I told you back at Half Moon Cross to stay away from me."

Willie paused, then turned. "Look, white man . . . I know you got your problems, folks out howlin' after your liver an' lights an' all. But I got a problem, too. Outside of Cap Freeman, there isn't a cowman in this whole solemn state of Texas that's likely to hire on a Comanche, an' Cap Freeman's gone. I got no claim up in the Nations, and over in the Territories there's folks that would shoot me on sight because they'd think I was Apache or Ute."

Stillwell raised a hand and the Indian stifled him. "Hear me out! I'm near on to forty years old and I don't own a thing in this world except a white education that gets me in trouble if I let on I have it, an' the pride of never havin' bent my head to any man I didn't respect. There isn't a place in this whole world that I belong, so nobody can tell me where not to go. Now you, you did a kindness back yonder, keepin' Cap Freeman's funeral halfway civilized. I was beholden for that, but I paid my debt an' from here on I go wherever I damn well please and if it gets me killed then maybe I'll find out if *hell* will have me."

He turned away again, stiff-shouldered and angry.

"My God," Stillwell shook his head. "Where did you ever learn to lecture like that?"

"From a Methodist preacher," Willie said, not turning. "He couldn't ever bring himself to marry my mother, but he did take some pains to see after us. Maybe he felt guilty, I don't know."

The kid had tended his own horse, and wandered by on his way to the food. "Willie gets like that," he said.

They shared dinner—rabbit, beans and sourdough bread—in the shelter of the bunk shed. Like many such places along the expanding railroads, Buffalo Wells had been abandoned as an active station, but the buildings still stood to serve as quarters for periodic maintenance crews and occasional track inspectors. The bunk shed was a public facility. Its plank door had a hasp but no lock, and a working hand pump on the well. A painted sign beside the door said: "Stranger, rest here on your way. Stay as long as you will stay. Close the door before you go. As you have found it, leave it so."

Provision of a shelter was the best insurance the rail-

225

road company could have against passers-by breaking into the locked station house or vandalizing the storage barns.

Through the meal, Willie Birdsong was silent and aloof, his Comanche features expressing nothing. Then as they sipped at strong, black coffee the Indian grinned suddenly, his eyes sparkling with humor.

"Story they tell up in the Nations," he said. "White man's lookin' for strayed horses and he asks an Indian, 'You seen two stray horses around here? They're a matched pair, real valuable. Best matched team I ever had. Sure would hate to lose 'em.' Indian says, 'If they're matched that way, how do you tell 'em apart?' White man says, 'well, if you look close, you'll notice the white one is a hand taller than the black one.'"

Stillwell and the kid both stared at him.

Willie looked from one to the other, then shrugged. "Well, in Comanche it's funny."

The kid emptied his cup and went out, not looking back. After a time Stillwell said, "I guess I owe you an apology."

"Don't owe me anything," Willie said. "Just don't tell me where to go. Kid said there were five of those owlhoots out there. Any of them left?"

"No."

"That's good. I don't suppose one of them was that Goldie Locke?"

"These were a different bunch. Double D hands. They came straight from Dawes. Goldie Locke works alone."

"Then you still got that'n to worry about."

"Maybe not for long. There's a message on the wire today telling him where I am. I don't expect it will take him long to get here."

The Indian gazed at him, thoughtfully. "A

challenge?"

"Bait," Stillwell said. "This is the only place I know this side of the Scarp where I might have a chance of seeing him before he sees me. It's the best idea I have, right now, short of getting to Mobeetie and settling with that old man up there."

"That's why you don't want company," Willie allowed.

"Locke doesn't care who he kills. But it's me he wants. If anybody else is here he'll just hang back and wait for a better time. Or maybe just kill everybody here, I don't know. Either way, I'm better off alone."

"I see that," Willie nodded. "Maybe you could use some lookout, though?" He waggled a thumb toward the caprock bluff rising beyond the station grounds.

The kid appeared at the door. "Somebody comin'," he said. "Anybody want to take a look?"

The rain had diminished for a time, and in the distance—vague in the mist—a lone rider was plodding toward them.

Stillwell squinted, then scowled. "Looks like I've got a regular parade," he muttered.

"If that's who's after you, no problem," the kid said. "That big rifle I found can pick him off from here."

"Let him come." Stillwell sighed, irritated. "His name's Coby Shanks and he's about as hard to get shed of as you two are."

At a place where the railroad ran through a dredged cut in the hills above the Brazos, a closed carriage stood beneath the telegraph line—a sleek, reinforced carriage with a powerful horse in its traces. Below the canopy, out of the misting rain, gloved hands held a neatly penciled sheet of paper, just copied from the

227

coded impulses of the wires.

The message read: "B . . . Wait for escort . . . Buffalo Wells . . . be careful . . . M."

The broadside had just come over the wires, encoded from Waxahachie and ordered for public posting at every receiving point west of there.

A trap? Possibly. Yet they *would* be trying to contact Stillwell now. The dead typewriter would have been found, and they would know that Goldie Locke had the itinerary the drifter had given Ed Rice. They would be trying to warn him, to somehow protect him. Buffalo Wells had not been on the route he intended, according to that itinerary.

Escort? Rangers, probably. To take him to Waco or somewhere, maybe to make a plan for entrapment . . . if there wasn't already such a plan.

But Stillwell should be heading for Mobeetie. The killer had seen to that. The threat against his women left him no other real choice. Would he change his mind now? Or would he go ahead, westward.

Whichever, he would be at Buffalo Wells . . . soon, if he was as smart as the killer knew he was. And if his "escort" was coming all the way from Waxahachie, then he might have a while to wait.

Goldie Locke didn't care in the slightest whether Byron Stillwell made it to Mobeetie and killed Peter Lewellyn Dawes. The old man had paid in advance, as all of the assassin's clients did. What happened to him now didn't matter. The primary consideration now was simply a professional ethic—when a job is paid for, the job must be completed.

Byron Stillwell's death had been paid for. So Byron Stillwell must die, as promptly and as neatly as possible. And the killer of Byron Stillwell must be Goldie Locke. Anything less would jeopardize a reputation that had taken more than five years to build: Goldie Locke never failed to fulfill a contract.

And right now, Goldie Locke didn't want to have to follow Stillwell all the way to Mobeetie to discharge this obligation. That incredible accident in Waxahachie—the horse that had reared and taken the bullet meant for Stillwell—had necessitated a rapid changing of plans, had disrupted a calculated schedule and had cost far too much in resources. Too much to tolerate any further delay.

It was time for the drifter's luck to run out.

Buffalo Wells was nearby. Only a few miles, along the graded road paralleling the railroad. Not much farther by back trails, one of which offered a concealed approach to within rifle-shot.

Gloved hands pulled a long, black-leather sheath from beneath the carriage's cushioned seat and laid it across a tailored lap. With the flap unbuckled and opened, the rifle inside gleamed coldly in the gray light. A big rifle, but sleek and honed down to trim lines. A long, fitted barrel with a mount forward of its breech for the setting of its telescope sight.

Alexander Henry, caliber .453, magazine-fed. The breech clicked open and the first of the big gun's seven brass cartridges lay exposed—a long, powerfully-loaded shell with a finely-swaged, prow-molded bullet seated in its neck. Alexander Henry—the finest long-range rifle of its time.

Gloved hands closed the sheath and put it away, then picked up the carriage's reins and snapped them smartly. The assassin known as Goldie Locke headed for Buffalo Wells.

At Buffalo Wells, Byron Stillwell ignored the yellow

cat spiraling around his ankles and stared at Coby Shanks.

"That's what I was goin' to tell you before you took out back yonder," the redhead said. "I recollect where I heard that name Goldie Locke before. I wasn't but a tad then, but I remember. But the Goldie Locke I knew of can't be the Goldie Locke that's after you, 'cause the one I knew of is dead. Feller beat her to death better'n five years ago, out in Colorado."

Chapter Twenty-one

The last place Taffy Bates really wanted to go was to the sheriff's office, but as far as he could see there was no choice in the matter. Dimly, he realized that Miss Daisy would be furious with him for doing such a thing. But as the days passed he had become frantic with worry. So he rode into town and went to the courthouse.

"We . . . uh . . . we don't know where she is," the big man told Chief Deputy Jim Logan. "Been several days now, since she's gone. I . . . uh . . . I been hearin' things, like about people gettin' murdered around here. So when Ling come . . . uh . . . out to th' place to see if Miss Daisy was there, I got to thinkin' . . . uh, well, uh . . . maybe somebody might have done somethin' to Miss Daisy . . ."

Logan waved Taffy to a chair, and sent Buck Mabry to bring the sheriff. If there was another murder—or even just the possibility of it—Kingman would want the details fresh. Logan doubted whether the sheriff had even slept since that latest thing, the stabbing of Ed Rice's pretty typewriter.

Kingman arrived within minutes, and they took Taffy into the office.

"Tell me about it," Kingman said, bluntly.

"Daisy Walcott," Logan said. "You know her? Lives

231

up on Grover, the old McIntyre house. She owns the Cotillion Club, out on Gingerbread Hill."

"I know who she is," Kingman grunted. "From every gossip in town. What about her?"

"Well, Mr. Bates here works for her. He's a . . . what? Overseer, Mr. Bates?"

"I look after the club for Miss Daisy," Taffy nodded. "I . . . uh . . . make sure nobody makes no trouble on her property. Miss Daisy don't like trouble, Sheriff. She . . . uh . . . she runs a nice, clean house."

"Miss Walcott has been missing for several days, according to Mr. Bates," Logan explained. "He's worried about her."

"Missing for how long?"

"Oh . . . four days, I think." Taffy's gnarled and rutted face twisted in difficult thought. "Maybe it's five. See, uh, Ling thought Miss Daisy was maybe stayin' over out at the club, an' I thought she was prob'ly at home. So neither one of us . . . uh . . . knew she was gone 'til Ling come out . . ."

"Ling?"

"Chinese woman," Logan said. "Miss Walcott's housekeeper. At the McIntyre house."

"Miss Daisy shouldn't go off like she does," Taffy said, something like tears glistening in his eyes. "I tell her she shouldn't. Somebody might . . . uh . . . hurt her, y'know? Woman out alone that way. But she just says she . . . uh . . . can take care of herself. But I got a real bad feelin' this time, Sheriff. I been hearin' things."

"What things?"

"Like killin's. Like fellas say somebody killed a law down at Ennis, an' . . . uh . . . I don't remember, but they say somebody killed a . . . uh . . . a *woman* . . ." He paused, looking stricken. ". . . right around here someplace."

232

"It was another woman, Taffy," Logan said gently. "It wasn't Miss Daisy."

"I got a real bad feelin'." Taffy scuffed his shoes, big fingers mangling the brim of his hat. "Ever since that Stillwell come to see . . . uh . . . Miss Daisy, I had this bad feelin'. Kinda like somebody was about to die."

Kingman and Logan glanced at each other. "Stillwell?" the sheriff asked. "Byron Stillwell?"

"Yeah."

"Does Stillwell know Miss Wal . . . Miss Daisy?"

"Yeah. Miss Daisy, she said . . . uh . . . they was old friends. Seems like from about when I first knew of him, too. Out at . . . uh . . . Leadville. He busted me up pretty good out there, but he said it wasn't . . . uh . . . personal. He said I was in with the wrong crowd, was all."

Kingman frowned. "Sounds to me like you have a score to settle. Is that right?"

Taffy shook his head. "No, sir. I don't guess so. I guess he's . . . uh, Stillwell . . . he maybe did me a kindness. I might'a got killed with all the rest of 'em, I guess. 'Cept I wasn't with 'em in the canyon. That Stillwell, he . . . uh . . . he busted me up so bad, I wasn't there."

Kingman squinted at him. "When was the last time you saw Daisy Walcott, Mr. Bates?"

"Me? Uh . . . not since that mornin' he come. She left right after . . . uh . . . he did. I got her carriage for her. It was around back, still hitched up."

"Then he left, and she left, and you haven't seen her since?"

"She don't . . . uh . . . come out to the club much any more. I guess she went on home from there." He scowled in thought, then added, helpfully, "That was the day they had that big funeral. Cowboys was . . . uh . . . talkin' about it."

233

Logan and the sheriff exchanged looks and Kingman nodded. Logan got up and went out, closing the door behind him. To duty deputy Hank Spicer he said, "Get some of the boys to look around for Daisy Walcott. Here in town . . . out at the Hill . . . see if anybody has seen her lately or knows where she might have gone. Put the two probationers on it, maybe a ride-around outside town. It'll give them something to do."

"Right away," Spicer nodded. You goin' out, Chief?"

"To the telegraph office. We need some information from the authorities at Leadville, Colorado. You need something?"

"We just got a wire from Ranger headquarters in Waco, for Captain Mitchell. But he left yesterday on the westbound. Do I hold this for him or give it to the sheriff?"

"I don't know. What's it say?"

The deputy shrugged. "Some big rancher died, up in the Panhandle. Name of Dawes. Somethin' Mitchell was workin' on, I guess."

"Dawes?" Logan held out his hand and Spicer handed him the folded sheet. He read it through. Peter Lewellyn Dawes had been found dead at his ranch headquarters, the Double D north of Mobeetie. Cause of death . . . natural causes. A stroke. "The sheriff will want this as soon as he's done talking to Mr. Bates," he said. "Be sure he gets it. And get on that search for Daisy Walcott." Striding from the office, he shook his head. "My God," he breathed. "What next?"

In the closed office, Kingman was asking Taffy, "Who else was around the club that morning, Mr. Bates? I mean when Byron Stillwell visited Miss Daisy?"

"Nobody much right then." The big man worked at remembering. "It was early. Me an' cook. Some of th' . . . uh . . . girls, but they was upstairs. That Stillwell,

234

he had a cat with him. Yellow cat. I told him I never saw nobody bring a cat to a cathouse before."

"Anybody else? Think hard."

"No, I . . . uh . . . oh, yeah. That constable was there, nosin' around. That Zeke Albert. But he left right away."

Kingman's mustache twitched. One of the names on his "private inquiry" list was Zeke Albert.

At Paducah Crossing Zeke Albert stepped down from a coach car and accepted his buckled case from the day porter. Stiff from long travel, he stepped away from the train, set his bag on the depot porch and stretched his arms to relieve the soreness in his shoulders.

He looked around, saw a few familiar faces and some unfamiliar ones—places like this kept changing, always the same but never the same from one visit to the next. A bleak, windswept place where it seldom rained and the hills were coated with gray shrub and buffalo grass. All around, the land was dry, featureless and desolate. Tired-looking hills climbed northward toward the flat high plains, receded southward toward the scrub country and the distant desert.

Tired-looking land, and it always made him feel tired to come here . . . especially when he looked across at the squat, fieldstone building that still housed the Cattlemen's Bank. A bitterness lay in the memories associated with that building, a bitterness as old and time-scoured as the faint dimples of bullet-scars on the building's face. Worn-over scars from a time long ago—but like the scars, the memories and the bitterness were still there.

Just like the old bullet lodged in his own back was still there after all the years, and still caused him the dull, unending grief of its presence.

Down the street from the bank was a lesser building that had once been the town marshal's office. It was a feed store now, but he knew the interior of it. Every crack in the plaster . . . every warp in the creaky floor.

The same way he knew the little house at the end of the street—not visible from here, and he was glad it wasn't—where a young town marshal had once lived with his bride. Lived there, worked out of the town office, and dreamed of a better future.

Until the day the drifter came.

A down-at-heels drifter from the south someplace, a man on the wander or maybe on the run, stopping for a day at this town for no more reason than that he happened to be passing through. A drifter who might have meant no harm. No one would ever know what his intentions were. But of those following him, who caught up with him there, there was no question.

Old memories that tasted of acid, salt, and dust rose within him as he looked across at that bank building. Right there, the drifter's enemies had found him. And right there they had opened fire.

People had died on that street. On a lazy afternoon in a sleepy little town gunfire had erupted and the memories would always haunt him.

The drifter had put up a fight. He hadn't died easily, and the gun he carried exacted its toll even as he fell. But there were many guns facing him—guns that chattered and thundered and sent hot lead singing and ricocheting everywhere.

Zeke Albert's frown seamed his face with lines almost like myriad scars.

All those bullets flying . . . the drifter falling, some of the others sprawled on the dirt street, the rest still shooting.

I didn't even shoot back until the first bullet hit me, he thought bitterly. Maybe if I had . . .

The second shot that took him had knocked him down. He remembered lying there in front of his marshal's office, looking up at the dusty sky. He remembered the sound of the bushwhackers' hoofbeats as they raced away—those still living. He remembered shouts and screams, and wondering what it was all about, and managing to raise himself to look around.

Fallen people in the street, people who were no part of what had occurred because a drifter had happened by . . . but who were part of it now. People who happened to get in the way.

And among them a calico dress and a spilled picnic basket. She had been coming to share her supper with him.

A voice nearby brought him around, and for a moment he simply stared at the man standing there. A man older than himself, wearing faded clothing and scuffed shoes. The man smiled, and Zeke nodded.

"Hello, Mike," he said. "Sorry, I was just lookin' around. Nothing's changed much, has it?"

"Never does," Mike shrugged. "Haven't seen you in a while, Zeke."

"Been busy." He picked up his suitcase. "Helen and the kids all right?"

"Doin' fair," Mike nodded. "Just a drop-by again, Zeke?"

"Overnight, or 'til the next eastbound." He started toward the two-story hotel beyond the depot, then hesitated, his eyes narrowing. Some distance away, in the shadow of a livery barn, a man stood watching the train. A stranger, whose clothing contrasted oddly with that of others along the street. Not a trace of dust on the man, he looked freshly-scrubbed and totally out of place. And somehow familiar.

"Who is that?" he asked the townsman.

"Him? He's been here a couple of days, watchin' th'

roads and th' trains. Spooky-like jasper. Whispery voice an' the softest-lookin' pair of hands I ever seen on a man. Word is he's a gunfighter, but he don't say a word to anybody. Likely he's just waitin' for somebody."

"Come on, Mike. I know you hear everything there is to hear. What's his name?"

"Minter," Mike shrugged. "King Minter. Hotel register says that, anyway."

Albert frowned, trying to remember where he had heard that name. It meant something, but he wasn't sure what.

He headed for the hotel again, Mike trudging along beside him. After a moment the man asked, "You ever think about comin' back here, Zeke? I mean, to live here again? There's some that would welcome you."

Albert strode on, not answering.

Mike shrugged. "Guess I can see why not, though you do keep comin' back, Zeke."

"I come back here for one reason, Mike. Only one." Albert kept his voice level, fighting the old tightness that always came into his throat. "I'm just here long enough to go out and spend a little time at Tillie's grave."

At the hotel door he hesitated and turned. *"Minter?"*

"King Minter," Mike nodded. "You know him?"

"Heard of him. He's a gunfighter . . . some say the fastest man with a handgun since Jace McCoy." He looked back toward the depot. There was something about the gunfighter . . . something oddly familiar. "Why's he here, Mike?"

"Now, Zeke, how would I . . . ?"

"Mike!"

The man shrugged. "He asked the depot agent about somebody named Stillwell, Zeke. That's all I know about it. Honest."

Stillwell. Abruptly the old, dusty memories came

flooding back, and Zeke Albert felt again the pain of that day just as he had felt it then.

Byron Stillwell. A drifter with enemies. Not the same drifter, but the same situation. The same mindless, bloody facing-down of men whose guns were faster than the eye . . . in the same place where it had happened before. It would happen again now, if Stillwell came here, and innocent people would fall like sheep in the hellfire of pinging, howling lead.

"Bill Selman still the law here, Mike?" he asked.

"He's it, but he ain't here. Be gone a week or two, I reckon. Why?"

"Any other law around?"

"Not right now. Nothin' much happens here, Zeke."

Albert looked along the dusty streets, his eyes as bleak as the hills beyond. "There was a time," he muttered. "Something happened that time."

Far to the east, at Buffalo Wells, Byron Stillwell looked down at the yellow cat winding about his boots, and muttered an oath.

Coby Shanks glanced around, frowning. "If you don't like that cat, then I'll take him with me," he rasped. "I think that cat's good luck. That's his name. Luck. I named him."

"Take him with you," the drifter husked. "I don't need a cat, I don't want a cat and I don't *have* a cat. Do what you like, but get that saddle on that horse and get out of here. I told you, Goldie Locke knows I'm here and might show up any time."

"You're a real pain to try to get along with," Coby shrugged, returning to his cinches. "That Indian would have stayed and sided with you, you know. If you'd let him. Maybe I would, too, if I thought you'd ever once thank me for it. But no. Face it yourself, all by yourself, I guess that's your way."

"That's Goldie Locke out there," Stillwell said, shaking his head in irritation. The redhead just refused to understand, it seemed, that there were dangers far worse than he had ever even imagined.

"Goldie Locke," the youngster taunted. "Some damn gunny usin' a dead whore's name. I may not be up to what you're used to, Stillwell, but I *do* know a thing or two about takin' care of myself."

Stillwell turned away. It was useless to say anything more. Shanks wouldn't understand, and if he stayed he would die not understanding. At least Willie Birdsong hadn't argued about it so much. He had just saddled and gone away, when Stillwell told him to. The pale kid was already gone, without a word to anybody. It was just as well. If Goldie Locke showed up . . . *when* Goldie Locke showed up, and Stillwell's shoulders were tight now with an intuition that said the killer was near . . . anybody else around would be so much slaughter meat.

Just as he would be, probably, though he didn't intend to go down without one hell of a fight.

Coby Shanks finished saddling his horse in the shelter of the tack shed and swung aboard, raking Stillwell with accusing eyes. His glare said he would never forgive the man for not letting him prove himself a man.

Damn fool kid, Stillwell thought. Get out of here and live a long life. You'd just be in my way here. "Go on," he rasped. "Get away from here."

Coby glanced down, then leaned from his saddle. "Come on, Luck. I reckon we know where we ain't wanted."

The cat hesitated, then responded to the signal. It crouched and leapt, scrabbling onto Shanks' saddle-skirt. At the unaccustomed sound the horse glanced around, and Coby held its reins against shying.

Pointedly not looking toward Stillwell, the redhead pulled his hat low and flipped his reins, sidling his horse away, turning westward, clearing the shelter of the shed. "Hang on, Luck," he gritted, "we'll find a place where we're . . ."

Stillwell stepped to the corner of the shed, a sudden uneasiness gripping him. There was something . . . something in the wind.

A half mile north, where brush obscured a gully at the base of the mesa, mourning doves winged outward from their shelter, tiny dark dots against the rising hills beyond.

"Coby!" Stillwell shouted, "Down!"

The redhead turned, surprised . . . then was flung from his saddle as though a heavy fist had struck him. He skidded on the hard ground, sprawled there and didn't move. Bright blood began to pool beneath him. For an instant the horse stood, then it shied and turned to run. The cat bailed off its saddle and ran for cover.

And from the distance drifted the flat, hard report of a long-range rifle. Stillwell hugged the shadows of the shed, realizing that his Colt was in his hand and realizing that it was useless here. "A thousand yards," he breathed. "One clean shot . . . what kind of gun *is* that?"

Coby Shanks lay a dozen yards away, but there was nothing to be done for him. Dark anger burned in Stillwell's shadowed eyes. Just at the moment, it seemed, when the young tough was ready to change his directions—to get out of the gunslinger business—he had paid the gunslinger's price. Coby Shanks would never have the chance to change his ways, to choose a better path in life. Coby Shanks was dead.

More than a half mile away across rising, open land, Goldie Locke peered through the telescope mounted on the Alexander Henry and frowned. The rider had seemed to be Byron Stillwell. At this distance, in this light—and with a cat on his saddle—he had seemed so. But now he lay dead, and the telescope perused the body. It was someone else. Not Stillwell. Methodically, Goldie Locke jacked a second shell into the big rifle's chamber and rested it again on its tripod shooting stand. Stillwell was down there, and would have to show himself. Another clear shot, and it would be ended. This had taken far too much time and effort. It had cost too much for what it paid. It must be ended.

At the edge of the shed below, a face showed itself. But only for a moment. The face appeared and was withdrawn, too quickly for the full second that a bullet would take to reach there, at this range. The killer held fire, waiting. But there was no question this time. The features had been clear in the telescope's eye. Wide-set, hat-shaded dark eyes, hard, square chin, trimmed mustache . . . It was Byron Stillwell. The big rifle leveled on that edge of the shed and waited.

The sleek, swaged bullet from the Alexander Henry would require one full second to travel a thousand yards.

That was all Goldie Locke needed from Byron Stillwell now. One second of exposed target.

But soon. Far away, drifting up from the lowlands eastward, the thin wail of a train whistle drifted on the still air.

Chapter Twenty-two

Stillwell crouched behind the shed, realizing that the only cover it offered was invisibility. A bullet from a heavy rifle wouldn't even slow down going through the lap-board walls of the little building.

He had chanced one glance around the corner, trying to see movement or reflection in the distant brushy cut, knowing that he would not. He looked, then shifted position. Just in that split second, a bullet could be on its way. But it would take a second or so to arrive. He dodged back and crouched low. Nothing happened. The killer up there wasn't trigger-happy, wasn't wasting lead. There was no need to. Whoever that was up there was a professional, and knew that he had no place to go.

What would he do now? Wait for a clear shot? One clear shot, and it would be over. Nothing would stop a bullet from a rifle like that, and there was little chance of a miss. He knew that, and wondered again, what *kind* of rifle? Something in the flat, decisive crack of its report—he had heard it twice now—tugged at memories. It had a familiar song. Not quite the heavy thump of the Sharps the kid had found, this was a tighter, more ringing report. Like the cracking of a whip.

Like the fine ranging rifle that outlaw "officer of the court" up in Kansas had used. He remembered now.

243

Sturdevant. Sturdevant, the judge's man, up where they were trying to bring law to a lawless land despite some of the "law" that faced them. Sturdevant was outlaw law.

Sturdevant had carried an Alexander Henry rifle, the second of its kind that Stillwell had seen. And it had sounded like the cracking of a whip.

But such shooting, at such a range? At least a thousand yards. More than half a mile. Sturdevant had been good, but not that good.

A telescope, then, he thought. Locke uses a telescope. And for a telescope sight to perform, the rifle must be rested. On a shooting stand or tripod mount. Not as quickly adjustable as a free-hand hold.

It was time to gamble. Stillwell stood, holstered his gun and hugged the wall of the shed. With two fingers on his opposite wrist he counted his heartbeats, then he swung around the corner and stood, in full view, peering up the incline. One . . . two . . . three! He dropped and hugged the ground as an angry hornet sang over him, a few feet above his head—exactly where his heart would have been if he were still standing.

He scrambled back into the shelter of the shed, turned and sprinted for the depot building fifty yards away, clearing from cover—on the opposite side of the shed from where he had been—as the whip-crack of the passed shot echoed down the slope.

Another bullet whined past him as he ran, and he knew he was right. Without a set-stand, at that distance, the Alexander Henry was still deadly but it lost some of its accuracy.

Rounding the front corner of the depot he wheeled and stepped back out, again counting heartbeats, straining for a view of the assailant up there in the draw. This time he saw a little puff of smoke among the scrub branches, and noted its position for two heartbeats before he spun back to the shelter of the building. A high-powered bullet whanged off the stone corner, spreading a shower of little shards and dust.

Again the report came tardily, drifting down behind the bullet. But this time it was a double report, the hard thump of a Sharps .50 overlapping the flat crack of the Alexander Henry.

He stepped out again and shifted his view, up and to the right, knowing what he would see even before he did. On the mesa's lip was the pale-haired kid, the kid with no name, just raising the muzzle of his found rifle. Even at this distance, Stillwell could see the silhouette of him up there, see him working in a fresh load, raising the Sharps for another shot. He wasn't as far from the killer's hiding place as Stillwell was, but he was still a good five hundred yards from it, firing downward.

"Drop, Kid," Stillwell hissed through clenched teeth. "Don't try it again."

Again the Sharps spoke, atop the mesa, and the Alexander Henry answered it from the brushy draw. The kid spun like a rag doll in a wind, his rifle flying away from him. He toppled, dropping out of sight. A moment passed and there was a smoke again in the brushy cut. The bullet that followed ricocheted angrily off stone and howled away into the distance, flattened and tumbling through the air. At its sound the yellow cat came from somewhere near the bunk-shed, streaking across the open ground to disappear beneath the depot's porch. He could hear it down there, snarling and keening in fine feline outrage, and the sound reminded him—oddly—of how the cat had looked that morning on Gingerbread Hill when it let Daisy pet it.

It isn't angry, he realized suddenly. *It's afraid.*

Faint with distance, a train whistle wailed, and Stillwell realized there was a chance. The situation here

was a stand-off, as long as he kept to cover. All the
killer could do from up there was wait for a clear shot.
Would he wait, with a train coming? Or would he come
down, closer, seeking a kill?

Close enough for Stillwell's Peacemaker to have a
chance at him?

Despite its knock-down power, the big Colt was a
"hundred yard gun," with an effective range that might
be stretched to twice that by an expert. He looked
around again, at the open terrain, and his heart sank.
The killer could come down from the draw, all right—
come right out into the open and seek out his target—
without ever closing in to where the Peacemaker would
be effective. At three hundred yards; or four or five
hundred, Locke could circle the entire station area,
looking for a clear shot. And he would get his shot
eventually . . . if he had time. The train was still distant.

The cat came out from under the porch and
crouched near his feet, ears back, whiskered cheeks
curled above white fangs. It was staring at the corner
beyond which the land rose toward the draw. The end
of its tail twitched rhythmically, and its nose wrinkled.

"Do you know who's up there?" Stillwell muttered.

Again the train shrilled in the distance and Stillwell
judged its location. There was time, he decided. If the
killer wanted to come down and flush him out, there
was still time to do it.

Then a gunshot rang down from above, and Stillwell
raised his head. The Sharps .50 again! The kid was still
alive up there, alive and shooting.

"Keep your head down, son," Stillwell muttered.
"Maybe this isn't over yet."

Thirty yards away was the old barn, where his paint
horse waited. And in its saddle boot was the Winchester the kid had taken off a Double D bushwhacker. Not

a big gun, or a long-range one, but a better range piece than any handgun. If he could get to that rifle . . .

The Sharps thundered again atop the mesa, and its thump was answered by the crack of the Alexander Henry. Stillwell leapt from the depot porch and ran. Distantly he heard the Sharps fire again, but no bullets came his way. At the barn he ducked inside, drew the Winchester from its boot and went out the way he had come in, levering a cartridge into the receiver.

Caliber 44-40. Not a big gun, not any kind of match for an Alexander Henry—or even for the kid's old Sharps. But still, a rifle. He ducked around the corner of the barn, leveled the rifle at the impossibly distant draw, raised its front bead at least a foot and fired. He wouldn't hit anything that way, but now Goldie Locke would have something to think about. No Winchester was of much use at ranges like a thousand yards, but it could be deadly at three hundred.

"Don't bother coming down here, Goldie," he muttered. "Just hold tight where you are. I'll come to you." God bless that wild kid up there. He had turned the tables, just by being where he was.

Goldie Locke was no fighter. The realization came, and he knew it was right. Goldie Locke was a ruthless killer, but not one to face a confrontation. Goldie Locke's kills were neat and tidy. Always neat and tidy.

There had been no firing from the Alexander Henry for a minute or more, not since before the last report of the kid's Sharps. Stillwell fired the Winchester once more, hoping to drop a .44 slug in the killer's vicinity, then darted to the far side of the barn and broke cover, running as fast as pumping long legs could push him, zig-zagging and watching for any sign of smoke in the distant draw. Up the rise he ran, ready at any instant to swerve aside or drop face-down. Ahead was a shallow gully, a tiny wash barely two feet deep, and he made for it expecting at any instant to hear the deadly whine of a high-power rifle's bullet seeking him out.

He veered, swerved and ran, and dropped into the cover of the wash, trying not to think about the silence around him. Had the kid managed to shoot Goldie Locke? Something told him that had not happened. But then why hadn't the killer fired? Now that Stillwell had cover, Locke's chances of a clean kill were fading.

The distance between them wasn't a thousand yards now. It was no more than seven hundred, and though Stillwell's approach would be slower from here, there was cover. There would be no more chances at a clean, long-range shot to bring him down.

Crouching, he headed up the wash. Another hundred yards, then two hundred. From here, he could use the Winchester if he could see a target. Still extreme range for the 44-40, but no longer impossible range.

Switching from the wash to a dry-bed cut that came down from above, he dashed another hundred yards, paused and went over its side, into the near edge of the same wide patch of brush from which Goldie Locke had fired. He raised his head for an instant to get his bearings, then ducked and went on. And still there was silence.

Bleak intuition tugged at him, and when he looked up and to his right—toward the mesa top—he wasn't surprised to see the silhouette of the kid up there, waving at him.

The signal was clear. Goldie Locke wasn't here any more. Faced with an unfavorable situation, the killer had backed off and gone away . . . away, for now. Yet still out there somewhere, still faceless and invisible, still ruthless, still determined and just waiting for another chance.

Atop the mesa, the kid was on his feet and hobbling away. A moment later he reappeared there, on horseback, and waved again. Stillwell waved back.

He found where the killer had been. A little hollow in the brush, just at the edge of a drop-off that afforded a clear view of everything below. He found the peg-marks of the tripod shooting stand, a few scuffed prints that told him nothing of immediate use, and a couple of the brass cases from the Alexander Henry. Long, slightly-tapered, bottle-neck shell cases of a rifle tailored for precision shooting at extreme range. A big-game rifle, the finest of its time.

He picked up the cases, looked at them and raised them to his nose. Acrid stench of freshly-fired nitro-cellulose powder. Powder scent and—as the cases warmed in his hand, a hint of something else.

In the distance, the approaching train wailed, nearer now and coming on, westbound. Stillwell prowled the site for a few minutes, then headed back down toward the abandoned station of Buffalo Wells.

The kid had circled eastward to find an easy path down from the mesa, and as Stillwell reached the station yard he saw him coming, slumped in his saddle but hanging on.

In the open yard the yellow cat was circling around the still body of Coby Shanks, wary and curious. Stillwell walked to the fallen redhead and squatted beside him. He had died instantly, that much was clear. Shot from half a mile away, he didn't live long enough to hear the sound of the shot that killed him.

Stillwell thumbed shut the staring eyes, and lay Coby's hat over his dead face, waving the curious cat away as it came near.

"Luck, huh?" he said. "A cat named Luck." He stood, still looking down at the dead youngster. He would have another grave to dig now, for another young man handy with a gun. But it would be different this time. Not easier, but different. He hadn't killed this one. This one had died in his place.

"Doesn't seem like Luck was your luck, Coby," he murmured. "Seems like maybe he was mine, instead."

The kid had a hole in his side, but the only thing coming out of it was blood and not too much of that. "Man, I never seen a body shoot like that," he marveled as Stillwell tied a compress onto him. "How far was that, he got me from? Quarter of a mile, maybe?"

"Something like that. Did you see who it was?"

"Couldn't see a thing, except *where* he was. An' who he was shootin' at. Lord, what kind of rifle was that thing?"

"It's called an Alexander Henry. Kind of rare. I've only seen two of them. One in Kansas . . . and another one, a while back, in Colorado."

"Sorry I didn't do any more good than I did," the kid said. "I thought this ol' big rifle was really something . . . until that jasper opened up with his."

Stillwell finished the bandaging and let the kid sit on the porch. "Did you see where *that jasper* went?"

"He had a horse an' carriage waitin'," the kid nodded. "Way back up above that draw. There's an old road over yonder, I seen it before. I didn't know he was gone 'til he broke cover way off up there, an' there wasn't much I could do about it by then. Didn't even hardly get a look. Too far away. But he drove off in that carriage."

"Going east?"

"Yeah." The kid glanced up. "How'd you know that?"

"It doesn't matter. You just rest here. There's a train coming, a mile or so away. I've run up the flag, so it will stop here. I'll be over there," he pointed, "burying a friend."

The kid sighed. "Willie Birdsong will prob'ly be expectin' me to show up someplace west of here. I never told him I'd catch up to him, but I usually do. I guess he expects it."

"You'll find him," Stillwell said. "The train's a westbound."

He broke open the tool box, found a pick and a spade, and looked around for a suitable place for a young outlaw to rest. Up on the rise, he decided. Within sight of the trains going by.

And bury his gun with him. It was probably the only thing that ever made him feel worthwhile. He didn't live to learn how much more there is to life . . . than a gun.

Goldie Locke was headed east now. He didn't have the typewritten paper that the killer had left at Half Moon Cross. The sheriff in Waxahachie had it. But he had memorized it.

"To Byron Stillwell," it said. "You cannot run or hide. Come out."

Then two names, with addresses. Mattie Stillwell and Patricia Mills.

And a final line: "You . . . or them. Come out."

There was something about the way the words were placed, the spacing of separated thoughts instead of proper punctuation, that had puzzled him. It was telegrapher style wording, but done on a typewriting machine. An odd blend.

And now Goldie Locke was eastbound. Stillwell had eluded the killer, and so the threat must be made good. Goldie Locke was a professional, with a reputation that was worth money. A lot of money, he realized. Goldie Locke wouldn't bluff. Goldie Locke wouldn't back down. A professional reputation was at stake.

And a fortune, built on that reputation and a dead whore's name.

He knew where he had first seen an Alexander Henry rifle, and it was the same rifle he had heard today. He had no doubt of it.

The westbound train was at Buffalo Wells depot when he finished the grave and went for Coby's body. Men were there—passengers and crew—to help him finish the job. Among them was Ranger Captain Walter Mitchell.

"I don't expect you'll be going on to Mobeetie." the Ranger said. "They relayed word. Peter Lewellyn Dawes is dead."

Stillwell just looked at him.

"Natural causes," Mitchell shrugged. "Had a funny thing in his hand, though. My man out there said it was a mashed-out copper badge. Looked like a train had run over it."

"Little memento," Stillwell said.

"Yeah, I know. They found the note you sent with it."

Stillwell looked at the fresh grave, the people standing around it, and turned to gaze eastward. "You going on west, Captain?"

Mitchell shrugged. "No hurry now. You got a better direction?"

"I know where I'm going."

"My horse is in that stock car," the ranger pointed.

They had helped the kid into a parlor car, and Mitchell followed Stillwell down to see him.

"You saved my life today, Kid," the drifter said. "That makes twice. I'm beholden." He turned to Mitchell. "What will become of that ranch out there?"

"Double D?" The ranger shrugged. "Go up for sale, I reckon. Not much to sell, with its stock mostly gone and nobody to work it."

"Can your people keep it off the block for a little while?"

"I suppose we could. Ongoing investigation, something like that. What do you have in mind?"

Stillwell turned to the kid again. "You find Willie Birdsong, and the two of you get on up to Double D Ranch. It's north of Mobeetie. I wouldn't be surprised if Stoke Winburn and some of the Half Moon Cross outfit showed up there, too. Ranch shouldn't be left to go to ruin. Place like that needs some real cowboys to work it."

The ranger and the drifter watched the train pull out, then saddled their horses. "You still want Goldie Locke?" Stillwell asked as he swung aboard the paint.

"Of course I do. That's why I'm tagging along with you, Mister."

"All right. But I get first chance. My score to settle comes first."

"I believe the state of Texas' business with Goldie Locke takes precedence over yours, Stillwell," Mitchell glared at him.

"Meaning what?"

"Meaning that if you have an idea how to find him, then it gets to be ranger business."

"I *am* a ranger," Stillwell reminded him. "You made me one, remember?"

"You know where to find that killer?"

"I hope so." Stillwell dropped a half-length of his serape and the cat climbed aboard. "With a little luck, I think I do."

Chapter Twenty-three

Buck and John Henry, riding periphery patrol in the search for Daisy Walcott, found the unattended carriage at the edge of town, in that area above the creek commonly called Gin Alley. It was late evening when they found it, and Buck scoured the area while John Henry investigated the carriage. The area where it stood, its big draft horse still in harness, was a hidden lot between two warehouses.

When Buck returned, they compared notes.

"Can't find a thing in it or on it," John Henry shook his head. "Best I can tell, it's been here for a while. That poor damn horse was pretty dry. You can see where he's dragged this wagon around here, lookin' for a way out. I gave him water an' some grain from that stable yonder."

"Nothin' in the carriage?" Buck peered inside, then squatted to look beneath the rig. It was a finely-made, expensive carriage, and he admired its oiled leather springs and its polished running gear.

"Nothin' I could see," John Henry repeated. "I looked all over it. It wasn't a runaway. The reins were tied up like somebody left it here. What did you find?"

"Nothin'. Not a sign of Miss Walcott anyplace. Or any other female, for that matter. I *did* find some kind of a high-stakes gamblin' game goin' on in one of them

254

closed sheds past the warehouse. Sounds like plenty of folks inside, an' they got some fellers guardin' the door, but I asked an' they ain't seen Miss Walcott."

"We best take this rig in," John Henry decided. "If it's hers, I'd say somebody stole it."

Riding abreast of the draft horse, one on each side, they maneuvered the rig out of its confined space and back into town, where they turned it over to swampers at the county barn, a block from the courthouse.

"You go report," John Henry said. "I'll take a ride out to Gingerbread Hill."

Buck's eyes narrowed. "You can't go to Gingerbread Hill when you're on duty, don't you know that?"

"This is official business," John Henry said archly. "We're gonna need somebody to identify that rig. I'll find somebody at the Cotillion Club to do that."

"Well, then, why you?" Buck snapped. "I tell you what, you go over to the courthouse and *I'll* go to the Cotillion Club."

"Use your head, Buck." John Henry explained. "Yonder when we found that rig, you were the one that scouted around, so they'll need your report on what you found . . ."

"I didn't find anything. I told you that."

"Yeah, but you did the ride-around, and you interviewed citizens on the scene."

"They were a couple of boys watchin' the door on a highstakes game two blocks away! You're the one that investigated the carriage and watered the horse."

"You see," John Henry countered smugly, "They don't need me to tell about that because the carriage and the horse is both right yonder in the barn and anybody that wants to can look for hisself. Now you go in and tell 'em. I'll be at Gingerbread Hill."

Fuming, Buck watched his partner ride away, heading for the lights and delights of the Hill. He turned toward the courthouse, then thought better of it. "We don't need somebody from the Cotillion Club to identify that rig," he muttered. "Miss Walcott's house is just up yonder. I bet that Chinee woman knows her rig when she sees it."

Matching the action to the thought, Buck Mabry headed for the McIntyre house.

The place was dark when he arrived. He tied his horse out front, climbed the steps and knocked at the front door.

When there was no response he knocked again, then tried the latch. It was locked. He wandered around the enclosed area of the porch, peering at dark windows, testing them, then went down the steps and circled around to the back of the house. A smaller enclosed porch framed the back door, and he went in, reached for the latch, then stopped, listening. He had heard a sound, but wasn't sure where it came from. Cautiously he drew his revolver, then tried the door latch. It opened easily, and he peered into darkness beyond. Again he heard a furtive sound, as of someone in the room beyond. He pushed the door wide, hesitated and stepped through.

"Hello?" he called. "Anybody here?"

When there was no response he raised his gun, holding it in both hands, and took another step into darkness. "Sheriff's officer!" he said. "Whoever's here, speak up and show yourself!"

Again the furtive sound, this time behind him. He started to turn, had a glimpse of a man silhouetted against the doorway, then something collided with his skull and everything went dark.

Each night of the past four, the man in the long linen coat had ridden quietly into town a little past sundown, hard eyes under a slouch hat taking in every-thing around him in the manner of a predator on the prowl. He spoke to no one, and held to the shadows where he could. Long-boned, slope-shouldered and un-kempt, he had the look of hard country and the scent of woodsmoke about him.

And each night after he had made a circuit of the main square he selected a tavern, tied his horse and went inside. He would be there as long as there were men within who traded news and gossip, though he took no part in it himself. He simply sat back in some dark corner, nursed a mug of watered rye, and listened.

On this night the stranger sat in the Liberty Bell, and his patience paid off.

Observation told him the four men at the end of the plank bar were regulars—the bartender knew them by first name or nickname—and that they were courthouse people having a drink after work. One was a janitor, one a file clerk, one might have maintained the coun-ty's legal library and one was named Ned.

Experience told him that one of the best constant sources for local gossip, anywhere, was from those who worked within earshot of lawmen, lawyers, judges and record clerks.

He tuned himself to their conversation and was re-warded within minutes.

"That drifter's gonna be comin' back," the librarian announced to his chums. "Heard it from the chief his-self, he was tellin' Mr. Rice."

Ned sipped his beer, then asked, "What drifter?"

"Well, the one all the shootin' was about, o'course. That Stillwell. He's on his way back."

"That a fact?" The librarian looked concerned. "Con-stable won't like that. I heard him say, right in front of everybody, that Stillwell draws trouble like a lightnin' rod draws bolts."

"Albert ain't in town," Ned said. "He's took another trip out west: I keep wonderin' where he goes out there, and what for."

"Just as well," the janitor allowed. "He'd have a fit if he knowed they're bringin' that jasper back to this town. I was right yonder in th' main hall when Zeke Albert told the sheriff that big shoot-up was Stillwell's fault."

"Don't see how it could have been, though," the clerk said judiciously. "He wasn't anyplace around when it happened. Besides, I saw most of the reports on that. Bunch of them Tightwadders an' some owlhoot young'uns from over around Ennis got into it, that's all that was. Just plain trigger-happy, the whole mess of 'em."

The conversation continued, but after a time the man at the back table got up and left. He had heard enough.

Pack Folger had a camp down by the creek, and a reason to hang around Waxahachie. He had three brothers dead back in Mullinsville and a score to settle with Byron Stillwell, and now he knew. Stillwell had been here and gone. But Stillwell was coming back.

The sun was high when Sheriff Matt Kingman arrived at the courthouse, to find pandemonium reigning in his territory in the south wing. The outer office was filled with people—more than he had expected.

Some were witnesses and complainants in the various court cases arising from what the newspaper had called "The Great Waxahachie Shootout," of the previous week—that bizarre few minutes when gunfire had crashed in the dark street east of the square. There were a few Tightwadders there, a pair of lawyers from Ennis and several local lawyers, as well as various staff people from several of the local saloons and some sheriff's reserves in the court suits.

Both of the courtrooms upstairs would be in use today, with two judges and various juries trying to unravel what it had all been about.

Ed Rice was in a frenzy, trying to sort documents for all the cases set to be called on two full dockets.

Kingman identified most of those involved in the court cases, but was surprised to see the Mayor Fuller, Commissioner Taylor and a dozen or so townspeople in the crowd in the anteroom. He nodded to some of them and hurried into his office, Jim Logan following him.

"You finally get a night's sleep, Sheriff?" the chief of deputies asked.

"I did," Kingman nodded. "Maybe I should have stayed around, though. What's going on out there?"

"Mostly court business," Logan said, then handed the sheriff some typewritten reports. "Few other things, though. Somebody stole the mayor's horse and carriage, and he's upset about that."

"Any leads?"

"Nothin' yet. Haven't had time to look. He just found out it was gone an hour ago."

"What did they do, take it out of his barn?"

"No, sir, he'd left the rig in a fenced lot down on Gin Alley. That's where it was stolen." Logan was trying hard to keep his face straight.

"What was the mayor's rig doing down in Gin Alley at that hour?"

Logan lost his battle with his face and grinned wolfishly. "So far, His Honor has declined to comment on that, sir. But he *is* some upset about losin' that nice rig of his."

Kingman sighed and shook his head. "Never a dull day. What else?"

"Probationer problems," Logan offered.

"Probationer . . . as in probational deputy?" Kingman frowned.

"Yes, sir. But make that deputies. It's both of 'em. They may be off shift for a couple of days. Deputy Taylor went out to Gingerbread Hill for some reason last night — we don't know why, yet — and wound up in a fist fight with the Loftus boys."

"Which ones?"

"All of 'em. But they swear he jumped them and all they did was defend themselves. An impartial witness says the boy took offense at something somebody said about one of the typewriters."

Kingman gritted his teeth. "What kind of shape is he in?"

"Beat up. But he'll mend. Then there's Buck Mabry; he's over at Doc's with a knot on his head an' a bad set of the dizzies. Best we can figure out, he went up to the McIntyre house last night and walked into Daisy Walcott's servants' quarters. With his gun drawn. That deaf gardener of hers thought he was a burglar or somethin' — it was dark — and brained him with a shovel."

"Jesus," Kingman whispered. "What in God's name did those two think they were doing?"

"I guess we'll know when they're up to talkin'," Logan shrugged. "Right now we haven't got any idea."

"Is that the worst of it, yet?"

"Far as I know. We've got several planters up in arms because Tim Sullivan's disappeared. Nobody's seen him since the shoot-up, and these gentlemen are worried about gettin' the Tightwad gin to bid on their fall crops. They want us to drop everything else and go find Sullivan."

Once more, the sheriff sighed. "What else?"

"Mostly just the usual," Logan reported. "The bank

threatening to sue you for letting the Half Moon Cross crew sell some of the ranch's horses before they vacated the premises . . ."

"The bank got the money!"

"Yeah, but the banker says he might have got a higher price at auction. He's also upset because everybody went off and left the place untended."

"Bastard!" Kingman muttered. The ranch had been unattended because the banker's eviction order specified that.

"And Miz Whickert's raisin' cane again. This time she says there are Tonkawa Indians sneakin' into town every night so they can look in her windows when she gets ready for bed . . ."

"Last time it was nigras, wasn't it?"

"That was the time before. Last time she said it was drunken cowboys up from the trail."

"Lord love Miz Whickert," Kingman muttered. "I saw Commissioner Taylor out there. What does he want?"

"Well, he tried to get Ed Rice to have his typewriters write campaign letters for him, and Ed refused, so the commissioner wants you to order him to."

Kingman went to his window and stood, looking out. "Is there *anybody* out there about anything important, Sam?"

"No, sir. Just two court dockets and the usual."

"All right. Now tell me something interesting."

Logan had been waiting. "Message from the ranger, Sheriff. Goldie Locke showed up at Buffalo Wells, just like y'all figured. One man dead and one hurt, but Stillwell's all right. He and the ranger are on their way back here, and Stillwell's got an idea where Goldie Locke is."

Kingman spun around. "Where?"

"He hasn't said. But around here, somewhere. Mitchell asks for a couple of your best, on standby."

261

"All right." Kingman nodded. "If that's what it takes. Our two best."

"You and me, Sheriff?"

"That's right," Kingman nodded. "You and me."

There was a knock at the door, and it opene[d] slightly. The duty deputy stuck his head in. "'Scus[e] me, Sheriff. Whose horse and carriage do we have i[n] custody, over at the barn?"

Both of them looked at the duty deputy, blankly.

"It's the stablekeep, sir. Somebody brought in a hors[e] and carriage last night, sheriff's authority, but he hasn[']t got any hold warrant or anything, and he wants t[o] know what he's supposed to do about the rig."

Logan shrugged and Kingman shook his head. "[I] don't know a thing about it, Joe. Check around. Some[-]body's bound to."

"Yes, sir. Oh, an' about the lady that was gone? Al[l] Daisy Walcott? She's safe and sound, sir. Been away o[n] some business, seems like. But she sent a message t[o] her housekeeper that she'll be back shortly. Housekee[p]er's a Chinee woman named Ling. She brought th[e] message over last night. I've already called off the boy[s] on that one."

"All right, Joe." Kingman seemed distant. Loga[n] knew he was thinking about the ranger and Stillwell . . . and about Goldie Locke. It had become almost an ob[-]session with the sheriff, this thing about the assassi[n] who shot down a Texas Ranger on the street, right ou[t]side the sheriff's office.

Joe hesitated at the door. "We got a query from Co[n]stable Zeke Albert, little bit ago. He's out at Paduca[h] Crossing, wants a rundown on a gunman named Ki[m] Minter. Also wants to know what we know about [a] Panhandle outfit that brands Double D. We got a Colo[-]rado poster on this Minter, an' the same informatio[n] you sent to Ranger Mitchell about Double D. Want m[ore]

262

send it to him? He's waitin' for an answer."

"Send it," Kingman said, again looking out the big double-hung window.

He was looking at the place where a lawman had died three years before.

Chapter Twenty-four

Zeke Albert had not slept well. But then, he nev
slept well when he came to visit Paducah Crossing. Th
memories lived here, and for him the nightmares
them were always alive. Memories of gunfire an
blood—of senseless combat on a quiet street, mindles
bullets flying wild, useless death and pointless agon
Calico and blood, and an end to all things good in h
life.

The dreams kept him restless and tossing, as they a
ways did, and each time he awoke—sweat-damp an
aching—he saw faces in the dark. The face of an u
known drifter, faces of those who gunned him dow
. . . and the dead face of his own young wife, lying i
the dust of a bullet-riddled street.

Then, strangely, he had seen the dark, sardonic fa
of Byron Stillwell. The drifter, Stillwell, whom he ha
never seen except just recently in Waxahachie and hope
never to see again.

But in his dreams, just before waking, he saw him
not at Waxahachie but here, in Paducah Crossing. A
though Stillwell stood on that dusty street in front
the Cattlemen's Bank, as though there were bullets fl
ing, as though killers were cutting him down as th
had cut down that other drifter years ago.

This time, the drifter a killer stalked was Stillwell.

As he came awake, the dream fading, Zeke saw again the faces of the killers, so long ago. And recognized one of them. He hadn't known the man then, but he had a name for him now.

King Minter.

It had not been a good night's sleep, but that didn't matter this time. Zeke Albert recalled the dreams and knew there was a thing he had to do.

He washed his face and hands and got dressed, then locked the hotel-room door behind him and stepped out onto the morning street. The sun was just topping the hills to the east, and the air still felt cool and clear from the night. He walked along the street and turned, then turned again at the depot complex.

A barn and stables were there, just as they had been years before—a place that catered to travelers and passersby.

"Noticed a slick-dressed feller around here yesterday," he told the yawning night man. "Mike Larson said his name was Minter. He have a horse here, does he?"

"That'n yonder," the man pointed. "The blaze sorrel. Nice piece of horseflesh."

Zeke had a look at the horse, briefly, then told the stablekeep, "I'll be needin' a saddle horse for a while today, Billy."

The man looked sympathetic. "Sure, Zeke. Like always, huh?"

"Like always." He strolled out of the stable, feeling oddly removed, as though he really weren't in his body at all but rather were floating along with it, beside and above it. He glanced upward at the telegraph wires nearby. There hadn't been a wire at Paducah Crossing when he had lived here, but the wires told him where the key was.

The Western Union office was just opening, a sleepy operator just lifting the blinds to let the morning in.

Zeke nodded and went to the counter where he printed a message on a pad of paper. To Ellis County Sheriff Matt Kingman, two questions. He handed it across. "Can you get this out right away?"

"Sure," the operator glanced at it and sat down to open his key. "I guess you'll be waiting for a reply?"

"I'll be around," Zeke nodded. "You have the name there. Albert. Zeke Albert."

He found breakfast at a smoky little place near the hotel, then went back to the stables. The attendant had a saddled horse ready for him and he swung aboard without a word and rode out of the little town, heading south of west.

It was only a mile to the old cemetery, but he always rode there when he went. It reminded him of those times long ago when she had been with him, when they rode together on Sunday afternoons, out past the cemetery and on down to the little creek where the cottonwood thicket was. It was where they had their picnics.

At the cemetery he dismounted, walked across to the grave where she was buried, and took off his hat. Squatting there, he said, "It's me, honey. I just had to come, to talk to you one more time."

The only sounds were the scuff of the horse's hoof, the whispering of the constant, lonely wind and the calls of meadowlarks across the way. But in his memories he heard her voice as clearly as if it had never been stilled.

"Probably the last time," he said. "One way or another. Lord knows I've tried to turn you loose, honey. I've tried to just let go and get on with the days that are, instead of the ones that were. I've tried, but I just never could, so I keep comin' back here to talk to you like this. We both know that's no good, but it's all I can do."

The wind whispered, and he bowed his head.

"But maybe I won't be back again, after this time," he said softly. "There's a man in town yonder. I know who he is. I don't know if it was him killed you, honey, but he was there and I saw him. And I'm thinkin', maybe the reason I can't let you go on like I should, is because I just can't stand it that I never could do anything about what they did that day.

"All the time, I see a drifter with a gun, and I know there are people lookin' for him and I'm afraid they'll find him in my town. Then more people will die ... like you died, honey. An' if it happens there won't be anything for me to do about it then, either. So I know what I need to do, you see."

The wind and the meadowlarks ... and somewhere within them, her sweet long-gone voice.

"That man," he said, "he's waiting there for a drifter. If the drifter shows up, that man will try to kill him. Maybe he can do that, and maybe not, but who else will die while they find out about that? I just don't believe I want that to happen this time, honey. Maybe I won't live to see what happens next, or maybe I might just be better than that man in town, and put him out of business. Either way," he raised a strained, haggard face to the sky, holding back emotions, "either way, maybe I won't ever be coming back here again. So I'm saying goodbye, honey. You and me, we've held on too long and now I've got to let you go."

He stood, abruptly, and crammed his hat onto his head. Without looking back he strode to the waiting horse, swung into its saddle and headed back toward Paducah Crossing.

There was a response waiting for him at the Western Union. It was a long message, and the telegrapher watched him curiously as he read it.

"You a lawman, Mr. Albert?" the man asked.

"I was once," he admitted. "But not any more. Not

here. Right now, I'm just a private citizen."

Which is all any lawman is, he thought, heading back to the hotel. Outside of his own jurisdiction, a lawman is just a private citizen.

And what difference does that make? Even within his jurisdiction, where he wears a badge and carries the authority of a town, a county or a state, a lawman is still only a citizen.

A citizen being paid to concern himself with exactly those matters that *any* citizen should concern himself with, paid or not.

In his hotel room he opened his valise, put on a clean shirt and strapped on his gun. For a moment he looked at the badge lying there—*Constable,* it said. *City of Waxahachie, Texas.*

Waxahachie was a long way from Paducah Crossing. He left the badge where it was and closed the valise. It seemed right, somehow, to be just a private citizen.

He was waiting at the stables when King Minter came to get his horse for his day's patrol of the roadways along which Stillwell might come. As Minter started for the stalls, Zeke stepped in front of him.

"Mr. Minter?" he asked, quietly. "King Minter?"

The gunman studied him, a smile toying with his cheeks. In a voice that was a purr he asked, "Who wants to know?"

"Just me," Zeke said evenly. "Let's go down by the switchbox yonder and talk a little bit."

"I'm not interested in you," Minter purred. "Get out of my way."

"You're interested in Byron Stillwell, aren't you?"

The gunman eyed him coldly. "Enough to know that you aren't him. What do you want?"

"Like I said, let's walk down there to that switchbox and talk about it."

268

Sudden suspicion glinted in the gunman's eyes. "Why there?"

"It's out of earshot," Zeke said. And maybe out of gun range of the town, he thought.

Minter hesitated, then shrugged and turned, totally confident. He led the way, the two hundred yards to the bleak siding where rails joined at a gate box. Zeke followed silently, noticing that the gunman didn't once look back and showed no slightest sign of fear.

On the street and at the depot, a few people gathered to watch them, wondering what this could be about.

Beside the switchbox Minter stopped, then turned. "You want to tell me what this is about?" he purred. "Who are you?"

Zeke pushed back his coat tail. "My name is Zeke Albert," he said calmly. "And what it's about is, I am arresting you for murder."

Minter blinked, then began to grin. "You? You intend to arrest *me?*"

"I do." Only Zeke's lips moved. "I have reason to believe you murdered my wife, Mr. Minter. Now I'd like for you to just unbuckle that gunbelt and let it drop. I strongly advise you to do that."

Minter's grin widened. He could hardly believe what he was hearing—a yokel in a wool vest telling him to lay down his guns. It was preposterous. "You don't know who you're bracing, mister," he purred. "If I decide to be done with you, you'll never even know it. Even if you had that gun in your hand instead of in that holster . . . go ahead," he taunted. "Take it out. I'll give you that, just so there's no question at all in the minds of those good folks yonder, who drew first. Go on, take it out!"

Obligingly, Zeke drew his gun, though he didn't yet point it at Minter. He held it casually, pointed at the sky, and said, "Let me tell you what's about to happen here, Mr. Minter. No. Hear me out, then you can do what you want to. One of two things is about to happen here. Most likely, you're going to draw on me and shoot me. Oh, I expect you're right, I'll never even see you do it. Maybe you'll shoot two or three times, and most likely you'll kill me. But my dying is the last thing you'll ever see, Mr. Minter. Because I've been shot before, and I know what I can take.

"I'm slow with a gun, Mr. Minter. Slower than you are, at least. But that won't matter. You see, I really don't care if you shoot me. All I care about is that you never shoot anyone else, ever again. And I've got a bullet here that will see to that, even if it's the last thing I ever do."

Minter's smile faded and he stared at Zeke. "You're crazy!"

"Most likely," Zeke said in the iciest, calmest voice King Minter had ever heard. "Most likely I am. Do you think you can kill a crazy man, Minter? Before he kills you?"

Still holding his gun upward, he stepped toward the gunman. A step, then another and another. "I'm ready, Minter. Shoot, if that's what you mean to do."

Minter's hand twitched, then hesitated. The man was barely ten feet from him now . . . then eight, then five. The gunman's lips felt dry. His eyes blinked furiously. All his reflexes seemed to be off. This was all wrong, not how it always was, how it was supposed to be. "Wait . . ." his voice cracked.

Zeke took another step. They were an arm's length from each other now, and Minter's bulging eyes focused on the man's gun. Why didn't he level it? Just start to level it, then maybe he could react.

"Other thing that might happen here," Zeke said evenly, "is you unbuckle that gunbelt an' drop it, like I said. That way neither of us dies. The other way we

270

both do. Your choice."

Minter tore his eyes from the man's gun . . . and wished he hadn't. Zeke's eyes held him, eyes that said nothing at all. Eyes like a dead man's eyes. Abruptly, King Minter knew that what the man said was true. Neither of them . . . or both, and those dead eyes didn't care a bit either way. Slowly, with suddenly trembling hands, King Minter unbuckled his polished gunbelt and let it drop in the dust at his feet.

Zeke stepped aside and pointed. "Now put your hands on that switchbox there. Wide apart, where I can see them. That's right. Now just slide your feet back a little bit . . ."

The gunman spreadeagled, bracing against the switchbox.

Zeke stepped back another pace, hesitated for a moment, then methodically lowered his gun and fired twice, one bullet for each of those soft, skilled hands.

Minter fell against the switchbox, rolled off and lit on the dusty ground, staring at his ruined hands. A faint sound built at his lips, a sound that wasn't human at all. A faint, husky purr that built and climbed until it was an eerie, wailing scream.

Zeke Albert put his gun away, picked up the gunman's rig and said, "I told you, Minter. Either way, you won't ever gun down innocent people again."

Minutes passed before he got Minter to his feet and headed back toward town. "By the way," he told him as he half-carried him along, "you're out of work. Your boss at Double D, he died. But you have a home anyway. That little rock building yonder, that's the jail. We'll just put you in there, an' somebody can come an' bandage your hands. My, but don't a .45 make a mess of a man's hands? 'Specially when they're restin' on steel? I guess it just splatters or somethin'. I don't expect you'll ever get much use out of those hands again."

"You had no right!" Minter hissed through clenched jaws. "What kind of law . . . ?"

"I'm not law, Mr. Minter," Jake said. "Not here, anyway. I don't even live around here any more."

"Not . . . law? Then what . . . ?"

"Just a private citizen, Mr. Minter. That's all I am, just a private citizen."

"You're crazy as a loon!"

"Maybe," Zeke admitted. But the melancholy wind whispered about them and he thought: then again, maybe I'm not. Maybe not any more.

Goodbye, honey. I loved you and I'll never forget you. But you're gone and it's time for me to let you go.

Chapter Twenty-five

"These horses both need a feed," Walter Mitchell noted as he and Byron Stillwell rode up the street toward the courthouse at Waxahachie. Evening twilight rested on the town, blue shadows deepening toward nightfall. "Lot of miles from Buffalo Wells. Lot of miles in a short time."

Both the paint and Mitchell's big black were looking gaunt, though they still walked with heads up and ears high.

"I can tend to that," Stillwell offered. "You go on over to the courthouse and do whatever you need to do. I'll wait."

"Your word?" Mitchell looked aside at him, his eyes narrowed.

"My word," Stillwell agreed.

"I don't like this, you not saying who you think Goldie Locke is."

"You already told me that."

"Sheriff's not going to like it, either."

"You said that, too."

"Well, if you go off on your own and get killed, how are we supposed to know then who you thought the killer was, if you never told us?"

"You have my word I'll wait," Stillwell repeated. "But

273

we do it my way, as we agreed."

Mitchell drew a deep breath and blew it out. There was no way he could force the damned drifter to talk. Stillwell had made that clear the past two hard-riding days. What was he going to do, take away his ranger's badge? And what did that matter to Stillwell?

What had it ever mattered, for that matter?

Lamps were being lit along Rogers Street as they turned toward the courthouse. The ranger gestured ahead. "The county barn is right yonder. Take the horses there. There'll be somebody to feed them and rub them down. Save you doin' it yourself. Your badge will get you in."

Across from the courthouse Mitchell dismounted and handed his reins to Stillwell. "I won't be long. But I wish you'd at least say where we're going."

"Not exactly sure," the drifter said casually. "Maybe I'll know by the time you and the horses are ready."

Mitchell scowled in irritation, then turned and stalked stiffly away, heading for the sheriff's office. Stillwell rode on to the fenced yard of the county barn and showed his badge at the gate, realizing that it was the first time he had used it for anything, and likely would be the last . . . if he was right.

A Texas Ranger badge, and its only claim to fame was that it got a pair of horses grained and flanneled for free.

"We'll be needin' these mounts again in a bit," he told the stable attendant, then hesitated as he looked beyond him, into the barn's lamplit interior. Inside, various county vehicles, implements and animals were kept. Near the door a strong horse waited in a holding stall. Next to it sat a closed carriage. "Whose is that?" he pointed.

The man shrugged. "Damned if I know. Somebody brought it in for impounding, but nobody tells us anything. Might have been stole, or a runaway. You want to know anything about anything here, you'll have to check over at the courthouse."

"Have these horses ready in an hour," Stillwell said. "Ranger business."

The man glanced at him, grumpily. "You want the cat rubbed down, too?"

From the barn he walked north, past the courthouse, then cut east to Jackson Avenue and turned north again. Big, ornate houses lined the avenue here, houses with scrollwork porches and stained-glass windows, where seedling trees stood in little whitewashed enclosures, waiting to grow.

In deepening dusk he walked the quiet, elegant street, looking at houses here and there. After several blocks he turned and started back the other way, this time walking down an alleyway bounded by gardens, chicken pens, horse lots and carriage sheds. After a time he headed downtown again, satisfied. He knew—instinct and logic and unarguable hunch told him—where he would find Goldie Locke.

He knew, and a part of him wished he had never figured it out. Or wished he had never been forced to.

He paused on the stone walk outside the courthouse, half expecting to see Walter Mitchell waiting for him somewhere. But the area around the courthouse was silent. Not the south wing, though. Lamps blazed inside, beyond the big double-hung windows, and there were people there. A shrill voice came dimly, strident with anger, but he could not hear the words.

At every corner around the courthouse, bright lights and the lazy traffic of off-season saloons, relatively tame on a night when there were no herds on the trails and no drovers coming in to let off steam. Between the saloons, and beyond, the dark streets were quiet. A faint smile touched the drifter's cheeks. Waxahachie. Boisterous and pretentious, stateliness and raw exuberance reigned equally in the little city. Garish, lavish, ostentatious and bawdy, prim propriety dwelt side by side here with rowdy mayhem and each turned its back on the other and pretended to be alone.

The sun had set and prim, proper Waxahachie had rolled up its streets and taken refuge behind its ornate paneled doors. The sun had set, and the bars were open and what revelry was to be had on this night was in full swing.

Waxahachie—a town where anyone could be invisible simply by wearing both kinds of camouflage. A perfect base of operations for a cold-blooded assassin.

Past the Liberty Bell, the street was dark and silent, only the lights from the county barn ahead relieving the gloom.

He walked the block and stopped at the county barn gate. It was open, hanging on its hinges, and there was no attendant in sight.

He heard a slight sound then, and turned. In weeds beside the gate a booted foot twitched feebly and someone moaned softly. It was the gate attendant. Stillwell crouched, touching the man's throat. He was alive, but unconscious.

Carefully, Stillwell came upright and looked around. There were lights in the barn, and sounds from there—the routine sounds of animals being tended, of people forking hay and sweeping stalls, greasing axles and patching tackle.

Soundlessly he crossed the yard, toward the main door. It was closed, but lamplight came through the cracks around it. He approached, paused to listen and reached for the latch.

Something hard and cold prodded his back and a low voice said, "Just stand still, Mister Gunfighter. This pistol is loaded and cocked."

Stillwell froze, his hands outward, away from his sides. "Who are you?" he asked, not turning.

"You don't know me, but I know you," the low voice

said. "I had three brothers a month ago. Now I don't have any. But I have you, an' I'm fixin' to send you straight to hell. When you get there you can tell 'em Pack Folger sent . . ."

The man's boot scuffed gravel as he eased closer to muffle the sound of his gun, and suddenly a sharp, shrill, spitting yowl pierced the air. He heard Folger's surprised gasp and felt the gun in his back waver. Instantly he ducked, pivoted around, pushed the gun-arm aside with his forearm and grasped the man's wrist in a grip like a bear trap. The gun roared and chips exploded from the barn's doorframe. Folger tried to twist away, started to kick, then seemed to hang in air as Stillwell drove a rock-hard fist into his yielding breadbasket—quick, stunning blows, two and then another—and a final, chopping uppercut to the chin that lifted the man off his feet. Folger sagged and fell, limp and dangling from his trapped right hand which remained motionless in the grip of Byron Stillwell.

There were shouts in the distance, and a babble of voices beyond the door. Stillwell removed the six-gun from Pack Folger's limp fingers and dropped his arm, then knelt to check for any other weapons. He found three—a pocket gun and two long knives, one at the man's belt, the second in a boot.

As he stood, the barn's door opened a crack, then opened wide and people came to stare at the fallen man. Moments later others arrived, from the courthouse.

"Somehow I just knew it was you," Walter Mitchell said. "Is he dead?"

"Just restin'," Stillwell assured him.

Matt Kingman peered at the fallen man and asked. "Locke?"

"No, his name's Pack Folger," Stillwell said. "Those three up at Mullinsville, that I told you about, they were his brothers. He came to get even. Might have,

277

too, if he hadn't stepped on a cat's tail doin' it."

In shadows by the open door, the yellow cat preened itself, pointedly ignoring them all.

"Well, that was luck," Kingman said.

"Yes," Stillwell nodded. "It was."

More people had come pounding into the yard, and a crowd was forming. Kingman motioned. "Some of you boys pick this man up and carry him across to the jail. We'll . . ." he glanced at Stillwell. "Attempted murder?"

"Assault. He knocked that gate attendant in the head, he's over there in the weeds."

"But he tried to murder you! You're a witness, Stillwell!"

"I didn't see him try to murder me. Didn't see him at all until I apprehended him. For assaulting that man over there."

Kingman squinted at him. "Damn it, Stillwell, you . . . !"

A dapper-dressed man shouldered through the crowd, heading for the open barn door. His right arm was stuck straight out ahead of him, his index finger pointing and wagging, and his voice was the same shrill, irritated voice Stillwell had heard coming from the sheriff's office.

"There it is!" he shouted. "That's my horse and . . . and my carriage! What's my rig doing in the county barn? Where'd you find it?"

Sheriff Matt Kingman shook his head, then stepped out to head the man off. Keeping his face very straight, he said, "You see, Mayor? I told you we'd find your rig. And from now on I'd appreciate a little bit more respect when you discuss your county sheriff in public. Otherwise I might want to talk about where we found it."

When the mayor was gone with his carriage, Mitchell asked Kingman, "You didn't know that was his, did you?"

"Not 'til this very minute," the sheriff admitted. "Meant to tell you, Captain . . . you recollect that little shootout in town here, that the Tightwadders were involved in?"

"What about it?"

"Well, I guess we'll never get to the bottom of that one. We got word yesterday, they found Tim Sullivan and some of his men out west of here—couple of counties over. They were dead, and from the looks of it there's been a shootin' war. Don't know who it was they jumped, but the trails said it was them that started it and somebody else finished it."

"So?"

"Well, it's out of my jurisdiction, but I just wondered if any rangers want to be involved."

Mitchell glanced quickly at Stillwell, then shook his head. "One already was, I imagine," he shrugged.

"Well, then," Kingman squared his shoulders, "I can't say I like what you told me over yonder, but I guess that's how it's got to be." Though he spoke to Mitchell, he was looking at Stillwell.

"No other way," the drifter said. "Take it or leave it."

"I want Goldie Locke," Kingman said, pointedly.

Stillwell turned away and walked to the barn door. "The paint and the black," he pointed. "Are they ready?"

"Ready an' waitin'," the attendant said. He signalled a pair of helpers to saddle the two horses.

Stillwell stepped out again and faced the ranger. "My way," he said.

"Your way," Mitchell conceded. "I just hope you're right."

Stillwell gazed at him for a moment, then looked beyond him, narrowed dark eyes distant and melancholy. "And I wish I were wrong, Captain. I really do."

279

Chapter Twenty-six

It was the nature of Gingerbread Hill, business was seasonal and traffic erratic. On this night, with no herds on the trails and no crews in from Ennis, the gaudy street of taverns, casinos and elaborate bawdy houses was quiet. For an hour or more, no one had entered the Cotillion Club, and the mounts at its hitch rails had thinned down to three, then two, then none as departing customers swung into their saddles to go somewhere else.

Byron Stillwell watched the place for a time, then approached and stepped up onto the boardwalk. At the batwing doors he hesitated, looking in, then he stepped through. In the grand parlor only two people could be seen, and both looked up at him as he entered. He walked across to the mirrored bar, leaned an elbow on it and pointed his thumb toward the aproned man behind it. "You," he said. "Outside. Now."

The man hesitated, and Stillwell swept aside his serape to reveal the Peacemaker ready at his hip. "Leave," he repeated, quietly. "Go to the front door and outside. I mean *right now.*"

A few feet away, standing at the bar, Taffy Bates stared at him, motionless.

The bartender hesitated only a moment longer, then scurried around the end of the bar and sprinted for the door. The batwings swung closed behind him.

Taffy stared dumbly at the man in the serape.

"Hello, Taffy," Stillwell said.

"Uh . . . hello, Mr. . . . uh . . . Stillwell. What do you want?"

"Open your coat, Taffy," he ordered. "Slow and easy. Just do like I say. Open it and hold the lapels wide. That's right."

The big man opened his coat and Stillwell stepped to him, reached to a vest pocket and withdrew a small, two-barreled pistol. Using his left hand he dropped it into his own pocket, holding Taffy's eyes with his own. "Don't think about it, Taffy," he warned. "Remember last time."

The creased, battered face nodded, the eyes seeming immensely puzzled. "You uh . . . you mad at me, Mr. Stillwell? I don't . . . uh . . ."

"Just stand still, Taffy. Don't move at all. Do you understand?"

"Oh . . . yes, sir."

"That's fine." He backed away, went to the door and glanced out, then walked to the foot of the curving staircase and looked up. Satisfied, he returned to the bar. Beyond and behind it was a closed door. He tipped his head toward it. "The office?"

"Uh . . . yeah, that's . . ."

"Door locked?"

"Sure it is. Uh . . . it has to be, all the time."

"Open it, Taffy."

Bates' eyes narrowed with great worry. "I can't do that, Mr. . . . uh . . . Stillwell. It ain't allowed. But you could knock."

"I said, open it. Now."

Bates shook his head, stubbornly, then winced as Stillwell moved toward him. "But I'm not s'posed to . . ."

"Open the door."

With a sigh of resignation, Taffy walked around the bar, Stillwell behind him, and took a key from his vest. Carefully he inserted it in the lock, turned it, and

281

reached for the latch. A hard hand closed on his arm. "That's good, Taffy," Stillwell said. "Now just move away."

Bates backed off.

"And stay out of this," Stillwell ordered. "It isn't your concern."

He opened the door, stepped through and closed it behind him.

Daisy Walcott wore a handsomely-fitted evening dress of dark maroon satin with lace collar and cuffs the color of her strawberry-gold hair, and intricate embroidered designs that matched her blue eyes. The air in the tapestried room was rich with the scent of her fine perfume. She was at a polished desk, working with papers and stacks of currency under a cut-glass shaded lamp that duplicated the colors of the many-paned stained-glass French window behind her.

As the door opened she looked up, anger touching her wide-set eyes. "Taffy, how many times have I told you . . ." Then she shaded her eyes to see beyond the lamp, and stood. For a moment she only stared at him, then she smiled and came around the desk. "By! What a pleasant surprise. I thought you had gone, days ago."

"Hello, Daisy," he said. "I came back. You knew I'd have to."

She paused at the corner of the big desk, looking surprised, then the smile returned—a dazzling smile on a delicately chiseled face that reminded him of other beautiful faces he had seen. "Well, I don't know how I could have known any such thing, but I'm glad to see you again. Are you feeling better?"

"Better than I was. And thinking better, too, I guess. You knew I'd come, Daisy, because you knew I had to find you. The note about Mattie, and Patty Mills . . . that note was a leash to keep me on, wasn't it, Daisy? If you couldn't find me, you knew I'd have to come to you. And that I'd find you somehow."

"You are talking such nonsense, By," she smiled. "What on earth are . . ."

"I remember Slick," he said evenly. "Five years ago in Colorado. Maybe I did save your life when I stopped him from roughing up his girls. But I didn't kill him. It wasn't necessary. He wasn't going to hurt any more women . . . or kill any more, the way he killed your friend Goldie. That was her name, wasn't it, Daisy? Goldie Locke?"

She stared at him, the smile fading little by little, her bright eyes seeming to change, to darken as he spoke.

"Was Slick the first one, Daisy? The first you ever killed? I have to admit, it's poetic, killing him like that with his own rifle. Do you know, that's the first time I ever saw an Alexander Henry rifle. When I noticed the one he kept behind his desk."

She stood very still, her eyes dark and unreadable.

"You said you'd come into money, Daisy. I expect you did, at that. Ten thousand dollars is a lot of money, for simply killing a man. And there have been so many! Is it just the money, Daisy? Or is there some pleasure in your profession, too? Goldie Locke was your friend. A very good friend, I imagine, wasn't she? The kind of friend no man could ever be? Is that part of it, Daisy, all the killings these past five years? Have you come into money by being paid to do something you would gladly have done for free, because they were men?"

"Stop it!" she screamed, her eyes blazing at him. "How dare you . . ."

"This had to come, Daisy. I had to come and find you. You left me no choice."

"Damn you!" she shouted, her hands writhing in the folds of her maroon gown. "You could have been different, By! I told you so. I even offered, when you were here, to let you off the list. But you were too stupid to understand! I still can, you know. You could still be someone special to me . . . someone I'd never . . ."

Tears welled in her eyes as she stepped toward him, her hand reaching for him.

There was a crash as the door flew open. Taffy Bates seemed to almost fill the room as he rushed between them, rounding on Stillwell. "You leave her alone! You just get away from Miss . . ."

His eyes bulged, his mouth dropped open and a gasp escaped his throat, then died. For a moment his eyes stared at Stillwell, then they slid away. The big man half-turned, making strangling sounds. He swayed, then fell, and the little wound in his back was just the width of the slim stiletto gleaming red in Daisy's hand.

Stillwell grasped her wrist, twisted and the knife fell to the floor beside the body of Taffy Bates. She twisted away from him, and backed off, glaring with eyes that were like cat's eyes — bright and feral, and deadly.

Stillwell looked at the body of Taffy Bates. "Now that is a shame," he said quietly. "A real shame. Taffy loved you, Daisy. He would have died for you . . . and I guess he did."

"Damn you!" Her voice was a hiss, spitting fury.

"Even that cat tried to warn me about you, Daisy," he said. "I've never seen that cat show fear of anything. But he was afraid of you. And out there at Buffalo Wells . . . he knew who was up there, shooting. I wonder how he knew. Maybe it was your perfume. The same perfume that little typewriter girl wore, the perfume I guess you gave her. The same perfume I smelled on a couple of spent rifle cases. Brass is a sticky metal, Daisy. It will hold a scent. I understand why you killed Roy Pye. He was in your way. And about the telegraph operator. He wouldn't have given you those names willingly. But why the girl, Daisy? Did you *have* to kill her? Had she figured out why you wanted all those files?"

"Yes!" she hissed, backing farther away, around the desk. "She heard what those men were saying, about Goldie Locke being after you. And she knew which files I wanted. She wanted money . . ."

"And you couldn't let her live," he nodded. "I have to hand it to you, Daisy. Five years, and no one ever suspected who Goldie Locke really was. Smart. Very, very smart."

She eased back another step and he shook his head. "You can't get out that way, Daisy. Sheriff Kingman and his deputies have this house surrounded, and there is a captain of rangers upstairs, waiting. There are a couple of things I'd like to know, though, before they take you into town. Why, Daisy? Why all this *Goldie Locke* business? Why that name?"

She glared at him, a glare of pure, hot hatred. "Because I loved her!"

"I expected so." He nodded. "And one other thing. If I hadn't come back . . . would you really have gone after Patty Mills, and my mother?"

Fury raged in her eyes. Abruptly she turned toward the French doors, swept aside a drape and spun around, strong arms raising a big rifle, leveling it at him. A rifle with a long, telescope sight. "Yes!" she spat. "Yes, I would!"

The rifle came level, then jerked aside as thunder crashed and rebounded in the little room. The Peacemaker spoke only once, but its message was final. Daisy Walcott lurched back against the French doors and crashed through, falling into darkness beyond.

Byron Stillwell stood for a long moment, the pain of years sorting itself behind his dark, melancholy eyes, putting itself away in the niches of him where it always lived. Finally he slid the Peacemaker back into its holster and let his serape fall over it.

"Goodbye, Daisy," he whispered.

He turned away, and behind him the night wind murmured through broken doors, "Goodbye, Goldie Locke."

Epilogue

An odd dozen men assembled on the platform at
Waxahachie depot as the westbound Midlands Express
pulled in. Eight of them had various luggage and bag-
gage, waiting to be loaded aboard. All of them had
worn saddles and bits of tackle—the trappings of men
who worked hard when there was work and traveled
light when they traveled. One among them, Frenchy
Boudreau, leaned on a crutch—a legacy from the breed
bull that killed Cap Freeman.

"You boys know where you're going and what you're
supposed to do," Ranger Captain Walter Mitchell told
them. "That ranch out there is called Double D, and
it's goin' to be tied up in court for a while. So you'll be
workin' for the county district court out there and
drawing your wages from the judge, until everything's
settled and new owners take possession. After that,
well, what you all do then is between you and the owners. But that may be a while yet."

Stoke Winburn gazed at the ranger, faint amusement
in his eyes. "Be the first time any of us worked for a
court," he said. "But I reckon cowboyin' is cowboyin'
no matter who opens the chute."

"Heard tell there might be buyers waitin' when that
spread goes on the block," Frenchy allowed. "Heard

there might even be a few folks around here puttin' up some money."

"I don't know a thing about any of that," Mitchell shook his head. "And neither do you boys. All you got to do is get on out there and tend that place the way a spread ought to be tended, and keep doin' it 'til somebody tells you otherwise. Oh, and by the way, Stoke, you may find a couple of folks you know already out there. An Indian and a kid. Put them on the payroll, too."

Winburn nodded. "I got a feelin' that Stillwell has somethin' to do with all this," he said.

"Could be," the ranger shrugged. "That drifter's a real busybody when it comes to getting involved in other folks' business."

"Where is he? Still around?"

"I doubt it. He was saddling that paint horse last I saw of him. I expect he's pushed on by now."

"Where to?"

Mitchell stepped back as jets of steam shot from the Midlands Express' valves. "I don't believe he said. Now y'all get aboard. This train's ready to roll."

At the edge of town, Byron Stillwell stood in his stirrups, breathing the good west wind that blew down fresh and clean from the rising lands beyond the Forks of the Brazos, and scanned the wide country ahead. Morning sun was warm on his shoulders and his shadow pointed the way as he settled himself and patted the neck of the big paint.

Nice day for it, he thought. Whatever it is, it's a nice day for it.

Hope all's well with you, Mother. I'm doing some traveling, seeing the sights.

Patty, take care of yourself. Maybe when I get back to Kansas we can find a train going east, all the way to

Philadelphia. *Scheherazade* and sherbet at the Pavillion . . . then maybe a walk along that rain-wet street where the hansoms parade by and all the little shops have gaslights at their doors for the after-theater trade. We'll have that, Patty. I promise you.

"But there's still a ways to go," he told the horse.

He lifted his reins, then hesitated as a scurrying sound came from behind.

"You don't give up, do you?" he asked, looking down at a furry orange face with slitted yellow eyes. "What's the matter, can't you find anybody in that whole town who's up to your standards?"

The cat stared at him, then crouched and sprang and he helped it get its footing on his saddleskirt.

"Luck," he murmured, putting heels to the paint horse. "I don't know, maybe you are at that."